Abdullah Hussein was born in 1931 in Rawalpindi. He published his first novel, *The Weary Generations*, in 1963, for which he won the prestigious Pakistani Adamji Prize. His novels and short fiction have been published in Urdu as well as being translated into several languages of the sub-continent and into English and Chinese. In 1996 the BBC based a feature film, *Brothers in Trouble*, on one of his novellas. *Emigré Journeys* is his first novel in English. Regarded as the leading novelist in the Urdu language, he has lived in Britain since 1967.

émigré journeys

Abdullah Hussein

Acknowledgement is due to Yaasir Aslam who gave help with computer work in the preparation of this manuscript.

Library of Congress Catalog Card Number: 99–65189

A complete catalogue record for this book can be obtained from the British Library on request

The right of Abdullah Hussein to be identified as the author of this work has been asserted by him in accordance with the Copyright, Designs and Patents Act 1988

First published in 2000 by Serpent's Tail,
4 Blackstock Mews, London N4
website: www.serpentstail.com

Phototypeset by Intype London Ltd

Printed in Italy by Chromo Litho Ltd

10 9 8 7 6 5 4 3 2 1

For Clare Pearson
who helped give this novel a shape and form

1

Breath sticks in my throat, I do not know where to turn, yet I turn – like a fish caught up in the eddy, with no power in my limbs.

It was the eddy that first gave me the dying feeling.

'Do you see that, son?' said my father, pointing with his finger stiff with arthritis. 'It will swallow you up.'

The monsoon had caused the waters to swell and my father was warning me off bathing in the flooded canal. But my father had only one leg. He never swam. And it was the month of August, hot, windless, drawing sweat from every pore of the body.

Outside the flooding season the eddies were small and no stronger than me. I dived into them without fear and caught with my hands little trapped fishes, which my mother fried whole in ghee for me to eat. But when the floods came the currents dug holes in the earth underneath, making room for big water-whirlwinds with a dip in the middle going down and down. Older boys said that you could catch fish as big as a spread hand that spun powerless in the centre of them. I could sit on the branch of a tree by the canal bank or float out of reach and look at the big mud-coloured conch in constant motion folding back on itself for hours, dreaming of the silver fish within it. It threw an invisible ring of rope like a lasso round my head, pulling me in. After my father left me standing there on that day, I jumped into the canal. I would swim to the edge of the circle, I thought, and look at the fish suspended upright on their tails and turning and turning as the boys had said. I swam too near. Spinning in that black and breathless spiral, I lost my own centre of wind and sank, till my feet touched the muddy earth below. My arms and legs were beating the water like those of a puny frog with no escape, when a bottom current slapped me out of reach of the eddy's strike. I saw no fish. But the waters fell short and above me was the sky. I vomited streams of water, lying flat on the bank and weeping, begging for God's face to appear in the sky and save me. With nosefuls of water still dense in my head, I could not breathe. I rolled over and knew that I was dying. Some bigger boys picked me off the ground and hung me upside down from the tree and I lived.

At the age of nine, I had crossed my first black water and glimpsed the end of life. Nineteen more years were to pass before I crossed my second, and was hurled into another vortex where for years I drew no breath of the living, only that of the half-dead, unseen and unheard. But never, not even when my very existence on this earth was denied by other men did I have the wind taken from my chest. In my forty-four years of life I have fought through much and made progress. Today, they have shut the door on me and locked it and give me no answer. And to think that they are none other than my very own wife and daughter who love me, and whom I love from the depth of my heart. What have I done wrong? My breath is trapped in my throat. Did I ever think that after thirty-five years of life's endeavours I would once again have a knife in my gut and in my heart a dying feeling? What do I do, wait till they return and then tell them what I have crossed and uncrossed, passed and not passed?

I cannot think. But I can remember. It is all in here,

wrapped up within the sheets of my body. Anybody can think, but to remember is to face one's own existence. I had qualities. Never put off till tomorrow what I could do on the day. If a floorboard creaked or a knob fell off the door, I got down to it right there and then, unmindful of my need for rest after a hard day at work. I earned to provide all necessary requirements, and some even that were not essential. I had qualities of education, for a start: at school I was the special favourite of my English master who daily asked me to recite the poem of golden daffodils, lonely as a cloud I wandered and so on, while he shut his eyes the more to enjoy the scenery of the poem on his brain. After I had finished the poem I was told to read a page from the book of essays and was held up before the whole class as having command of language, grammar, vocabulary, which no-one else attained. That was the one shining time of my life. There have been other good times, victories over tall barriers against which I had to push and strive, but no great and golden time again; for when you are in the tenth class and all the boys look up to you, that is a victory which is no longer an achievement and has not even a reason for being, it is a miracle. I was destined to pass the matriculation examination in the first division, said the English master, and then seek a position in the government department, with benefits for self and family accruing to such position. But I was thwarted.

Half-way through my tenth year in school my father sat me down and spoke.

'I am only a third-share tenant with one good leg on four acres of land, you know, son. I cannot pay for school fees and books and pencils and feed you on top. You have to work.'

I had respect for my father, but I did not want to toil on a few acres of no-rain land as he had done. So I made my first choice: I wanted to work with iron tools. I went and sat at the blacksmith's hut, just looking and running occasional errands for him. After a few days, the blacksmith had a word with my father and took me in as an apprentice. There was no money in it at first, but I ate from his hearth twice a day. Four years I spent there, learning all the skills. When the old blacksmith had nothing more to teach me, I began to think of working independently of him. I needed a hut of my own. But where? That was the first big question. I literally dug up the answer to that one in due course. There was a little strip of land on which no-one would dare to set foot.

A long time ago, someone went mad on that land. The plot, measuring approximately six yards by seven, was under the 'shadow', it was said, of a jinn. One night a passing lad emptied his impatient bladder on the spot. Enraged by this, the jinn pounced on him. The boy fell on the ground and lay there, shivering, for two whole days, uttering squeals of suffering. By the time he rose to his feet on the third day, the boy had jumped several ages. He had the face of an old man, creased and set as if in stone. He had lost his natural faculties; the jinn, having taken over his earthly body, had entered his spirit. Forever afterwards, this boy-man wandered from village to village, begging for food, inhabiting wild places, speaking in tongues. In the world's eyes, he had gone out of his mind. But even at the age of nine when I first heard the story, I thought differently: having surrendered his person to a foreign being, he had actually become one himself. This seemed at the time to round up the picture in my mind. It took me another five years to bring the story to a satisfactory end: this man, having lost human abilities, was denied in return the special powers that went with the foreign being. As a result, the change in his existence occurred only to the extent of bodily dysfunction, while the soul got consumed altogether; he had suffered a living death. No wonder then that he roamed the earth like a man with no destination, as if exiled from the world. Inside me, this story never died, and as the time came for me to contemplate moving to my own place, it came to my aid in the form of a blessed thought: the boy-man had been punished for desecrating the land over which lingered the shadow of the jinn, but conversely, what if the jinn, his shadow and the land were honoured in some way?

'There is the shadow on it, do you not know?' the owner said to me. 'If you want the weight of it on your neck, then it is your neck. The land is no longer mine, it is "his".'

'I only want to provide him with shade from the sun,' I said. 'It will please him.'

The landlord moved away as if already certain of seeing me come to a bad end. My mother went to the mosque Imam and got a taveez from him. She had it threaded and bound in leather, and slung it round my neck. It was to protect me from the doings of all the beings foreign to human kind. Thus armed, I went and put my foot on the jinn's land. This was to be my first conquest. From all the trees available to me, I chose the seeds of the dhrake, for this tree's rapid growth and the dark shade of its crowded top, and for the whistling sound the wind makes through its thin leaves, pointing to a life of its own. I sowed twelve dhrake seeds all round the plot of land. Around each one of them, once they had broken surface, I constructed brick shelters to provide protection from the cruel sun and from the herds of goats that laid waste to every green leaf in their path. Every single day, after finishing work at the blacksmith's forge, I went to water the plants, staying there longer and longer, never tiring. Seeing them suck up nourishment from the soil and become heavier, taller, greener, I already felt as if, at the age of twenty, I were the father of twelve children. Every

night, I would sit there until late, growing familiar with
the dark, driving the fear of the jinn from my heart, until
I began to feel that I had made the land my very own.
Within a year, the trees were six feet tall and thick at the
top. Among them, with every penny that I had saved
during five years of working at the forge, I built a hut with
my own hands.

I soon found that carrying on an independent trade was
a different matter. There was much fearful talk: no way
was the jinn, they said, going to allow a fire to be lighted
on his territory. But the mosque Imam had already told
me that just as humans are made of dust and angels from
light, so jinns are composed of fire: my jinn would not
object. Day by day, I passed this knowledge on to the
people of the village. Eventually, my endeavours bore fruit
and the village folk began to come to me with work. In
time, I grew to be more than a blacksmith in their eyes; I
was the one who had banished fear of the unseen creatures
of fire from their hearts. I had attained a stature which,
though not as high as the landlord or the mosque Imam,
was nevertheless deserving of some respect. Within three
years, I had saved enough money to build two extra rooms
in my father's house. Then I was ready to fulfil the desire
of my heart – to make Salma my wife.

It had started many years before when we were children.
We were playing in the fields. Wild boars, scourge of crops,
had dug up hollows in the earth. Moles had then burrowed
into the sides of these dips to lay tunnels under the surface.
Rabbits and hedgehogs followed the moles and we, the
children of the village, followed the animals, scraping
the soil off the walls of their passages for days with our
fingers, until they were wide enough to crawl into. We
called these 'graves'. I was lying on my back, hiding in my
favourite grave, looking up at a spot of the sky through
the air hole, when a delighted shriek of discovery shot

through the earth. Above me, the small round patch of the sky had disappeared. In its place were two eyes, a nose and a mouth. This face, with no ears, cheeks, chin or a head of hair, had filled my grave with a yell that was mingled with a whiff of sweet and sour fruit. She had been eating a pear. For the first time in all my playing days, I shivered with happiness at being found. The smell of fresh, ripe pears, wherever I come across it, at whatever time, reminds me of her half-face framed within a hole in the ground. During the years before I was ready to wed I saw my cousin Salma nearly every day in the village, but nothing in my vision replaced that first picture and the breath bearing the fragrance of pears, as though it were the beginning of the whole of my remembrance. In my twenty-fourth year, we were married.

I would still be sitting in my hut today, working among my trees, not getting rich but feeding and clothing my family, earning the respect of many for whom I'd done good, sound work, often on credit, had it not been for the man who appeared one day in the village, dressed in nice, English clothes, looking prosperous and happy. He was, it turned out, an agent of the agents in the city, who under-took, in return for 'expenses', to send anyone who wanted to go, to England. There, he said, we could earn ten, twenty, a hundred times the amount of money we were earning here, and buy with it merchandise like English electrical goods. There was no electricity in our village, but it was no matter. I remember going on one occasion to another village as part of a wedding party. The room where one group of us was seated before the start of the feast was furnished with items of electrical application bought from England. They were placed neatly on the wooden shelves fixed to the wall and appeared, from the shine on their surface, regularly dusted: a shaver, a small food mixer, a power drill. There was even a sewing machine and a record player, sitting side by side on a large table by the wall. There was no electricity in that village either. But these things were meant for purposes other than their usage; they were possessions which indicated enterprise and success. We knew that people had been going to England for years, although no-one from our own village had yet taken this step. I was the first to make up my mind to go. I am not a religious man, but I was happy in the belief that in return for my labours in this world and my success in the occupation of feared land, I was being offered by God almighty another world of bright prospects. I consulted my father. He, as usual, clenched his fist and brought it down on his bad leg.

'You are a grown man of full years, are you not? If your mind is made up, it is made up.' He rapped his leg again, producing the familiar sound of knuckles on wood. 'There used to be a leg here. I left it in Burma during the war.'

'I know,' I said.

'What do you know?'

'You have told me many times.'

'You do not know the whole of it, do you?' he said. 'We ate rats, snakes, scorpions, worms and grass. Most did not come back. I did. Do you know how? I kept my head down and my mouth shut, that is how. So here is the trick: when you are not among your own people, keep your head down, let everything pass over you, and you will stay alive. Go and fight your war.'

Next, I came to the main question: money. Five thousand rupees, to be exact, as the down payment. No-one would buy my hut, or the tools or the trees, for as the news of my leaving spread, the fear of the jinn returned to the people. What was I to do?

Long before we were married, Salma knew that the gold was hers. I used to go to my uncle's house when I was small and once, as we were looking in the secret places of the house, Salma had pointed it out to me. It was buried under sheets at the bottom of a trunk, tied up with a rough white cloth at the neck, making the shape of a fist. It had belonged to her mother, who had died. On her death-bed, my aunt, Salma's mother, had got her husband to utter a pledge that the gold would go to her only daughter. During all the time of pouring sweat over hot irons to make horseshoes, shovels, spades and sickles, axles for bullockcarts and hinges and hoes, there were no more gold ornaments for Salma other than those she had brought with her as dowry, still tied up, fist-like, in the same rough cloth with a piece of string, now a little whiter on account of being washed on the occasion of our marriage. There was no way I could pay the agents' fee; the gold had to be sold.

I had decided upon the time: the night. I was going to make my wife happy in the night by the power of my loins, and then ask for gold. It was a tough night. I tried many ways, many angles, used all my strength and stayed long with her but could not make her happy. She had sensed it; she would not close her eyes, or utter a sound, or go to sleep. In the end, I left her side and went to the trunk. There was no gold. In anger, I looked to my wife. She was half sitting up in bed with her eyes wide open and both hands at once holding and covering up the top of her stomach. I had to force open her hands: the little bundle of gold; it was as if it took birth from her body at that very moment. She did not open her mouth or say anything when I took it from her, but there was a terror in her eyes worse than death, or birth. The gold was not the only thing she possessed; she had me, and the children, and some other things. She had even accepted my going away for a while. But the gold was another matter. She had not had to work for it, or suffer for its sake; it was simply hers, like her hands or feet or childhood – a gift. I said to myself, let the time pass, it will heal. In the following four weeks, during which I got five thousand rupees from the goldsmith in town and, upon the payment of the sum to the agent, a false passport plus details of travel arrangements, her face gradually adopted the look of a barren field, as if her features, having taken in the terror of that night, were left only as solitary objects upon her front. I vowed to myself that I would restore, with money, with gold, the life that would put her face together again. A face with its inheritance taken away is no face. For her first face – my dearest possession – I had overcome a strip of land that would give itself to no-one; for her second, I was going to win another world.

My father was only half right. It was a war all right, but there were no medals. I worked ten, twelve hours a day, six, sometimes seven days a week. For the room, which I shared, and the provision of a mattress and three blankets, I paid one pound. I limited my food expenditure to one pound. After that I had to put aside three pounds each week for the rest of the agent's 'expenses' money, a procedure which had been agreed upon and contracted for at the outset. Whatever was then left of my total weekly wage I sent straight back to Salma once a month through Baba Rehman, who dealt in black currency and gave a good rate of exchange. In every letter to my wife, I impressed upon her to buy land in the village so that by the time I made my return there were enough acres to my home on which we could live in comfort. This was the final goal of all of us at the time – although there was always a question mark to it. Whether hidden under crates of frozen fish in big lorries or spat on to a deserted beach like washed-up drowned men with itineraries in their pockets, we got here one way or the other. What none of us knew was how to go back. Each night, as I lay down on the mattress after a long day's work and closed my eyes, I pictured Salma as I had seen her at the moment of my departing from home.

She was standing outside the door of the house, her shiny black hair washed, massaged and combed tightly back, carrying my daughter Parvin, who was eight months old then, in the crook of her right elbow. My son Hasan, already grown beyond his twenty months, stood by her side, holding his mother's hand and looking up at her. She looked clean, smelled of mustard oil and soap, and there was desolation in her face. Each night, my heart bled. She loved me. She has always loved me. And I love her too. In the few years that I spent over here away from her, time neither passed nor stopped altogether but seemed to slip, hour by hour, into a hole in the ground and disappear. It was only at night, viewing the scene of my departure from home in the back of my shut eyelids that I had the feeling for a few minutes that I existed, before sleep overcame my tired limbs and carried me away. The rest of the time we, all seventeen of us, lived our half-lives in the daylight hours, coming fully into our own for a short while only when we came home to the dark of that cave-like house, to sit and talk and do as real men do everywhere, dream of lumpsums of money and ways of escaping.

My wife and my son and daughter gave to me each night the gift of a brief life parallel to the one I had all those years ago, so why do they not help me now? My son, though he too has turned away from me, is a boy and can be no cause of disrepute no matter what he does. A daughter is a different matter. She bears the honour of my name and that of my forefathers. So beautiful, so able, who would have thought that she would turn out like this, stand in front of me and answer back, say no to what is required of her?

2

No, I say to him, I'll run away from home.

The moment the fingers close round my neck and my back gets a shove down the dark steps I feel the warm damp ants crawling down my legs. I can't believe it, I've had my period and it finished two days ago. I know where the light switch is. Luckily there's a bulb at the end of the wire from the ceiling, which there isn't always. I see that it isn't blood; I've only wet myself. What do I dry myself with? There isn't even a rag down here. An old mattress stands bent-backed by the wall. I try pulling out a piece of fabric with my fingernails and then with my teeth. Can't put a rent in the bloody denim. I get out of my shalwar and throw my pants into a corner. There's only my yellow polkadot scarf, with which I dry myself, rubbing and pressing it on the damp spots on my shalwar to soak up the wet. The flimsy silk doesn't absorb much of anything. I drag the mattress down and sit on it. My insides are cut up and rising to the base of my throat, forming little spheres of trapped gas. Desperately I try swallowing them. But I can't. Panic. I get up and run but am sick in the middle of the floor before I reach the small heap of coaldust in the other corner. My chest empties. I take up the coaldust in the scuttle that lies there and cover my sick. The smell stays. I pour more dust on it. Perhaps it's only my imagination, I tell myself. But the smell won't go, making me feel more sick. In the end I have to tear the scarf in two, right down the middle. I gather up the mess with the help of the scuttle in one half of the scarf, wrap it tightly round threefold and bury it deep in the coaldust heap. Then I come back and sit on the mattress with an empty heart. It was the scarf that Martin gave me.

Shit, bulb's gone. What do I do now in this black hole? Black Hole! Where's it from? Oh yes, from some history lesson back in school, black hole of something or other. Of what, though? It's coming! Got it, Black Hole of Calcutta, that's what, wherever that is. I can't even see my own hands. It's only eleven o'clock, I looked at my watch just before the bulb went and it was one minute to, have been looking at it since the morning as if just knowing what time it was will get me out of here. I can see it's a clear day from the tiny hole at the top of the coal chute. The coal man used to come once a fortnight and dump the coal in the mouth of the chute from where it slid down to here. When the gas came they closed it up flush with the pavement outside but not flush enough; there's a needlepoint hole on one side of the lid where the light comes and goes in trickles. The sun's out too. It doesn't show its face for weeks and when one day it does I get pushed down here, shit. Soon it will come up over the top of the houses on the other side of the street, and when it reaches a certain point in the sky a long thin sunray from the needlepoint will come lashing the darkness into waking and open its dim eye so I am able to just about make out things around me.

'Parvi – Parvee!'

My mother's quick panicky voice jumps like a spark in the black air, scrambling the darkness so I feel I can see things in this hellhole. Not true, but even when I was small and woke up by her side at midnight, she would utter a

sound in sleep and the room lit up, driving fear from my
heart.

I stay silent. She stumbles on the steps, balances herself
and calls out again. 'Parveee, what you doing in dark?'

My parents only speak Punjabi among themselves and
with all their friends, but when I got to senior school
and my friends started coming to my house, Mum began
slowly to speak to me in English. Now she does it all the
time. But no grammar. 'How much this?' 'Seventy-two
pence madam.' 'Too much, no?' 'I have a cheaper one.
Here, sixty-five pence.' 'No, no, no. That only. Sixty-five
pee?' 'No madam, seventy-two for that one.' 'No, sixty-
five. You my brother.' Pause, eye-contact in place, flabbergasted stallholder. 'All right, gimme seventy pence, only for
you.' 'No, sixty-five. Bus.' 'What?' 'Bus. Khlas,' waving of
her hands indicating the end, 'finish.' For me, the end
of the world, trying to hide, bending my legs to make an
invisible dwarf of me.

Slipping half-verbs like shifting prices. I too have lost
the verbs of the language that I came here speaking at five
years of age. Now we speak similar tongues, babytalking to
one another in different languages, she the one she has
picked up, me the one I have lost. It doesn't matter, she
has a voice like non-singeing sparklers.

'Parvi,' she cries, 'why you not speak? Speak.'

'The bulb's popped,' I answer.

'Bulb?'

'The light bulb, fused, can't you see?'

'No, all dark.'

'Yes, yes, for God's sake, get me a bulb.'

'You sit,' she says, 'I get bulb.'

She goes back up. She comes down with a bulb and my
baby torch in hand. We are forbidden by my father to do
anything electrical. I look back at her as she offers me the
bulb and she says she hasn't told him about it.

'Hasn't he gone to work?' I ask her.

'No,' she says. 'He very angry, sitting in front room, door shut.'

I have to drag up the chest of drawers and climb on top of it to change the bare bulb in the light of the torch while she holds the rickety chest in place. I take the torch off her as well when I get down and switch the light on. She sits down on the floor by the mattress.

'I go to maulvi saab,' she says.

'What for?' I ask her.

'He take jinn out.'

'Take jinn out? Out of what, me? You're joking.'

Her eyes are dry, but I know she's been crying in the electric light, I can see the glisten-marks where tears have freshly dried on the moles on her wheatskin cheeks.

'You mad,' she says quietly.

'I'll strangle the maulvi with his own huge bloody beard,' I say to her.

'Your father angry,' she says, and starts crying. She cries in Punjabi, no words, just the sound, a wail, stretched long and curled as a column of smoke from a hearth, that stays in the still air long after the dungcakes that produced it have burned out. How I have loved this face smelling of fresh cooked brown roti and semolina khir and how much hated it when she comes out in floods of tears, digging deep ravines in her flesh and mine.

'Don't cry,' I say to her, 'please stop. I love you, all right? Now go, I can't bear it. Please.'

'Achha, achha,' she says, getting up. 'I go. I come again.'

'Not yet, please. Later.'

She scrambles up the steps, locking the top door behind her. It is her weird crying that gets me down, sends me way back to where I have no wish to go. At least I have the light now. Two lights. If this cheap bulb pops off again, I've got my torch.

Jinns, in fuck's name! I feel like banging my head against the wall. Won't, though. Just wait, I tell myself, let the time pass.

3

The house resembled a cave, long and dark. It was divided
into two functional parts, with two separate kitchens. The
lower floors had their kitchen on the ground floor, complete
with shelves and tables and two chairs, plus a free-standing
almirah. The four of us who lived on the top floor had no
proper kitchen, just a gas stove on the landing, one small
table, one water tap sticking out of the wall and a sink
below it. Ghulam and I had a joint system. Ghulam did
not eat well, until I suggested that I could cook for both
of us, to which he agreed and started handing over his
share of the groceries to me. Hussain Shah cooked for
himself. He was a pathan from Campbellpur, short-statured
but stockily built with a long moustache and the two front
teeth missing. He had an authority about him; although
never harsh with anyone, he appeared all the time to be
on the brink of losing his temper. For this reason, and
because he was the most senior resident of the house
and had a single room under his sole occupation, Hussain
Shah's word was law.

My first night there was the toughest. I will never forget
it as long as I live. In my pocket I had the address of a
house which I found after walking miles until my feet
ached. Night had already fallen and I had difficulty finding
the light-switch in the dark. When I eventually found it
behind the door of the room and pressed, nothing

happened, so I had to get down on all fours until I came
to a mattress on the floor and sat down on it. The room,
the landing, the stairs, everything was in pitch dark. The
man who admitted me into the house came up to show
me the room but did no such thing. Pointing upwards into
the dark, he turned and went back from half-way up the
stairs. I climbed the stairs carefully but knocked into
the heavy stove, from which the long bone of my left leg
was still hurting when I found the mattress. I sat on it a
long time, one, maybe two hours. The door of the next
room, which I later discovered belonged to Hussain Shah,
was closed, although I could see the light on inside. Then
he switched it off, opened the door and went out of the
house. After a while, getting used to the dark, I was able
to see dimly round the room. There was a light bulb
hanging from the ceiling. It was probably burnt out; still,
I got up and tried the switch two or three times just to
make sure. Then I went back and sat on the mattress. It
was covered with thin blankets, all jumbled up. A low table
stood by its side, on top of which I could see some utensils.
My belly was empty and I started shivering. After some
time, a man came up the stairs carrying a mattress and
some blankets. He left these outside the door and went
back. I took a blanket from there and wrapped it all around
me, then came back to the mattress and sat on it. It was
strange that until then I had been travelling, with nowhere
to go. Then that evening I had the shelter of a roof over
my head and what happened? I was sitting in a safe place
and I could not stop shivering, my heart becoming
smaller and smaller from knowing nothing. All day I had
been walking about, then I got to a roof over my head and
nobody talked to me or asked me to eat, just left me in
this dark room. One by one, they all went off to work, or
came back from work and went to sleep. However much I
tried, I was unable to control the shivering spreading all

over my body. That is why I can still sometimes feel that hunger in my belly and the pain in my shin from hitting that old stove and wonder whether the past time is ever past.

Some time later, Ghulam came back from work. He stood in the doorway looking at me for a few seconds, then marched right past me without a word. He had heavy army-type boots on his feet, was wearing a thick overcoat, buttoned up to the chin, and on his head a hat with earflaps. He had just come in from outside but was walking about in the dark as if it made no difference. Pulling out a loaf of bread from one pocket of his coat and from the other a tin of baked beans, he put the two things on the table. He knew exactly where everything was. He picked up a can-opener and cut open the tin of beans, emptied it into a frying pan, carried the pan out to the landing and placed it on the stove. Expertly, he turned on the gas and lit it with a match using just one hand. As the beans began to simmer and crackle, he turned the gas off and brought the pan back into the room. He sat down on the blankets at the head of the mattress, placing the frying pan in front of him on the floor. Then he picked up the bread from the table, spread thick layers of butter on the slices with the help of a spoon. Doubling up the slices, he began to eat them with spoonfuls of beans.

In the middle of eating Ghulam stopped abruptly and, looking at me sideways, said, 'Come today?'

'Yes,' I replied.

'Eaten something?'

I had great hunger, but couldn't say, it being our first meeting.

'Thank you, and thanks be to God,' I said.

Within a minute or two, Ghulam wiped the pan clean. Pushing it to one side on the floor, he stood up. First he took his hat off, then his overcoat, and hung them both by a nail fixed to the back of the door. After that he sat down on the mattress and began removing his boots. While he was struggling with them, Ghulam stopped suddenly and spoke to me again.

'Get your mattress,' he said, pointing with his elbow to the landing. It was the last thing he uttered that night.

I brought the mattress in and lay it down on the floor by the opposite wall. On top of the one I already had, I wrapped the other two blankets tightly around me and sat down on the mattress. By now Ghulam had removed his boots. These he placed side by side on the floor by the lower end of his mattress, so that they were in line with his feet and right next to them as he lay down to sleep. Ghulam had slipped his trousers off and spread them on top of his boots. He had pyjamas underneath that he had tucked into thick woollen socks. He did not take off the socks nor the jumper he had on, only undid the collar button of his shirt and, pulling up the blankets around him, went to sleep. Almost immediately, he began to snore. I was sitting on the mattress and I could not lie down to sleep. It was as though if I dared to do that then something would happen, something that would be the cause of a kind of disturbance and would wake up the others and I would be blamed. I had fear in my heart.

When the alarm of Ghulam's clock went, it was still dark. I came to understand then the placing of Ghulam's boots and trousers. He slipped his legs straight into the trousers while still half-lying in bed, doing a little hop to pull them up to his waist, and did up his buttons. Sitting up where he had lain, he put his feet smoothly into the boots, tying the laces with quick movements of fingers. Then he stood up. He fastened the collar button, put on first his hat, then his overcoat and buttoned it up. At the back of the door beside the nail hung a tiny mirror. Ghulam bent at the waist to look at his face in the mirror, combed his moustache with his fingers and adjusted the hat. Before leaving he gave the dirty frying pan from the previous night a quick rinse under the tap and put it back on the table in the room. Then he was gone. I could see from the hands of the clock in the dark that it took him just three minutes to be up and out. All the time that we spent in that room, Ghulam did nothing other than repeat that first day's routine. His life was set. He was out of the house just after seven in the morning and back at half-past eight at night, seven days a week, most weeks. Within two years, he told me, he had already managed to buy four acres of arable land in his village. He met his needs of nature and ate during the day at the factory where he worked.

This used to be a good area once upon a time, it was said and considered a clean part of the city. 'Honest working people lived with their families in one or two-room accommodation,' said Ram, 'their women washing the footpaths in front of their houses every morning and dressing the children in clean clothes.' Ram had come here just after the war ended. But after 1950 many people from foreign countries began arriving, most from our countries and Negroes from Jamaica. Within a few years this country of white people had 'plenty of other colours of faces'. These people nearly killed themselves working and were able in time to buy their own homes. Ram, who came from Surat in South India, had started working on ships at the age of twelve and could speak many languages, his own and Bengali and Punjabi and some others. Once when his ship passed these shores, Ram left the ship and never went back. I always had the feeling that he was the first man to arrive here.

'The end came,' he told me, 'when the white people saw our people arriving in numbers and settling down. Then they began to leave. The price of property fell. Most white tenants left on their own, while tricks such as the burning of dried chilli drove the rest of them out. There was some trouble, but in the end the area was cleared.' Empty rooms were filled with newcomers at high rent, shops and cafés opened and everything began to be sold. 'Nowadays many white people go to our restaurants after pubs close,' Ram said, 'and stuff themselves with our food, drink glasses of water and have a good burp. In those days, they complained of the smell and covered their noses while passing by.'

The landlords made money, especially as the prostitutes, seeing ready demand, came and settled in the area in large numbers. When I arrived the general population there was just us and the prostitutes, plus a few students. We all lived peacefully together. Some of our more clever people, after getting permission from the local council, started small cafés in their front rooms. These were the places where all our people gathered in those days, passed the time and collected information about making a living. Men from the same village and town formed separate groups and sat at their own tables. A newcomer would join the group from his own area and be guided as to the ways and means of this country. All day long, Indian film songs were played on the gramophone, thus the cafés were the first places where the melodious sounds of our ghazals and quwalis arose in this land. Years later in one of these cafés I met Ram. By that time he was an old man. He worked nights and during the day he lived in the cafés, going from one to the other, not belonging to any one group but sitting wherever he wished. Ram had authority; he had knowledge of this country, procedures of government offices and every-thing, and when in difficulty, people asked him. He had made his way on his own and needed no-one's help, except for a chat and to pass the time.

Old Ram was a good man. Once or twice a year, when he had worked on the ships, he had visited his village and given money to his parents. On one such visit, his parents

had found a girl from the same village and married him
off to her. When I met him, Ram had a married daughter
back home, who had grown-up children of her own. He
showed me some photographs once, faded, cracked and
most of them of his youth with him standing on the decks
of ships or in the centre of foreign cities, in the company of
friends in sailors' uniforms with their arms around each
other's shoulders. Others were of his daughter, of her as a
child and as a young girl, of her being married, and of her
children when they were small whom Ram had never seen.
These photographs he kept with great care in an old
envelope secured with a rubber band. Ram told me that
he had been sending 'regular money' to his wife 'on the
first of every month without fail' for forty-five years, even
though he had lived with her only fifteen times at intervals,
and never more than a month at a time. He would spread
his fingers and count, 'fifteen times in all', he would say,
almost as though he were proud of it. But I don't think he
was. There was humour in his eyes, as if he understood
the nature of his life. Ram had been living in one room
for over twenty years – neither he nor anyone else knew
exactly for how long – and during this time had only been
to his village once, for a period of two weeks, when his
daughter was married. I once asked him why he did not
consider getting his wife over to England, and he said that
his wife was happy in her village, with her relatives and
neighbours and grandchildren, and what would she do over
here? In the beginning Ram took up with a white woman
and lived with her for a while, it was said, although it did
not last. I questioned him once about this and he said,
laughing, that it was true, but he missed his room where
he could mutter to himself and not have to explain who he
was talking to. Ram worked in cleaning jobs, in small
factories and large all over the city, and in the cafés he
talked without stopping in his low, slow voice of no special

tone. Day by day, he lived on like this, his life lacking pace, nonetheless looking as if it would go on for ever. But in the last days, his health suddenly failed. When I met him he was beginning to be ill. Within a month he was dead. Some people from the cafés got together and with the help of the social department, had him cremated. The government people burned his old clothes, made a packet of his photographs and letters and posted it to his home address back in his village. Old Ram had made no progress in life.

The youngest amongst us was Sakib, who lived in the attic. The big and dark attic had been cleverly converted into a kind of room by erecting hardboard walls, three feet apart, on the right- and left-hand sides, with planks of plywood fixed on them to serve as shelves. The third side had a small frosted glass window in the slanting roof that let in the light. Sakib used a step ladder to climb into the attic when he came back from work, crawling up the mattress that fitted snugly between the hardboard walls. On some days, as he heaved himself up into the square entrance in the ceiling, he sat there resting from the effort, pulling a magazine from one of the shelves and reading it. The others living with us in the house could not read or write very much but only looked at the pictures of film actresses in magazines, cut them out and pasted them on the walls. Apart from me, only Sakib had education, having matriculated and even spent a year or two in college before he came here. Back home, he could get a government post and, with hard work, rise to a good position, make progress in life. He had no family other than his mother, who had her own house in the big city of Lahore – inherited from her deceased husband, an official – and had enough to live on. Sakib did not need to come here at all. What brought him, he had told me, was that he had read the novels of Thomas Hardy and Robert Louis Stevenson, borrowed from a travelling British Council library that regularly visited his college, and was drawn to this country, which had nurtured such fine brains, and its 'beautiful language'. Now, I myself having been so good in the tenth class and read so well the English poems and essays, harboured no such feelings; my success had only served to make me feel proud in class and not much else. But Sakib looked at things differently. Many of our renowned people, he told me, came and lived in this country for many years, doing ordinary jobs and at the same time becoming writers and later the rulers of our countries. Sakib wanted to become a writer, and this was what made him throw away his career at home to come and work as a labourer in England. I still remember the day he talked about his plans.

'Writing in newspapers and magazines brings you into contact with important people,' he said, 'people who have power in society.'

'So you want to become a leader,' I said, laughing.

'I only want to become well-known.'

'What is the point of fame when you have no money,' I said to him.

'Once you are famous, money does not matter.'

'So you want to be famous and live in glory.'

'No, no,' he said, 'I want to go back home when I am well-known.'

I was left speechless. The vehemence in his voice, and the glitter of emotion in his eyes showed that he had faith in what he was saying. All he wanted to do was to make his name here and then to go back home. And no consideration for money! Sakib was nineteen years of age and because of this, and the fact that he had lost his father when very young, was treated by all of us in the house like a son. But he had ideas so different from all the rest.

'I will pray to God that you are able to do all this, Sakib, and go back with your head held high,' I said to him with sincerity.

'Yes, yes,' he said, laughing eagerly.

On the days Sakib was too tired to take his shoes off or crawl up the mattress and sat up reading in the trapdoor, Ghulam kept poking his head out of the door every few minutes, saying that it caused disturbance in his heart to see two legs hanging from the ceiling like a dead man's, until he could no longer bear it and shouted, 'Oye Sakiba, your feet will swell, take your shoes off.' Having to pay only ten shillings for rent, Sakib was quite happy in his attic. Besides, he said, when he switched off the light up there, it felt like any other place in the world. In that little place Sakib's thinking had a space that even I couldn't fully understand. In the light of the bare bulb that hung by a wire wound around a nail in the wall, he sometimes read half the night.

Then of course there was Roshan, who once almost made the sky fall on our heads. We escaped, but only just. Roshan Hafizabadi came from a village out in the far interior of the Punjab, where he had worked as a share-cropper on small tracts of land. At the age of thirty, he borrowed money from his father and two older brothers and took it to the agents. Inside of two months, from the wilderness of his village he arrived, confused, in the centre of Birmingham. The first time he ventured outside the house he lost his way. After roaming all day long, dressed in clothes unfamiliar with his body and shoes that were strangers to his feet, he came back to the house looking like a person at death's door, the yellow colour of fear breaking through his dark skin, his eyes fixed at some point above everybody's head. He lay on a mattress under a heap of blankets, shivering through the night. Thereafter, this man of wild open spaces fell victim to a terror of the outdoors. For six days he refused to step outside the house.

Finally, as he was shown a slip of paper – obtained through our usual channels – which offered the opportunity of a job, Roshan took no notice. It made me sad to behold this stalwart, who may have fought singlehanded many an enemy – man and animal – in the broad fields of his village, cowering in a corner of the room and diminishing day by day, disabled by the loss of his world. We had to coax and push him out to go in the company of Zia Mirpuri for an interview with the foreman. He got a job as a labourer. Every morning the two of them would go to work together, Zia leading the way, Roshan dragging his feet behind. After he had attended the factory for two weeks and come in possession of some real money, Roshan's fear of the outdoors began to lift. He was just returning to full health of mind and body when he was ordered to go to another branch of the factory a mile away, to take up the job of general cleaner and sweeper of the foundry floors. He was told of this on a Saturday, and that evening we saw Roshan's old fear returning. He immediately lost his appetite as well as his tongue. We rose early on Sunday and held a meeting, coming up in the end with a workable plan. Roshan could not read or write, but he could count. The proposal I put forward was that, as a trial run, Zia would accompany Roshan that same afternoon to the new workplace and Roshan would count his steps there and back, memorising the various turnings on the way. Poor Zia had to go back and forth three times before Roshan gained enough confidence to take up the route on his own. Within a few days, Roshan had perfected a method: each hundred paces were treated as one unit and ascribed to a finger of his hand. Once he ran out of the ten fingers, he would start with the first finger over again. There were fifteen hundred and forty-nine paces. Many of us saw him walking back from work in the evenings, looking straight ahead of him with eyes vacant, lips moving without making a sound, hands spread and twitching, a man in his own world, the one he had created for himself.

One day, Roshan missed a finger. With that he missed the house. Whether it was a finger less or a finger more, we never knew. But the result was that he arrived at the door of a house which looked exactly the same as ours, as almost all of the street did. Roshan first tried the key, then knocked at the door. The door was opened by an elderly man. Confronted by a strange white face, Roshan turned and ran. He was still running down the street when he met Sher Baz returning from work and came back with him to the house. With one look at his face, its thin skin tightly quivering, we knew something terrible had happened.

'What is the matter?' I asked him.

Without words, Roshan kept looking at his hands, turning them round and pulling at the fingers, flicking them one by one as if to see they were still there. We were still asking questions and receiving no answers when there was a knock at the door. We all froze. Another knock. Someone was tapping at the door with the help of what seemed to be a stick. Panic was now beginning to get hold of us. We had visions of the police having seen Roshan running on the street and come knocking at the door with their batons to negotiate arrests. Whoever it was, would not go away. There was a third knock, and then a fourth Finally, I decided to act on my own. Approaching the door, I pushed a finger into the letter box and lifted the flap, from which I could only see the middle part of a man wearing a suit. The man bent down to take a peep back at me through the opening.

'Is everything all right?' he asked in a kindly, old voice.

'Yes,' I answered.

'A gentleman came to our door,' he said.

'No, no,' I said, without thinking.

After a brief pause, the man said uncertainly, 'He did come – a coloured gentleman.'

'No. Nobody lives here,' I said to him.

'Oh,' he said. Another pause. '*Some*body does,' he muttered to himself, then to me, 'thought I might ask. The fellow looked in some distress. Are you sure . . .'

'Yes, yes,' I said, 'No problem.'

'I am sure I saw . . .'

'Nobody lives here,' I shouted to him through the letter box, 'no-one.'

I dropped the flap and came away. Everyone sighed with relief when we heard the man's footsteps drawing away from the house. In the middle of the discussion that followed as to what was to be done in order to prevent the same thing happening again, Sher Baz jumped up and rushed to his room. He appeared after a few minutes with a green rag in his hand.

'This,' he said, dangling the rag in front of our faces.

'What is it?' someone asked him.

'The sign,' he said, 'the sign. Tie to the door.'

'Why,' said Hussain Shah slapping his thigh, 'did we not think of it before?'

The front door, we decided, was too open a place and would attract attention. Instead, later that night, Sher Baz crept out of the house under cover of darkness and tied the small green rag (green being also the Islami colour, said Sher Baz) to a twig of the thin, half-dry hedge in the tiny patch of our front garden.

After a few weeks, Roshan did not need the rag to locate the house, though the rag stayed, signifying our dwelling but forgotten by the residents, until one night it flew away in a big storm.

4

'Peeng, peeng, peeng,' we shouted.

'Swings,' my father said, 'swings.'

'Peeng, abbaji, peeng.'

'No, no, no,' said my father severely. 'Swings. And daddy. Say swings, daddy, swings. Say it.'

We parrotted after him: 'Swings, daddy, swings.'

It sounded funny and meaningless. It was the first Saturday after we got here and my father had taken me and my brother to the park. There was no sun, the sky was dark and spitting. There were swings and slides and roundabouts in the park and we started shouting 'peeng, peeng' and my father told us to say swings and call him daddy. Once on the swing, we forgot about it. 'Hootay, hootay,' we cried, 'abbaji, hootay.'

My father threw a quick glance at the other kids playing there. 'Not hootay, not peeng, not abbaji,' he said, raising an admonishing finger. 'If you do not say swings, then no push. No daddy, no push. Remember, it is of the paramount importance that you learn English. Forget Punjabi.'

Like rain-frightened birds, we repeated after him in small, fading voices, 'Swing, daddy, swing.' Then he gave us pushes, long and hard and high and we forgot everything else. On the way back I rode piggyback on my father with Hasan up on his arm while my father talked constantly, half in Punjabi and half in English, translating each sentence as he went along. Now that I have lost half of my first language, it has turned the whole way round. Everything I remember is in translation.

The day we got here was a Tuesday. Funny how I remember it after fourteen years. On Wednesday my father took us to the supermarket round the corner. My mother did not know what to pick up. My father got all the food items one by one, telling my mother what they were. At home, my mother just sat there staring at the stuff, which lay untouched all over the kitchen table, until my father put his hand over his heart, took an oath in the name of God, then finally held his head and, invoking both the Quran and the prophet, swore that nothing, not a single morsel was haraam, that each and every thing he had bought was halal, strictly complying with the laws of religion. 'Shops are full of one hundred and one haraam things,' he said to my mother. 'Would I deem it fit to even touch them?' My mother was not convinced. She approached the foodstuffs with halting steps as if learning to walk, hovering over the tins and packets, inspecting them first from one end of the table, then from the other, putting out her hand to touch them with tips of her fingers and quickly withdrawing, as if they contained serpents that would break out and bite her.

That is how I remember them myself. In our village there used to come a nagi, the snake man, carrying a wicker basket with its lid tightly shut. He would place the basket in the middle of a circle formed by all the children of the village out in a field and start to play on the bein, a kind of flute, only thicker and always of orangey-yellow colour. He played it for a long time, blowing hard on it, his cheeks inflating and deflating like two little bladderballs stuck on his face and the blood veins standing on his skin like thick strings, getting thicker and thicker, until suddenly, with a quick movement of the hand, he flipped open the lid and the blackhooded head appeared over the rim of the basket. Slowly it rose, uncoiling its arched shiny back, the great swivelling fan of the head looking nervously to the right and to the left as if astonished by the first light. Within moments, it had fixed its gaze on its master. Two tiny points of the eyes glittering on top of its head, it stood absolutely still for several minutes, as if suspended in the air, before it began to sway from side to side in a wide arc following the movements of the bein, tingling the nerves of our spines with a delicious fear, putting the itch in our fingers for a touch of that beautiful skin. It had nothing to do with things that were haraam, but that is how I always saw them, secret, sinister, with a smooth, silky skin. Even today, having tasted most of that which is haraam, if I see a sign saying 'Wet Paint' I have got to touch it with the tip of my finger, not to defy the notice but merely to have the feeling that I am here, alive and present, perhaps looking still for the serpents.

My mother starved for two whole days, swallowing nothing but gulps of water from the tap. My father cooked our meals for us. My mother would turn her face away from the food while we ate. My father, gripping a morsel of food between his fingers, would walk round to the other side and kneel, facing my mother. Opening his mouth as wide as he could, exposing to our view his tongue, his teeth and the roof of his mouth right to the back of the throat, he would, after first holding it up in front of my mother's eyes, put the morsel in his mouth and start to chew, mumbling, even as he chewed, some verses from the Quran to sanctify the food, and then swallow hard, spreading his hands before her to announce, 'Halal, all halal'. Time after time he repeated it while a slow bewilderment spread over my mother's face. She had a great source of it somewhere behind her face, which I first saw when we were in the aeroplane and I asked her, 'Is it a hundred miles away?'

'Yes,' she said. 'Is it a thousand miles away?' 'Yes, yes.' 'Is it a hundred or a thousand miles away?' 'A thousand, a thousand,' said my mother impatiently, her face lost in great desolation.

So it was a thousand miles away.

It was Thursday evening before my mother finally gave in. She accepted a mouthful from my father's hand and, shutting her eyes tight, swallowed it straight, as if to taste it would desecrate her tongue. So pleased was my father with his success that he took her face in his hands and let out a scream of a laugh, happy and sudden.

That was also the first day we spent at school. The day before that, Wednesday, we went to meet the headmistress with my father.

'N-A-M-E. NAME,' said my father, 'when you hear this word from her mouth, say Parvin, say Hasan. All right? Say it.'

We rehearsed. Easy, the word for name in my language is 'naam', so no problem.

'And when you see her hand in front of you,' he instructed, put your hand in her hand. Like this.'

No problem there either. We spoke our names and shook hands. Then we were off to the clothes shop for my uniform.

At home, shedding my shalwar to try the uniform on, I felt lame, as if a part of my body had fallen off. The socks didn't hide my legs nor stop the wind going up my bum. Looking at myself in the mirror, I saw someone else standing in my place.

It was like the first time I saw my father over here.

Outside the village, between the last of the mud walls of houses and the fields, lay the blacksmith's hut, permanently locked up. It had belonged to my father, mother said. A year before we came here, it was sold off to someone else. Not for me, though. For me the hut and everything in it, including the man who ran it, *was* my father. Playing outside, I always stopped there and looked. Inside, whether it was the morning or evening, the hut was boiling hot. A hole in the ground was full of great lumps of amber which was glowing coal, kept alight with the help of bellows. The rawhide bellows had a nozzle that went into a rabbit hole and stopped just short of the bottom of the coal pit. Every so often the blacksmith, sitting straight-backed, would get hold of the bellows by the scruff of the neck and pull them up, filling them with air, then push down, pumping air into the coal fire, producing, with long blasts through the nozzle, small leaping flames of blue at the top. Into the fire went pieces of iron of various shapes, gradually changing colour until red hot, when they were taken out with the help of tongs and beaten. The flames, in a frenzy for being chased by gusts of wind, escaped into the irons and got trapped, making the irons glow. Then, as the irons got beaten mercilessly, they slowly died. I had pity for the flames.

There were always men sitting around, most of them peasants who had come to have their implements mended, joined, sharpened, beaten into shape. Even at the height of summer, clad only in kurta and shalwar that ended above my ankles, running barefoot as most children of the village, I would still go to stand by the door of the smithy and look. The dirt tracks, strewn with clods of dried earth which were like hot coals, burned the soles of my feet and, from above, the shining silver-sheet of white hot sky boiled my brain. But it was as nothing compared with the hut, inside which burned the same flames leaping fiercely to be consumed by the irons. The men would all be naked above the waist, their bodies burned the colour of mud by the sun and drenched in sweat, streams of it running down like tears from every pore, soaking the folds of rough cloth wound round their hips. They seemed unmoved. Like heavy rocks they sat upon the ground waiting patiently for their work to be done, talking in heavy, slow peasant voices about the land, the rains, the cattle, the cost of seed, the feuds, the living, the dead and the dying, things that were of consequence to them. That sound, though not the words, remains still with me, lodged in a corner of my brain where such things live. And along with that, the smell! As the hour came, the men would undo the knots of their little bundles and spread the cloth on the ground. Inside would be thick roti folded foursquare which they would open out to lay on the cloth, revealing a lump of mango achaar wrapped in the centre, a spot of chutney made of pounded green chilli and salt, sometimes a little earthen cup half-full of daal with a lid on, other times nothing but the roti which they would eat with lassi given them in brown earthen bowls by the blacksmith, who had a pitcherful of it by his side. Accepting the bowls of lassi, they would thank not the blacksmith but God and sit eating, motionless, the muscles and bones of their jaws and foreheads working, appearing and disappearing under the skin, chewing lazily like oxen, as if there was nothing ahead of them and nothing behind but only the eating of this day, within which lived all memory of their bodies at one and the same time. The smell was not of anything, not of the gas from the burning coal nor of sparks from the hot iron nor of sweating bodies nor achaar nor leaves of fresh coriander floating on top of the daal. Neither was it a mixture of all these. It was the smell of heat – of hot earth and bodies black with toil but at rest, not hurried, willing as if for an unbroken passage of days and nights, bullocks, ploughs, crops, the sun. This smell had a shape in my mind and it was the shape of my father because he had built and owned the hut and for me it was all that there was left of him.

'Parvin, Hasan, bolo assalam alaikam abbaji,' said my mother to us at the airport. 'Parvin! Bolo, bolo.'

I didn't. I clung to my mother. My father picked my brother up and kissed him. This man, come to collect us at the airport, looked like nothing I had imagined. He wore a suit and a tie and polished black shoes and he smelled of perfume. We took a taxi. I sat by the window and looked outside, afraid to turn my face to him. If he was my father, then he was in disguise. Standing in the place of my father was someone else – just as here in the mirror stood someone else in my barelegged uniform.

Walking out on the street in my uniform on Thursday I felt not a thousand but a hundred thousand miles away. Everything loomed as if out of a darkness: the houses loomed over the narrow streets, the sky, low and dense, loomed over the housetops. There were no distances. The earth was hard and cold, stiff with stone. This was the land of the jinns.

In our village, during the months of winter, we all sat in the long, narrow mudhut where the maulvi lived and prayed. In the summer we sat outside and, in between lessons, told stories.

'One cold evening, as it was getting dark, the maulvi asked the new boy to go and fetch the lantern nearer to the centre of the room. The boy did not move. Instead he lifted his hand and reached out, his arm getting longer and longer, till it touched the lantern hanging by the wall in the farthest corner of the hut. He plucked the lantern from there and swung it round to place it on the floor where the maulvi was sitting. Then his arm shrank back to its normal size. The new boy was a jinn.'

In the mosque, where all the children of the village went in the evening to learn a lesson from the Quran, we swapped the tales among us while we waited for the maulvi to finish his namaz. We sat on the ground in the broad courtyard in two rows, the boys on one side and we, the girls, on the other, face to face, holding our suparas in our

laps. We kissed and touched the suparas with our foreheads
before we opened them and, later, did the same again before
shutting them at the end of the lesson, although we
understood nothing of the Arabic words written in them,
except that it was good to read and memorise them as they
came straight from God, and if one of us stopped or
stumbled there would be punishment, as when the maulvi
would pull up the erring culprit's hand and bury it deep
in his lap for many minutes to make known God's long
hard staff of fearsome strength. We were in awe of the
words, but there was no love. It was the stories of jinns
that we loved and understood. We knew that jinns could
appear among us in any shape or form, man, woman or
animal, and do things which were not in our power, like
stretching their arm a mile long, or disappearing in front
of our eyes. We knew that there were good jinns and bad
ones, that the good came to the mosque to learn the Quran
and do good deeds, that the bad were ugly and stole
children from their homes and took them away. We were
scared by the stories, but also thrilled. They offered us the
glimpse of another life, running side by side with ours.
There was a feeling of the permanence of time, stretching
far and wide – a space in which nothing ended, lending to
us not just freedom but confidence in eternity. No such
spaces here. Coming straight as I did from the stories of
the village at five years of age, all the people, men, women
and children, wrapped up in many layers of clothing,
looming up suddenly in this half-light and hurrying away,
speaking another language, appeared to me as jinns. Only
they were different: they did not disappear into the air, or
fly in the sky, or fetch objects from afar with a stretch of
the hand. They lived beside me, eating, drinking, going
about, carrying a threat but no thrill, offering no view of
another life. A division, taking birth in my little mind,

took away the certainties from beneath my feet. There was no constancy of time.

On Friday we went to the supermarket. There my mother picked up a few things on her own and we were happy. Having lost my father at the airport on Tuesday, I got him back on Saturday on the swings in the park. That was when I was screaming to him 'oochay, oochay' – high, high. Pushing me with all his force, for a while he forgot about English and started answering my calls. 'Oochay?' he cried, 'oochay?', pushing and laughing, laughing and pushing me higher and higher and higher. Riding on the arc of that flight, flying with my head light as air and the drizzle-wind whizzing past my ears, I had regained him. Within weeks, I lost hold of him again . . .

So quiet in this dungeon. Sound of cars running above coming as if folded within thick fluid. Sixty-watt bulb too weak to penetrate the darkness, I can faintly see the bare bricks of the walls, black with coal dust.

5

Sunday used to be a busy day for us: two entertainments occurred on this day. First came the film show. It was not just a film show, it was the centre of our liberty too. Everyone went. The sick left their beds and the religious their afternoon prayers in order to be there. A crowd of hundreds. The show began at four and our starting time was three. We gathered in the Mirpuris' large room on the ground floor and started calling out to the lazy and the sluggish among us to hurry up. There was no question of going in twos and threes, we all went together – minus those who worked on Sundays. Dressed in clothes clean and pressed, with polished shoes, we started out to the cinema on time. On all the roads there were groups of us going the same way. The police and other white people had no way of knowing who was legal among us and who illegal; they knew that there was a film show on for our people and that all would go. On Sundays, we were all, legal and illegal, one people – although among ourselves we did not fail to recognise each other. Beside the men in our house, if I saw another group going down the street, I knew them at first sight. The illegals had a way about them; they walked very close together in tight groups, and were always trying to look busy talking to each other. They didn't look anyone straight in the eye, didn't look straight anywhere but walked with heads lowered and eyes sideways,

as if looking from behind some object. Even to this day,
though the illegals no longer come in such numbers, if I
see some going about I at once know their reality. I think
sometimes that perhaps, like a twenty- or thirty-year war,
it will one day come to an end, but what about these
people? They will always have these marks on them. It is
not a matter of wealth or poverty, but of respect. In their
own country they might eat three times a day or only once,
but they would give and get respect not because of that but
because their fathers and mothers knew each other's fathers
and mothers and grandfathers and so on. In the new
country there is no family of men to which they belong,
they only have their life and the labour that it makes. This
is the reason that I have a regard for the principle that we
should mix and mingle with the family that is our own
people. What is wrong with that? I have seen and I
remember everything. On Sundays, in those days, in the
middle of this city of white people, many hundreds of our
men gathered, walking and talking and mixing freely in
front of the cinema. Whatever we liked we wore on this day,
shalwar kameez, kurta, chaddar, turban, lungi, anything.
Loudspeakers played our songs at full volume. News was
exchanged: who was coming and who was going, who
was caught and locked up or held up in Germany or
Holland, waiting to come, whose agent was squeezing
whom and who was paying the top rate for black market
currency to send back home. Then the jobs: which factory
was looking for men and how to get in there and through
whom. All this. Some white people passing by stopped and
looked at our crowd and our clothes and listened to our
voices with blank faces and moved on. There were only
two policemen, but they stood on the side and did not
interfere, except when a popular film arrived and the queues
broke up and people started pushing and shoving and
jumping over the top to get to the ticket window just like

back home. Then the policemen came and formed up the queues once again. We had the old feeling within us of being one people out in the open together – it was a time and a place where we regained our lost respect.

Inside the hall, popular songs were played one after the other: Lata Mangeshkar, Rafi, Noor Jehan, all. When the lights went off, the world changed. On the screen were our actors and actresses, our jokes, romantic stories, the scenery of our land. The stories were mostly of the injustices suffered by the poor, the weak and the lovers at the hands of the rich and the heartless. In the end, those living in the huts with no worldly goods side by side with the palaces won their battles against the lords of the earth one way or the other. And although such things never happened in real life, the clever mixture of these plots with beautiful girls and their songs and dances was a culture of our dreams which at once entertained and wrenched our souls in this foreign land. Often I forgot where I was until a few seconds after the lights came back on. When the film had in it terrible things done to people and their families, many of us started to weep. One thing I have seen here, when we leave our country and come to another, our hearts grow soft. Here we can have women and even children, but it is not the same; our tongue and our talk, the way we meet and mix, the light of our skies, long suns and shadows on the ground, our sounds, the touch of our hands, warm; these things. I saw very strong men, they had skill in their hands and money in their pockets, but every once in a while, suddenly, in the middle of doing or saying something, they would break down and begin to cry, as if suffering from a terrible disease.

On the way back home, our faces glowing with health and wellbeing, we talked of the film's story and repeated its jokes. As we got back, home life resumed with the arrival of the prostitute. Many lived on our street, as they still do in that part of the city. Before I arrived there, everyone used to spend their money on their own and got their satisfaction outside. Then the suggestion was put forward by Hussain Shah that this was a waste of money and dangerous on account of the risk of being seen and caught; funds had to be pooled and put to better use. The proposal was accepted and a system established: money went into a kitty and the lot was paid to one girl, who called round to the house, and everyone got satisfaction within a fixed period of time, within the four walls of the house, without risk. Each newcomer was told of the system and was left to decide for himself. Nobody had refused to join except Sakib. But Sakib was only a child in our eyes and we were happy for him to stay out. Hussain Shah, being responsible for running the system, had an arrange-ment with three girls. The girls took turns on a three-week rota basis, and if the same girl came for two weeks running because of the other girl being busy or sick, then for the second week she was paid less than the fixed rate on account of offering no variety. This was agreed upon beforehand and Hussain Shah held them to it with strict discipline.

'Come on boys, feeding time,' called out the girl jokily upon entering the house, and went straight up to the first floor where one of the Hafizabadis' rooms had been earmarked for this purpose. The men followed and gathered outside on the landing and all the way down the stairs while the girl was making preparations inside. First they stood and talked in low voices, then as the proceedings began, joking and laughing started, voices getting gradually louder. I sometimes wondered about this. Perhaps it was because of old habits, formed over a lifetime of attending prayers and funerals. Upon entering a mosque, or at the start of a janaza before the burial, there were the same hushed tones of voices, which later got careless and loud because of quick familiarity. Sex and prayers and deaths

are occasions of the same likeness, so it seemed to me
sometimes.

On account of being the leader and organiser, besides
being a namazi, Hussain Shah had precedence over everybody else. He was the first to go, followed by the other
namazis – two Mirpuris and a Hafizabadi. Those who
prayed regularly, offering namaz five times a day, were
respected in the house, so no-one objected to their taking
priority with the girl and in the bathroom, where they had
already put their shillings in the gas meter for a hot bath
straight off afterwards. After them went the rest. Here the
seniority of residence counted – the longer one had lived
in the house, the higher his place in line. The last to go
were the Bengalis. Although the Bengalis had lived in the
house for longer than some others, they were only two
against fifteen Punjabis; there was no system for them.
Even the girls knew that their position was slight so while
the Bengalis were getting on with the proceedings, there
were shouts raised in the room which were heard
throughout the house. 'Animal,' yelled the girl, 'animal!'
and got rid of the Bengalis in half the normal time. Then
she came out demanding, 'Where is Hussain Shah?' beating
at the door of the bathroom. 'This is the last time, do you
hear me, Shah? They cost me dear if you pay me ten quid
each. Animals!' Every Sunday we enjoyed this little drama,
watching the Bengalis sneak back into their room without
offering any defence. I cannot deny, however, that some of
us felt a little bit jealous of them, thinking what sharp tools
they might possess which the rest of us did not.

It being a free day, the namazis poured their hearts into
the night prayers. Till late we heard their voices in prayer,
weepy and repentant, begging forgiveness. We sat in groups
in one or two rooms on the ground floor, gossiping, playing
cards and listening to the music of our songs on the tape
player. The agents came to receive their weekly installments.

Occasionally there was an argument, but the agents never left without their money. We talked sleepily of many things, of news on the radio, letters from home, families, the cost of land back in our villages, things like that. It was a strange and sad time; voices became weak, as if something, some form of life had left them. We went to bed thinking of the next day, the start of a new week. Factories were safe places, in the factories we walked free. The gaffers looked after our safety, us being handy for cleaning work, loading work, outdoor work in winter, and no sick leave, no casual leave, no absentees, no holidays and no demands for more money, only requests for overtime. The guvners were happy with us, knew our situation, false cards and all, but asked no questions and saved themselves insurance money. We were not, it was said, on their books at all. We were not there, in other words, and for this reason we felt free in the factories, and safe, even more than at home. It was a time like that. We were in the dark and it suited us to not be seen.

6

On the fourth day of our arrival here, the Friday that we went to the supermarket the second time, my father took Hasan and I to the toy shop. I got what my father chose for me – two dolls, clothes and all. Hasan picked up a torch, the biggest I had ever seen, as big as his arm. My father tried to take it away from him, luring him to other items, a football, a little plastic gun, a Dinky truck. Hasan wouldn't let go of the monster torch. Reluctantly, my father paid for it. 'He is not as foolish as he seems, Salma,' my father was to say later. 'I failed to see it at first, but a torch is a useful household item.' For the next three years, while he got through countless other toys, breaking them up, losing interest and throwing them away, the torch remained Hasan's main plaything – his weapon against the world. He was only six when he got it, but carrying it around he looked like a little man with a big stick. Anyone approaching him unawares would see him raising it like a truncheon for protection. In possession of it, even his walk changed – he began to roll on the balls of his feet, as if aping a character from the comics. The first day at home, he took the thing apart, poured out the batteries on the floor, put them in the wrong way round, took them out again, put them back, switched it on and off, on and off. He played unendingly with its four dry batteries, balancing one on top of the other, making shapes with them on his

bed, aiming and hitting them with one another like
conkers, rolling them up and down on pillows, the pavement, the park, wherever he found slopes. What with
constant use inside the torch casing and the abuse they
took outside it, the batteries would run out within weeks,
the light of the bulb growing dimmer and dimmer by the
day. Each time my father would happily buy him a new
set of batteries. Watching him play with the torch, taking
it apart and putting it together again, my father would say,
'Look, Salma, I told you, he is diligent, puts his mind to
a job and works it through to the end. Does not leave
work unfinished. Diligent I say he is. Once he gets going
at school, he will make good progress.'

Until we left the village, all three of us slept in one large
bed, my mother in the middle with Hasan on one side and
I on the other. On the very first night over here, my mother
went to sleep in my father's room. To have a room to
ourselves, with no-one in it but the two of us was like
nothing we had ever imagined. The first two nights I slept
badly; on the third I snuggled into the soft, narrow mattress
and made my peace with it. I arrived at things in this
country more quickly than Hasan, shedding and taking
them up as they came. Within two months, I was talking
to the other kids; at times I even spoke to Hasan in English
at home. It annoyed my mother but pleased my father no
end. 'You don't understand, Salma, for them to speak the
language of this country is of utmost importance.' Hasan,
despite my father's best efforts, stayed dumb for almost a
year, making no friends at school, answering my father
never directly but through me or my mother. My father
kept his faith. The boy needed time, he said. There was
not going to be another son for him, he knew that. 'This
boy,' my father would say proudly, 'has one quality essential
for progress: persistence. He puts his head down and gets
on with it. Don't you, my son?' In reply, Hasan would look

at my father and nod and go on doing tricks with whatever he had in front of him, the torch, the Lego, the football, in order to please, his eyes glittering with a fear, a distance, a love.

Hasan never slept. At first he wouldn't let me turn off the light. I couldn't stand it after a few days and threatened him with screaming my head off, which made him relent. In the dark room from then on he would cover himself with a blanket, making the shape of a small tent, and sit inside it with torch in hand. He would push up the button on the torch, lighting it up. After a few seconds, he would slide the button-hold down. Some moments would pass in the dark, after which he would repeat the process. I would be at the point of dozing off when the faint, dull click of the torch would wake me. I would open my eyes and see Hasan's tent of thin blanket lit up across the room. Noiselessly, I would stare at it, fascinated by this other-worldly sight of a conical shape glowing right in the middle of the dark room. My brain hovering on the edge of sleep, I shivered with excitement, until Hasan would push the torch button down and darkness would return. Then I closed my eyes, waiting for the click and that magical sight to appear. As if promptly granting the wish, the button would click and the luminous tent would come up again. Lying still, I would look at it for ages, dreaming of some other time and place, until I would be overcome by sheer tiredness and fall asleep. One night, having assured himself that I was asleep, Hasan got down and went out of the room. I left my bed and tiptoed after him. He was sitting on the floor of the landing, shining the torch light on the door behind which my mother and father slept. 'What are you doing, Hass?' I whispered to him fiercely. He looked up at me, stood up and came back to bed. Every night after that, I saw him go out of our room when he thought I had gone to sleep. Only once did I follow him again to the door to look, and found him sitting on the same spot in his new, blue-striped pyjamas, doing the very same thing, shining the light on the door of my father's room, as if trying to burn it with its rays. I now had this to contend with: staying awake each night, waiting for Hasan to go out on his nightly trip; waiting, too, for him to come back. After two months of this, my mind, my worn-out consciousness was ready to submit and I was able to go to sleep in my own time, never finding out what time Hasan slept. As we grew up we had separate rooms, and until about a year ago when Hasan started staying out most nights at Janet's flat, I would fall asleep each night listening, however late, to the noises of him moving about, fiddling with his things, rustling papers, tuning his radio, whistling under his breath on the other side of the wall that divided our rooms. Hasan is a creature of the night, living through the dark, yet fighting its element, the blackness.

In those early days, the most I did was complain to my mother, who told my father, and my father said, 'He is energetic, Salma, you must note that. After all, there are two things one requires in order to make progress: energy, and resources.'

My father would sit the two of us by him, my brother in his lap – always Hasan in his lap – and me under his arm, snug beside him, and talk to us.

Back in the village, we had grown attached to our grand-father.

'He was in the war, you know,' my father would tell us.

'What was he doing there?'

'Fighting, what else. In another country.'

'Which other country?'

'Burma.'

'Where is that?'

'Near our country.'

'Why was he fighting?'

'Because there was war. Your grandfather was fighting on our side, the British side. British, friends. Japanese, enemies.'

'Why were they enemies, dad?'

'On account of the Germans.'

I lost interest there.

'Does dada's leg hurt, dad?'

'Not dada. Grandfather.'

'Grandfather.'

'Yes, it hurts. Your leg hurts, does it not?'

'Yes, but he beats it with his stick to show us.'

'That leg, it is made of wood.'

'Grandfather said he had left it far away. Why did he do it?'

'It was cut off, on account of a battle wound.'

'Who made the leg, dad?'

'The hospital. All paid for by the British army. You have seen his medal, have you not?'

'Yes.'

'And not only that. He acquired the skill to till the land with one leg. Your grandfather prevailed over many such difficulties. He is a hero.'

My mind wandered. I missed my grandfather.

'Dad, did you build that hut yourself?'

'What hut?'

'The blacksmith's.'

'Yes. With my own hands, yes.'

'Did you go there every day?'

'Every day.'

'Did you work with fire, daddy?'

'Yes,' he laughed, 'I worked with fire. Every day in the morning I went there, when the sun was rising. The sun in my face, my shadow at the back. All day I had men in the hut. For some I performed work free, for others on promise of payment when the harvest comes. At the end of the day, I came back, the sun in front of me again, setting, and again my long shadow behind me, covering the earth.'

'Did they pay you when the harvest came?'

'If they had good crops.'

For a moment or two, when I was five years old, the two of us, my father and I, together had a glimpse of another world. I remembered those men sitting in the hut at the hour of noon and eating lazily, like oxen chewing cud, for whom nothing else seemed to exist, either before or after.

My mother spoke. 'Your father had hut after long battle.'

'Salma, make no mention of it,' my father said.

'It was battle,' my mother said forlornly. 'Now gone.'

'Forget, Salma, forget. All that lies in the past. We possess this now, this land under our feet, these walls, good, strong walls, roof, all the goods in it, I want to convey to you that this was a battle also. Perhaps one day we will have two houses in our possession. In this country you can do anything you want. No restrictions.'

On Saturdays, he took out his wage slip from his wallet and studied it closely. Then from his pocket he produced his diary. He had stacks of these little Woolworth diaries in the chest of drawers in his room. When one finished, he bought another. The diaries had different columns on their pages into which he entered figures of earnings and expenditure, adding them up each week, thus keeping track of his accounts. These columns had various headings. Income: pay, hours of overtime, total money earned, tax deducted, savings, take-home pay. Then expenses: mortgage, food, household, clothes, hire-purchase, milkman, bills, every other item, all meticulously recorded in his neat, loopy handwriting, many words and figures joined together. Over the years I invented a game that I often played. I would think of a time long past, like a few years before, and try to recall what kind and colour of, say, shoes I had in the summer holidays in that particular year. I would think hard and then go into my father's room in his absence and look it up in the diary of that year. Leafing through to the months of summer, suspense in my heart, as if on the verge of discovery, I would scan the lists in the column, eventually arriving at the correct entry: red shoes, size 5, for Parvin, £2-18s. And if I had guessed it right, it would be a great pleasure, a satisfaction, as though I had control of my life; if wrong, I would be dismayed, with a sense of defeat. The reading of those lists became, in a way, a picture of my life, of me growing up in front of my eyes, a history tabulated in dates, things and money.

On Saturdays then my father would place his diary upon his knee and, after painstakingly entering fresh figures in the columns, tell my mother how much he had 'picked up' that week. That was the main conversation between them each week, the talk of income and expenditure, and my mother waited for it. Every day except Sunday he would work nights.

'Why don't you come home, daddy?' I would ask him at times.

'I perform overtime,' he said.

'Why?'

'To acquire resources, my little dove. In order to provide you and your mother and your brother with all requirements we need resources.'

The first time I heard this I asked, 'What's resources, daddy?'

'Earnings. Everything is earnings-related. To furnish you with food and clothes and gas heating, resources have to be procured. And for good education.'

'It is free.'

'What?'

'School is free, daddy.'

'No, no, much better private education for your brother,'
– cuddling and squeezing my squirming brother to him –
'he will go to private school, and then for high education
to university. All the people who rise to a position go to
private school. The ones whom you see on the telly?
Famous people? Yes. Good education is of utmost
importance.'

'Can I go to private school?' I asked, though I had not
a clue at the time what a private school was, or even that
'resources' meant money.

'*Yeeees*,' he said vaguely. 'Later. You should first stay in
this school. Very nearby, just round the corner, convenient,
is it not?'

'Yes, daddy.'

But I knew even then that I would not go to private
school, whatever it was, now or later; and that Hasan was
different.

My father's lap was reserved for my brother, and for me
a place by his side, on the settee, the bed, the floor, apart,
although it was me who wanted to be in his lap and Hasan
to be out of it. But there he was, from the very first day,
constantly wriggling to escape. Every Sunday, and whatever
other time he found for it, my father would repeat, in
different ways, his two words to Hasan, 'resources' and
'progress': 'Leave the resources to me, just put your energy
into education.' 'We will make a good team, you and I, a
progressive team.' 'Progress depends on diligence. Keep at
it. Keep at it.'

The only progress Hasan made was by way of gradually
worsening reports. At the end of three years, even his torch
was confiscated. He had started carrying it in his bag to
school, and one day he hit a boy on the head with it. By
this time Hasan had taken to beating up other boys at
school. He would push a boy, always selecting one smaller
and weaker than himself, into a corner for no reason and

start attacking him, pulling his hair or hitting him with his bag. There were complaints from parents and the teachers were getting upset. My father ignored the written reports sent to him for some time. 'I blame only the teachers,' he said, 'teachers and other authorities, for negligence and bias.' Finally he was asked to come to the school to see the headmistress. My father returned home afterwards in a state of shock: it was requested that Hasan be kept at home for a week. On the Sundays either side of that week my father said nothing to Hasan about progress and resources. After the week was over, Hasan resumed school. For all the years he was there, Hasan paid no attention to his lessons and took no interest in his books, although by the time he left at sixteen he was able to read and write, eventually becoming an avid reader of newspapers. By then my father had changed to saying, 'He is a dreamer, Salma, you do not understand him, but you should take note that he shows keen interest in things, one day he will come good.' But there were no private schools for Hasan.

7

It was a time like that. The house dated back to the time of Queen Victoria and seemed to have been slowly falling apart since then. Decay had worked itself deep into the walls covered with great big patches where chunks of plaster had fallen off. The damp had made the mortar bulge out in the shape of half-melons and white dust floated down from the ceiling in a continuous drift, as if it were snowing indoors. Rumour was that the house had been on the council's condemned list for ten years. But it was still on its feet and in use, the cunning old landlord extorting rent from us on a regular basis, having both his hands in karahi and his head in halwa, so to speak. I must admit that many of these landlords were our own people. Yet who could blame them? They only did what they did to get their feet on the ground. Breathing in the air full of white lime dust made us ill. Chest colds and head colds and coughs and ache of joints spread to each one of us in turn. We had no medical cards, so no doctor. There was a telephone but it was an instrument of fear fixed to the wall on the ground floor which no-one touched, and if it rang, nobody answered. Ghulam had pneumonia, I think, and groaned from pain in the chest for days, keeping me awake many nights.

It was a long affair, it went on and on. When Ghulam died

we did not know what to do with him. At first everyone
ignored it, only I had to bring my mattress out on the
landing and shut the door on dead Ghulam. In the morning
we all went off to work. When we returned in the evening
and the body was still there, we knew something had to
be done. There was no question of making it known to the
outside world, so we had a big problem on our hands. We
had, in fact, three problems: how to dispose of the body,
how to give it the religious rites (for the pious among us
would not have it any other way), and most importantly,
how to do it without alerting anyone on the outside. First
of all it was decided that all should behave as if nothing
had happened, meaning everyone going to work as usual.
Nothing more was resolved that night and everybody went
off to sleep. The following evening, it was the same story:
nothing settled, because not even discussed. Next evening,
same again. A misfortune, combined with the urgency of
the situation, had put our brains to sleep, so that all we
did was to take our cooked meals to one place and sit
down to eat together – the first time that had happened in
the house. It was as if Ghulam, virtually non-existent in life,
in death had vanished without trace. My mattress remained
on the landing, and the body in the room, with the door
tightly shut on it. In the end, I decided to take steps, and
I advised Hussain Shah to bring Baba Rehman in on it.
Being the one who could read and write English, and of
mature years in comparison with Sakib, I was always consulted by Hussain Shah about important matters. Hussain
Shah took my counsel about dead Ghulam and readily
agreed.

Baba Rehman was not one of us. He was a free man
who lived two streets away and served as an elder to us in
matters requiring advice and help. He was the only outsider,
being not only pious but worldly and wise – having contacts
with the good as well as the bad – in whom we put our

full trust. There was only one drawback: he was forever going on about the political situation back home, whatever the occasion, and had shown enough activity in that direction to become an office-holder of the UK branch of one of the minor political parties in our country. He had left his homeland when still a young man and grown old here, never having gone back, his only connection with the old country being this active interest in the political scene back there. This was one thing we could never understand about him.

Baba Rehman was full of his old talk as he sat down to eat with us but was struck dumb as soon as he was told what the problem was. It was strange and upsetting to see him without words. After some time, as he regained his voice, he insisted upon seeing it for himself in order to make sure. Hussain Shah and I accompanied him upstairs. Hussain Shah opened the door a crack to let him take a peek. Through the slit, Baba Rehman called out Ghulam's name two or three times, gradually raising his voice, the last time almost shouting as though in admonishment. He was very pale and still without speech as he came downstairs. He sat down among us and began to pick crumbs off the floor, collecting them in a small heap. Encouraged by his presence, and assured afresh of the existence of the body by his visit upstairs, all the men started speaking at the same time. For the first time since the death a brief discussion on the matter ensued, quickly gaining breadth and speed, during which several unlikely suggestions were put forward – from hiding the body in the cellar (for how long, no-one said) to taking it to a graveyard, hospital, social security office, even to a railway station and leaving it there late at night. Many voices were raised simultaneously, and Baba Rehman started talking to Hussain Shah about the corrupt tactics being employed by the Selly Oak branch officers of the political party to oust him from the position of Assistant Joint Treasurer. Then just as suddenly, the discussion stopped.

The final proposal came not from Baba Rehman but, once again, from me: it struck me that we could not handle it on our own, it was too risky, so I put forward the suggestion that we ask the agents and their English friends for help. Everyone saw the proposal as reasonable and shrewd, since the agents would be as much concerned with keeping this matter quiet as the rest of us. All looked to Baba Rehman to arrange it for us, as he was the one in constant touch and, some said, himself a partner with the agents. Baba Rehman reluctantly agreed and quickly left.

Now we waited. A day passed, then two, but no sign of Baba Rehman. The body stayed in the room. No-one opened the door, and a slow fear began to rise among us. Various speculations surfaced – that swarms of little ants and insects, accompanied by a foul smell, would start pouring out of the cracks of the door any moment and attack us till we became ill and, like Ghulam, died; then there was the ghost: it was said that if not given a decent burial within three days, the dead man would rise and walk, attacking the attendants for revenge. No-one slept properly at night. The slightest noise, creak of a stair or rustle of the wind, and tired heads would jerk up from mattresses on the floor and peer into the dark. We were all becoming angry.

On the third evening – seventh since the death – Baba Rehman returned. He brought good news, and bad news. He had been able, he said, by begging and bullying, to persuade 'some friends' to undertake the task. But it would cost us money: a hundred and fifty pounds, no less. Considering the risk involved, Baba Rehman said, it was 'peanuts'. The news came as a total surprise. We had been so busy in first ignoring the corpse and then fearing it, going about as though it did not exist or thinking of schemes for getting rid of it, that the question of money had not entered our heads. Once we realised that funds had to be made available, all other concerns vanished from our thoughts. This, naturally, was the biggest problem.

One source of funds was the body: it had to be searched, it must have money on it, or underneath it, or somewhere close by. Where did Ghulam keep his money, they asked me, as if I had been in his confidence. Besides, no-one was prepared to go near the corpse, let alone touch it.

Sher Baz spoke. He was the most pious among us and the one who had insisted that proper religious functions be fulfilled over the body, with the threat that if denied these, the soul of the dead would forever pursue us like a curse and cut down our livelihood. He said that since the corpse had to be given a bath before the namaz and the burial could take place, someone had to handle it sooner or later, so why not now? Hussain Shah called upon the two Bengalis. The Bengalis had been telling us tales of how once, when there were Bengali–Bihari riots in their village, they had to hide in dark corners with the dead bodies of their nearest and dearest for days, until they found a gap in time to get out and bury them under cover of darkness with their own hands. Hussain Shah now said to them that they, being previously familiar with the task, were the ones best suited to perform this function and, he said sternly, to get on with it without further delay.

A thorough search of the body and the bed produced six pounds and fourteen shillings – notes from under the mattress and coins from the shirt pocket. There could be no question about the sum obtained as we were all present, first on account of the Bengalis' refusal to go into the room on their own, and secondly to prevent the possibility of theft. There were no swarms of ants or insects, although a strange smell filled the room. Luckily, it was a cold winter. As we closed the door behind us, our hearts were heavy with the thought that the body had given us a sum of no more than £6 14s. The Bengalis went into the bathroom to wash themselves and stayed there. Baba Rehman said immediately that he could not lift a finger without the full amount in his pocket. When everyone stared blankly back at him, he said, 'You are all involved in this.' I almost laughed. The way he said it was like he was accusing us of putting Ghulam to death.

'They are involved also,' Hussain Shah answered, meaning the agents. 'It is their responsibility.'

'Their responsibility, huh? Their responsibility?' said Baba Rehman angrily. 'Their responsibility is to get you here, then get you jobs and see that no harm comes to you when you are living and working, not when you are dead. There is nothing in the contract about that. You die, your problem. Don't forget that they are doing this as a favour to me, and to you through my good offices. They are not charging a penny, just taking a big risk through my good offices.' He got up to go. 'This money is for expenses, all expenses, petrol and such things.' I had visions of the body being burnt. But it transpired that he was talking about petrol for transportation. 'I cannot stay here talking, it is risky, and I cannot bear the smell. So make up your mind.' Saying this, he left.

At the time there was no smell in the house, other than that in the room. But after Baba Rehman mentioned it, we knew that it would soon spread, and that ants and insects might appear. Still, a hundred and fifty pounds was a large sum. Day and night, we lived for the money. All we ever bought was food and soap, minimum quantities at that, a tape player each for listening to our songs, and that was all. We could not imagine paying for something like this, which was money down the drain.

We all went off to work, some in the day, the others at night, and came back home, to eat and sleep without peace, while the body stayed in the room for the eighth day. Those on the night shift were lucky, for they at least had daylight on their side when they slept, with no fear of the dark, the silence or the ghost. Bad feelings about the body ran high among the men. Everybody began to be mixed up about its identity too: one moment they talked not of Ghulam but of the body, as if it were a separate item, holding it responsible for the trouble, next speaking of it as if it were alive, blaming Ghulam on account of not thinking ahead and providing for such an eventuality. Once again there were some last minute proposals for disposing of the matter, like all of us finding other accommodation and shifting there bag and baggage, leaving the body behind. Or sending a telegram to his family for money by return of post. Only no-one knew the address.

Here, at last, I came to the fore. Being educated and an advisor to Hussain Shah, my opinion carried much weight in the house. It seemed to me of utmost importance now that the matter not be let slip out of control. I said to Hussain Shah that I was prepared to pay my share of the money. It was as if everybody had been waiting for me to speak, Sakib being the first to say that he would pay his share too. Quickly, the matter was settled – although no-one else actually expressed agreement but just silently looked away, accepting fate. A message was sent to Baba Rehman and, on his arrival, the money paid.

There were two more days to wait, as it happened, before the body was to go. Difficult days, of which the memory makes me shudder. The day, or rather the night at last arrived when the religious functions had to be performed before the moment of final departing of the dead. Suddenly that evening, all the bad feelings disappeared – once the money had been paid, it was taken as spent and forgotten. The Bengalis again had to be coaxed into preparing the corpse. The clothes had to be cut away with a pair of scissors. The body had blue patches all over it. A bad smell, of rotting flesh mixed with sweat and urine, arose and spread in the room. The Bengalis, incapable on their own of hauling the body down to the bathroom on the ground floor, looked for help. No-one would volunteer, which meant that the three most respected men in the household, that is Hussain Shah, Sher Baz and I, were expected to lend a hand. The five of us wrapped the body in a sheet from Ghulam's bed and with much effort and care, brought it down two flights of stairs. There was only one mishap: on the second flight Sher Baz lost his foothold and let go of the cloth, causing the body to half slip out of its wrap, feet first, and slide on the bare steps like a bag of grain. Some men who were leading the passage managed to stop it by blocking its way with their legs and bodies, keeping their hands away from it. Several others began to recite verses from the Quran in order to ward off the evil spirits. It was they, the evil spirits, said Sher Baz, who were trying to snatch the body away and claim it for the devil. Be off with you, Satan, they were saying through the holy verses. The body was given a formal dip in cold soapy water in the bathtub, then dried and wrapped in a large clean white sheet. Placed on a mattress in the large room on the ground floor, the body was finally ready for the namaz janaza. Everyone performed ablutions, changed into clean clothes and congregated in the room. We sat in neat rows on the clean-swept floor, covering our heads with cloth caps or knotted handkerchiefs as in a mosque. About half the number among us remembered suras of the Quran by heart and recited them, while the rest sat listening in silence with their heads bowed, lost in the low rhythmic hum of the recitation familiar to us all from birth, though few of us understood the words, only that we were in the presence of God and overwhelmed by it.

The recitation over, we fell in line for the namaz janaza,

movements of which are different from the daily five prayers. Some men made mistakes but quickly learnt to keep their sights on Sher Baz, the Imam, and follow his motions. After the prayers, we sat down and offered fateha, followed by a long and loud prayer of forgiveness, ending with everyone blowing in the direction of the deceased for the sake of his redemption. Our task was done.

Some time after midnight, Baba Rehman arrived on foot. He made straight for Hussain Shah and told him excitedly that he had received from the vice-chairman of the party back home a letter of support, which meant that his position was now secure. Then he told us to wait. Shortly, three men drove up in an estate car that rattled and did not look in good order. Two of these were the agents, the third a white man. This man, stout though not flabby, had a rough voice and was called Fred. He had black hair grown low over his brow and wore a dark suit in which he looked tightly contained, arms held away from his body. It was apparent from the way the two agents kept looking at Fred with apprehension that he was not part of their group but was hired to do the job. He clearly had no feeling for the occasion, though in his own way he seemed competent. With his hands thrust into his trouser pockets, he slowly circled the body, peered at it, bent down and poked his finger into the body at two places, then parted the sheet at one point and took a quick peep.

'Where's the fuckin' garb,' he asked solemnly.

We all looked at him without answering.

'Don't you dress up your stiffs?' he said.

'This,' someone pointed to the sheet. Then as if to demonstrate the arrangement, two men kneeled down, one at each end, and quickly knotted up the sheet at both ends, properly bagging the body in the makeshift kafan. I had the feeling that whatever respect Fred had had for the dead until then, he lost at this moment.

'Well, it's your funeral,' he said, 'give us a hand.'

He clutched at the big knot with his huge paw and picked up the corpse at one end, while the other was carried by the two agents plus two men from the house. They took the body into the hall and waited inside the door. Baba Rehman stuck his head out to look up and down the street. The moment he said all clear, Fred tried to rush through the door with the two agents carrying the front end. But there were some men crowding round the door, just looking. In their haste the agents collided with the men and one of them fell, dropping his side of the body, half in and half out of the door. It struck the front steps of the house. Fred, who was still inside, began lashing out with one hand, pulling the men into the hall and away from the door, hissing with rage.

'What the fff—' he stammered, 'get out of the way, get out, fuck off.'

The light in the hall, as had been decided beforehand, was switched off. The three bearers raced to the car, lifted the back hatch and threw the body into the boot, then jumped in and sped off up the street in the dark without turning on the lights. We saw the brake lights come on at the bottom as the car hit the junction, took a turn and disappeared.

We only got an hour or two of sleep that night before it was time to rise and start for work. Ghulam had lived in that house for over two years. I, his room-mate for four months, was the only one who knew him at all. Ghulam was a quiet, hardworking man. He was only going to stop here for two more years, he told me. All he wanted, he said, was eight acres of arable land back in his village, and once he had bought that, he would go. How was he going to get out, I once asked him? 'Just the way I came,' he said to me with a cunning smile. Ghulam did not often smile, but that day I knew that he had a plan. I took note of it and meant to enquire of him at a later date as to what it was. Eight acres of arable land, that was the purpose of his life. I still feel for Ghulam, a man who desired not a lot and got half-way to it but in the end was thwarted through no fault of his. I grieved for him at the time because he was my room-mate and when he went we gave him none of the respect or honour a man deserves. Now as I remember him I begin to think of him as so close to my own self. Why does a man get defeated through no fault of his? There is no answer. All I want is an answer and there is no-one to give it to me, no voice coming through except my own. There is such silence. In this place I feel as I often did living with sixteen others in that house all those years ago – by myself with my memories. What happened there also happened because no answers were found by anyone, and it was no-one's fault, not Hussain Shah's, not Sakib's and in the end not the woman's either, although it was she who was the cause of it.

8

I was trying to hide, but my mother caught me quietly crying under the stairs. I told her about my bum. 'Kia?' she asked, raising my skirt at the back. Seeing the smudges, she knelt down to put her nose to my backside and made a terrible face. 'Kiyun?' she asked, slapping me on the head. I started crying again. Between sobs I told her about the loo at school. She slipped my pants off me, holding them by her thumb and forefinger away from her body, and went and dropped them in the rubbish bin. Then she gave me a bath, rubbing me all over with soap, mumbling some holy verses to make me clean. As I sat dried and dressed by the fire, she appeared with an empty milk bottle in her hand. This she packed snugly into my school bag. 'Yeh,' she said, telling me sternly to do it properly.

For four days, it went unnoticed. On the fifth they discovered it. As I was filling it up under the tap before going into the loo, Julie saw me. 'What is it?' she asked me. I did not answer her. The word went round. During break the next day, I was sitting inside when a crowd of them under Julie's leadership began to gather outside. Through the locked door I could hear it growing by the minute. They were pushing at the door, bending down to look from underneath, shuffling. I could feel their little fingers on the door like nails being driven through the wood, the air filling up with arrows, their tips gleaming like bats' eyes. Among the giggles, I could make out two spoken words: 'milk bottle'. Julie's voice called out once or twice, 'Hey, Parvin, come on out.' Inside the cubicle, as minutes ticked away, all life drained out of my legs, I couldn't move as if stuck to the seat with glue on my buttocks, couldn't even cry, fear had dried the tears in my hot eyes. I started trembling. It must have been no more than a couple of minutes but it felt like time had ceased at that point. My body was cold and wet and breath began to vanish in my chest. I couldn't stop trembling. The needles of noise in my ears finally came to an end with the voice of Miss Saunders, the PE teacher. 'What's going on?' she asked. Silence. 'Who is inside?' 'It's Parvin, Miss.' 'Parvin who?' 'Parvin Koreshi, Miss.' 'Oh, the new girl. What are you doing here, eh? Come on, move. Go on, it's class time soon.' The crowd moved but didn't go away, I could hear them dragging and shuffling their feet. Miss Saunders called out my name once, twice, three times, then pushed at the door. 'Are you all right? Answer me. Parvin, are you all right?' She started knocking at the door. I wished, prayed, for my mother to come, for my father to appear and stand between me and the door. Nobody came. The knocking got louder and louder, until I thought the door was going to break. Shouting my name, Miss Saunders's voice suddenly filled up with panic and cracked. On trembling legs, I got up and opened the door. Miss Saunders, her face pale and lips quivering, put her hands gently on my shoulders. 'Are you all right?' I nodded. 'You must never lock the door from inside like this,' she said. 'Why do you take your bag with you? You should leave it in the classroom. Here, let me carry it for you. Are you sure you are OK?' She tugged at the bag a couple of times. I wouldn't let go of it. Suddenly, Julie spoke.

'She's got a milk bottle, Miss.'

'Milk bottle? What milk bottle?'

Giggles rose again from the crowd of girls.

'All right, girls, off you go. Go on. Go. You come with me, Parvin.'

In an empty classroom, Miss Saunders shut the door behind us and sat down in a chair. 'Now what's this about a milk bottle? Is it in your bag, let me see, it's all right, I won't take it away. Just let me have a look.' She unzipped the bag.

Putting the bottle hurriedly back into the bag I had left a bit of water in it, which had flowed out.

'Aw,' Miss Saunders said, 'it's wet your bag. Oh, look, the books are wet as well.' She took out the slim books and pads and spread them on the desk, pressing the heels of her hand on the wet spots to dry them. 'What do you do with it?' she asked.

In the empty room, my trembling had stopped. But I was weak with the terror of not being able to express myself. Gesturing with my hands, making signs of slopping water over my bottom and pointing to the bottle, accompanying it with Punjabi words, I tried to explain.

'Oh,' Miss Saunders's eyes widened a little, 'oh.' She recovered quickly. 'I see. Good. Good. Nice. Look,' she kept pressing her elbow over the wet spots on the books, 'actually, you don't have to do that. There's paper in the lavatory, the rolls of tissue paper on the wall? Yes. You could clean yourself with it. Like this.' She used her hands, as I had done before, to mime the action of tearing the paper off, wiping herself with it, then dropping it into the loo and flushing it down. 'You can,' she spoke very slowly, 'clean yourself *completely*. I do it, every day. And I am clean, am I not?' she emitted a little laugh, 'everyone does it. Once you get used to it, it will be easy. You can bathe yourself when you get home, if you like. All right? Now, let's go back to the class.'

I shook my head violently, opened my mouth and started to bawl.

'You don't want to go to your class? All right, all right, all right, we don't go to the class. Right? We go home, all right? Now stop that. We don't want to keep crying now, do we? We go to my office and I'll phone home. No class. Home. Promise. Come.'

Miss Saunders took me home, had a few smiling words with my mother's mute face and left me with her. That evening I saw my father's anger.

'You took a highly foolish step,' he said to my mother, 'giving her a milk bottle. You must consult me about everything beforehand. E-v-e-r-y-t-h-i-n-g.'

My mother said she would not have me coming home with filthy knickers.

'Do you think everybody here is dirty, everyone goes about here with dirty bodies in your opinion? Definitely not. Everybody here is clean without milk bottles. Very particular about cleanliness. It is of paramount importance that she learns how to do it. Look, you do it like this.' He started to demonstrate in front of my face, moving his hands in the air. 'You tear the thin paper off, make a wad of it, grip it between your fingers and bring it behind you like this and then – oh, accompany me please to the bathroom, I will instruct you.'

In my mother's lap, tightening my hold on it, I began to sob. My mother said she would not send me to school if that was what I had to go through.

'What are you talking about? This is the law. Disregard the village and its ways. Here you have to comply with the law.'

It is God's law, said my mother, to wash yourself properly.

'God's law does not work here,' my father said. 'Entire laws here are tested and passed by science, by regulations of hygiene and everything. Good, clean laws. Look, in our home and hearth we can do what we like, nobody can come in and interfere. Outside these walls, we have to do as others do. This is the system.'

It went on like this. My mother wouldn't give. In the end, she had her way.

'All right, all right,' my father said. 'I will go and have a meeting with the headmistress.'

'No,' I screamed.

'What?'

'No.'

'You don't want me to go and speak to the headmistress?'

'No.'

'What do you want?'

'No, no, no.'

I did not wish to go to school, my mother said.

'She will be forced to comply,' my father said. 'This is the law, do you not understand? The law!'

By this time, I had lost him all over again, although I knew now that this was my real father and not someone standing in his place. Nobody was going to come and save me from that small room in the school. As weeks passed and I got through my difficulty as best I could with seized-up bowels, I developed a method for all the world's loos outside the home. I would wait until I had finished, then flush the toilet and pass my arm underneath me to put my hand against the stream of clear water coming down from the cistern. Quickly, I would take several scoops of it and splash myself. Then I would dry myself with the paper and flush again. I became expert at doing it. Julie the bully kept tabs on me, however. She and the other girls started asking me why I flushed two times instead of only once. By now I was able to ignore them, though I had something else to contend with. Although washing myself successfully to keep clean, I was not able to shake off the feeling of dirt that had stuck to me from the very first day. For a long time, through my furious bathing at home and everything, it built up and up before finally sloping off. Nine years later, my father came upon me one evening and made it return, permanently.

'Kafirs,' my father shouted as he slapped me. 'Kafirs!' I was sitting in the back room after my supper as he walked in. I didn't expect him home, he regularly worked overtime during the night. He looked at the television I was watching, then looked at me.

'What is this?' he said, 'what is this you are seeing?'

I suddenly realised it was two naked people making love. I will always remember that. My father grabbed me by the shoulders and pulled me up. I stood in front of him and what I wanted to say was, it's only a film, dad. Instead I said, 'Nothing.' Makes me mad, I can never say the right thing at the right time.

'Nothing,' he said, 'you call this nothing? Is this what you see on the telly when I am working outside like a slave? What happened to the rule, the rule I put down for you with which to comply, that is, no telly after nine?'

'Dad, I'm nearly sixt—'

He slapped me on the face. 'Go, go upstairs to your room.'

It was the first time he had raised his hand to me. It went like a cut through my body down to my feet and into the ground, leaving me standing still for a second with fear that if I moved I'd split in two equal slices from the head down. Then I ran upstairs. In my room, I hovered about the door. I knew what would happen next, and sure enough, my father settled down to watching television and eating hot food, hastily prepared by my mother while she put his sandwiches in the fridge for the next day. I changed into my nightie and climbed into bed, covering myself from head to foot with the quilt.

Why, I kept saying, why? I couldn't even form the question. Some time during the night, I awoke knowing what it was: there were kafirs about – pagans, heathens, non-believers in a Muslim God, the cursed and the condemned who infested this earth! At one time or the other all our people had said so. And I had something to do with it. I felt marked. It was as if a drop of some indelible liquid had seeped through my fabric and spread into a stain that would not be removed. I was sixteen years old then.

'Parvin the milk bottle' was the label that stuck, although I had stopped taking the bottle with me to school. At playtime, during halftime, in the corridors, dining hall, walking back at hometime, it was hurled at me like a rock, hardening me on the outside, beating the inside of me to a pulp. It was a prison in which I spent three whole years, from which I was freed with the arrival of Jenny.

Jenny was the biggest girl in the class and flung her arms and legs, even when walking and talking normally. She took on Julie on her very first day in school. She pushed her against the wall at playtime and said to her, 'I will fuck you.' There were about twenty girls in that corner of the field at the time and each one of them stopped in their tracks, stunned. For several minutes, nobody uttered a squeak. There were tears in Julie's eyes when Jenny let go of her. That was the end of Julie and her gang. The gang did not reform around Jenny. She was different. They stayed away from her big scary face and hammerblow voice, 'De bitches, don' take no shit from nobody' she announced. Only I attached myself to her, trailing after her everywhere, walking back with her from school. On the fourth or fifth day, Hasan and I went with her to her house, not far from mine, her brother Roy, a year older than her, accompanying us. Jenny got the four of us into the empty house with her key. We went into the front room. Roy switched on the television and we sat on the carpet watching the children's programmes. It was a cold house with shadows clinging to the walls and a strange, heavy smell, like rotting melons in the still air. Jenny went into the kitchen and spread some butter on bread for herself and her brother, which they ate with cups of orange squash. She gave a cup each of the orange drink to me and my brother. After a while, I started shivering. Jenny said, 'We're not allowed to light de fire, not fixed proper. George's brother fixed it, he's not a gas fitter. It moves.' She prodded it with a finger and the huge gas fire wobbled back and forth several inches. Two older girls, several shades lighter, let themselves into the house. 'Can't you put the light on, you morons?' one of them said.

Jenny and Roy looked at them and went back to watching the programme.

'Who are they?' I asked Jenny.

'Amelia and Marilyn.'

'They live here?'

'Yeah. Dey George's daughters.'

'Is George your dad?'

'No, my dad live in London.'

It was getting dark, so we got up and left.

Jenny and I were in each other's houses after that, she more in mine than I in hers. Her house scared me; there was never anyone there when we went after school. Her mother worked in a supermarket as a cleaner and came home late with food. Jenny was a big eater. In the end, she was eating in my house almost every day, chewing and slurping our food, chillies and all, just as we did, helping herself to it with her fingers, which she licked and sucked dry afterwards. She ate yam in her home. 'Yam an' beans,' she told me, 'yam an' sausage, yam an' yam, I hate it.' It was the smell of cooked yam, I discovered, left overs uncovered in a pan in the kitchen, that hung in her house.

My father, seeing that I had a friend, was happy at first. Then he became worried. 'Don't you have an English friend?' he asked me several times. Finally I told him, no, Jenny was my friend. He looked a bit dismayed, but stopped mentioning it. Jenny's dad had lived here for some time on his own, too, before he went back to fetch his wife and two small children from Jamaica. After a couple of years Jenny's mother had left her husband and come to live with George. George was a porter on the railways and had his own house. Jenny was terrified of George. 'He picks on us,' Jenny told me. 'He don' let us watch de telly, drinks rum all de time and changes from one side to de udder and back again. Sex and violence, he says, all sex and violence, even when it's de animals' programme wid dem fooling about in de jungle he goes on saying fuckin' sex and violence and changin' de channels. But it's him who does it. Yeah.'

'What?'

'Beats up my mudder and den dey go in de back room and have sex.'

Jenny was only eight months older than me, but she knew everything. She talked like older people, swear words and all. At school nobody dared mock me any more once they knew I was her friend. It was through her I got a partial release from fear and from shame. A time came when I boldly took the milk bottle back to school in my bag and used it openly. If anyone had the nerve to say to me, yuk, you smell, it's the milk bottle you take with you to the lav, I said yeah, because I don't want to carry my shit with me all day like you do. If they said I was filthy because I washed my bottom with my hands and then ate with the same fingers and not with a knife and fork, I said oho, so that's filthy, and what do you wash it with, with your tongue when you take a bath? And what is this you're eating, a sandwich? And what are you eating it with? Oh your fingers! So do you think the shit doesn't rub off on a sandwich but does on mashed potato? Sometimes they saw me wearing a shalwar on the street or wherever and said why do I wear baggy trousers. I said because I didn't want to have cold wind shoot up my arse and shiver with it all day like they did. They began to fear me. I owe this to Jenny and to no-one else. It's the kind of debt you never forget, no matter how long you live.

In the three years that Jenny was at junior and senior school with me, she shot up nearly a foot. It was as if her flesh and bones were jumping out of the earth in front of us. She developed breasts like a grown woman, although she was not yet thirteen. She had had sex. With Rufus, she said, her cousin who lived on the other side of town.

'What happe—' I lost my breath just sitting there as I took this in.

'Only as old as me is Rufus but looks twenty and has a prick equal to thirty-year-old, you know de alleyway by my house? He push me against de wall and he do it.'

'How – did you feel?'

'Fuckin' cold, wid de wind goin' up my legs an' all.'

'No,' I said, 'I mean it being, you know, the first time?'

'What first time, what you talkin' bout, virginity an' all? Are you joking? Dey only make a big thing of it in church and books an' all, it's for rich people, man, it's crap. I felt nothin'.'

One day, without warning, Jenny left. Nobody knew where she went. I went to her house after a few days and George just said 'they're gone' before shutting the door in my face. But only a few days before she left, Jenny had made me discover a state of half-virginity. It was a hot day during the half-term and we had been to the park, running around. Back in her room, Jenny took off her dress and threw it on the floor. 'I'm hot,' she said, spread-eagled and panting on the bed. With no-one else in the house, the afternoon was a total silence. I thought Jenny had dozed off. But she hadn't. She had slipped her hand inside her pants and was rubbing it between her legs with the slowest of movements and with her eyes closed.

'Jenny, what are you doing?'

'Fingerbowl,' she said very quietly.

'What?'

'Doin' my fingerbowl.'

'What in God's name is that?'

'You ever done it, Parvi?'

'Of course not.'

'It's lovely, come and lie down.'

'No.'

'Oh come on, you'll love it.'

'Of course I won't,' I said, but I was already half-way up from the chair.

In time, I grew fond of it. Later still, I became convinced of it. That summer of the year when I was twelve years old, I had discovered a certain power. I straightened my skirt and got up from Jenny's bed to sit in a chair by the window and there was stillness in the particles of my body. A conquest at my fingertips. I remember it with both shame and pride, as if I had finally recognised the mark of dirt-stain on me and accepted it. Jenny had helped free me first from the world, then from myself, so that I could be a little bit more at home in both places. Then she disappeared. I felt angry, raw and red, like some squelched fruit oozing from the splits. There were rumours later on that Jenny's transfer papers had arrived, that she was living and going to school on the other side of town, that was all. It's a big town, the second city they call it. Another seven years passed before I saw her again. By then, Jenny had changed almost beyond recognition.

9

Back from work, I found Sakib sitting on the floor in darkness with his ear pressed to the wall, listening. He made quick signs for me to turn off the light that I had switched on. Extremely quietly he whispered to me, 'Hussain Shah has brought a white woman with him.'

'Who is it?' I enquired, going to sit by his side in the dark.

'Don't know,' he said, making another sign to keep my voice low. After a minute, he said uncertainly, 'Prostitute?'

We sat there with our ears to the wall that divided the room from Hussain Shah's. Hussain Shah was barely literate but he had had enough practice to make conversation in half-English. Most sounds coming through the wall were his, with a few words now and then in the woman's voice. We could not make out what they were saying, but we waited for the woman's voice, and when she spoke, our hearts beat heavily. Our set routine of the night, the cooking and the eating and sleeping, not to speak of my tiredness, was totally put aside. We dared not make a move for fear that any sound or movement on our part might upset the situation and the woman would get up and leave. Every few minutes, Sakib turned his face to me and whispered, 'Prostitute?' and immediately put his ear back to the wall.

'Is she staying?' he asked finally. This was the question

uppermost in our minds: will she stay or go? It was too late for her to go, we silently said to ourselves. At the same time, it was hard for us to put our belief in it. No woman had ever spent the night in this house. Minute by minute, the question kept coming back in layers and settling on our hearts. Will she stay or go? Go or stay? What was going to happen? We sat there for nearly an hour, our bellies drying up with hunger.

Suddenly the voices stopped. For minutes there was no sound. I then tip-toed to my door to take a peep. There was no light coming from under Hussain Shah's door. He and the woman had switched off the light and gone to sleep for all we knew. As long as I had known him, Hussain Shah had not missed a single night from work. We were stunned.

Our limbs began to loosen up, we began to move, though still taking care not to make a sound. Our eyes and ears were fixed on Hussain Shah's door as we quietly started cooking on the landing. Nobody on the floors below had slept, everyone tiptoeing about the house. Several times it happened that someone came up to the bottom of our stairs, stopped there a minute or two, then went back in silence. Sounds of soft feather-like whispers filled the rooms. Even the food did not taste the same as we sat down on our mattresses to eat. It was as if the sanctity of the house had been violated. Sakib told me that earlier Hussain Shah had cooked food and taken it back to his room. This was the first time that Hussain Shah had not gargled his throat twelve times over the sink, nor taken ablutions or offered the evening prayers. He had not gone to work. He had missed everything.

The state of restlessness in the night was such that I could almost hear the tossing and turning of all the residents in beds up and down the floors. In the morning Hussain Shah sent a message through a Mirpuri to the foreman that he was sick. All of us were still gripped by anxiety, but the duties of work were not to be missed, so we went.

Returning in the evening, I was coming up the stairs when I saw the woman on the landing. She was speaking to Sakib. Before I reached the top, she quietly turned and went into her room. Sakib jumped on to the ladder and climbed into his attic like a swift monkey. Only a moment later he jumped back down and entered my room with face pale as turmeric and chest heaving as if he had run a mile. I questioned him.

'What was she saying to you?'

Sakib blanched and lost his tongue for a moment, then managed to blurt out 'Nothing.'

'Why nothing?' I persisted. 'She was talking to you.'

'Yes.'

'Yes what?'

'She was talking to me.'

'Are you stupid? This is what I am saying to you. What was she saying?'

Sakib caught his breath a bit, then said, 'Her name is Mary.'

'So what was she saying to you?'

'She said hello to me. She called me first,' Sakib explained.

'So she spoke to you first. But what was she *saying*?'

'She asked me what work I did, what time I went to work and what time came back. That is all.'

'Why she asked you this?'

'How would I know? Just talking, I suppose.'

'Why just talking?' I asked. 'What else was she saying?'

'Nothing.'

'Don't lie. She was talking to you for a long time.'

'How do you know? You only saw us when you were coming up the stairs before she went back into her room.'

'From the way she was standing in front of you it was

clear she talked more to you. Do you realise that she could be a shaitan sent by the police to inform on us?'

'No, no,' Sakib said agitatedly.

'So what more she asked you?'

Sakib tensed up, thinking. 'Her tummy is upset,' he said.

I kept my eyes fixed on him. Sakib only got more nervous, transferring his weight from one leg to the other in turn, looking blank. 'Her tummy is upset,' he repeated, 'that is all.'

He looked so funny saying this that I burst out laughing. Sakib calmed down a little, laughing with me.

'Our food has made her ill,' he said. 'She said she likes our curry and chapatis but the chillies make her belly burn.'

'Look,' I said to him gently, 'you are a young boy with a clear heart, but we have known the ways of the world. She could very well be an informer.'

'But that is not true,' Sakib said vehemently.

'How can you be so sure?'

'When she spoke to me, I could feel it.'

I shook my head at his innocence.

With our eyes on the landing outside, we sat down on the mattress, joined shortly after by Afzal Mirpuri. That the woman's stomach was bad was proved by her several trips to the lavatory. Each time Afzal followed her with his eyes, stretching his neck, until she closed the door behind her. Then he turned and spoke to us with certainty. 'Prostitute.'

She was young and thin, with hair that fell about her face in curling strings the colour of mice. She wore a loose gown-like dress that hung on her body down to her ankles. On her feet she had thick woollen socks and she wore slippers, walking weakly back and forth.

Hussain Shah returned from shopping. Besides the food, he had brought some new pots and pans. Some time later, the woman came out and cooked some English food for herself. She took the food in the new pans into the room.

After she had gone, we got up and started our own cooking. We were standing by the gas stove when she came out to wash her dishes and pots in the sink. She looked at us and smiled, then softly said, 'Hello.' Sakib responded by saying 'Hello' back to her. The woman stood by us and washed up. On her way back, she turned her head a little to us and again smiled. We stood there, hands idle and tongues silent. Only when the smell of burning food entered our nostrils did we come back to life, quickly pouring water into the pan. We ate in silence, all the things that we used to talk about gone from our heads, no thoughts, nothing. Now, we were familiar with prostitutes and their manners – hard and impatient. This woman, from the way she said hello and smiled at us, did not look to me like one of those. Still, the suspicions in our hearts were far from gone: she had come in from the outside as an unknown and spent a night with one of us. The atmosphere in the house had changed so entirely that all of us seemed to be floating in it, waiting for answers. If she was a prostitute, why was she staying; and if she was staying, then who was she? In our close, protected world a crack had opened and through it were looking two foreign eyes, shaking our foundations. Everyone looked to me, but I had no answers. Afzal Mirpuri, who joined us again after the meal, expressed his fears.

'My worry is that it will all cost us money.'

'Don't be a fool,' I said, 'she is not going to be dead, it is only a little belly upset. Even if she is, it will be Hussain Shah's responsibility. We will have nothing to do with it.'

This, though, was not enough to dispel his dark thoughts. Mary's stomach did not settle. We spent another night half-awake, listening to her going to and fro from the lavatory.

Next day was a Sunday. First thing in the morning, Mary did something that put the fear of God in us. Holding on to the banisters, she went down to the hall and picked up the phone. She leafed through the phonebook for a minute, put a coin into the box and rang the doctor. This was the first time that anyone in this house had dialled a number and spoken to someone. On a Sunday morning, people were usually running up and down the stairs, washing clothes, ironing, cooking, borrowing salt and chilli and other spices from one another, chatting. This morning, the whole house was hushed. On all three floors, we were sitting in our rooms silently waiting for the doctor to arrive. Suddenly the Bengalis jumped up and started cleaning the house. Within half an hour they had brushed, scrubbed and cleaned the kitchen, the bathroom, hall, stairs and all the landings. Then they went back and sat on their mattresses. Our eyes and ears were fixed on the front door. An hour passed. Long years have passed but I can hear in my ears the silence of the house on that day. Another hour went by before the doctor arrived. When the doorbell rang, nobody moved towards it. Hussain Shah went and locked himself in the lavatory. Sakib climbed into the attic and put the trapdoor back in place. I moved away to a corner of the room where I could not be seen by anyone out on the landing. The bell rang again. A Bengali was then pushed out of the room. He went to open the front door but kept walking backwards behind it so that the doctor saw no-one there. After waiting for a few seconds, the doctor called out, 'Hello?' No reply. The doctor stepped into the hall and called again.

'Hellooo.'

The Bengali poked his head out.

'Does Mary Johnson live here?' the doctor asked.

The Bengali dumbly pointed to the top of the house with his hand before quickly slipping back behind the door.

Within five minutes, the doctor had examined her, written the prescription and was finished. Before he left the house, however, a mishap occurred: the hen started to cackle. The hen belonged to Sher Baz.

Sher Baz, being religious, wanted to eat halal chicken and had asked Baba Rehman if he could procure some live chickens. Baba Rehman in turn put the request to a friend of his, a free man who went in his car every other Sunday to a farm to buy fresh vegetables and eggs. That was how Sher Baz came in possession of five live chickens. He slaughtered one straightaway according to the laws of our religion, with his own hands, over the sink in the bathroom. After cleaning and cooking it, he ate it over three days. The other four chickens he put in the cellar. As the cellar floor was flooded with water from God knows where, the chickens stood on the wooden steps, where Sher Baz fed them with pieces of bread on a plate twice a day. One died after two days. With that went Sher Baz's plans of making the chickens last over three or more weeks. He tried to sell them to others but got no purchase from us for the birds were of dubious health. They were becoming a nuisance to everybody. Any time of the day and night and without being given cause, they would start a racket, disturbing the sleep of the household. Since it was a matter of haraam and halal, no-one had the courage to demur. They were big chickens. Sher Baz could only eat half a chicken per day, and that with some difficulty, obliging him to run up and down the stairs several times in an attempt to digest it, causing further commotion. By the time of the doctor's visit, there was only one left.

The doctor was coming down the top stairs when the beast started to cackle with full throat. Two men, one of them Sher Baz, ran out of the ground-floor room carrying a blanket. Slipping through the back room, they tried to cover the cellar door, one of them holding the blanket at the top and the other stuffing it with his fingers into the holes all around the door. The sound got muffled, but the doctor had heard it. He stood by the bottom of the stairs, listening to it. Then he stepped out into the hall and stopped there for a minute, listening, craning his neck to look in the direction of the back room but seeing nothing there. Eventually he turned and went out of the house. The Bengali quickly shut the door. He was trembling.

Hussain Shah emerged from the lavatory and ran down the stairs, admonishing Sher Baz. 'You will land us all in prison, you and your chicken. You want the council to raid us? Eat it, you eat it now, I am going to get it.' Saying this, Hussain Shah pushed Sher Baz away and opened the cellar door. The chicken flew down the steps. Reaching the bottom rung, Hussain Shah slipped and fell into the water. The cellar had no light. In a few minutes, he came back up with curses on his lips and his clothes soaked, dripping with dirty black water. The chicken had disappeared into the darkness.

'You catch it and eat it. All right? Or I will throw it out,' Hussain Shah threatened and went into the bathroom.

The sounds of the house rose slowly at first, here and there, as in the early morning with people waking up. Then it was as if everybody got up and moved all at once, the noise rising like a howl from the pit of the house. Sunday had begun. Sounds of water running from all the taps, pots and pans clanging and smells of frying filled the rooms. Hussain Shah went off to look for an open chemist with the prescription slip. The rest of us got through our Sunday chores, dressed and left for the film show. Hussain Shah stayed behind with the woman.

That day, our feet fell on the ground more firmly and our eyes were bold. There was an invisible energy that propped up our hearts. Once back inside the house, we all went into the Mirpuris' room and sat down on the mattresses, silently waiting. None of us had mentioned it, though we all knew what it was. Sakib got up from among us and ran up the stairs. After only a minute, he ran down again. 'They are in their room,' he said.

We sat there while the minutes ticked away. When Hussain Shah came downstairs to sit with us for the first time in two days, everyone was relieved. He sat there without speaking, just twisting his moustache between his fingers and looking in the air. Then someone spoke to him.

'Shah ji, how is bibi now?'

Some other men mumbled words of sympathy. Hussain Shah nodded in reply. 'All right now,' he said. Immediately he stood up and moved his hand around. 'Here,' he said, 'do it here. And make no noise.'

After he left, the silence broke. A Bengali was got ready to go and open the door the moment the bell rang. He was to make a sign of silence to the girl and quietly take her to the room on the ground floor. There would be no queues outside, no pushing and shoving, no laughing or joking. This decided, everybody sat waiting. The business with the girl that evening went without a sound being raised. Afterwards, we cooked and had our meal. We were washing up when Mary came out of her room to warm some milk. She smiled and said 'Hello.' Sakib and I both said hello in reply at the same time. Sakib got bold and asked her how she was, to which she said she was feeling much better now. We left her at the stove and came back to my room. Returning to her room with the hot milk pan, Mary stopped at our door for just a moment, smiled and said 'Good night.'

We went downstairs to join the others. The agents came and went. We did the usual things – cards, songs – but we spoke in low voices as people did in their homes with other people present nearby doing other things.

10

My mother comes, her elbows out to keep her balance, a winged angel down the narrow stairwell, which is only half reached by the light of the bulb above me. She looks at me with her dry-weeping eyes and sits down in front of me.

'What you do?' she says.

'Do you think I have loads to do in this fff . . . in this dump? Did you speak to him?' I say to her, suddenly angry to hear the shuffling of feet by the door at the top of the steps.

A thick, harsh voice came through the top door. 'Forget, Salma, forget. Let her fall ill. Let her be better dead.'

'Your dad not listen to me,' my mother says.

'Why not? Why doesn't—' I hiss, but give up. I know he doesn't listen to her. Or talk to her even.

There were lots of times when he did. But they were a long time ago. For a year or more after we got here my father would talk constantly to my mother in the time that he was at home, and joke, and laugh. He would take her hand, hold it, touch her on the arm, the neck, the hair, and every once in a while, he would take her face in his hands, covering almost half of it, and bring it very close to his own face, causing my mother's face to turn red. I would be transfixed, unable to take my eyes off them, wishing my mother would do the same, take my father's face in her hands or touch him on the shoulders or somewhere, and laugh. My mother did no such thing. She just pushed my father away, blushing, almost as if in some danger.

My mother spent most of her time cooking, or praying, offering namaz every few hours, reading the Quran and watching television in between. Growing up, I saw my father go through various stages of what he called 'endeavours' to fill the gap between him and my mother. My mother kept having miscarriages one after the other and grew weak until she could hardly walk. The GP sent her to the hospital for an operation and that was that, no more sons for my father. Then he would come home from the night shift and after a big breakfast of parathas and chicken curry, go into the bedroom to sleep, calling out to my mother to come and press his tired legs. My mother would go in and emerge after only a few minutes, pursued by calls from my father to go back in. But with one excuse or the other, housework, washing up, brushing and making a ponytail of my hair and ironing my clothes to get me off to school, headaches and chestaches or whatever, she would stay out. That was the routine in the mornings throughout the week of his night shift: calls to my mother to come in, my mother disappearing for a short time then ducking out; more calls from the bedroom, ending in a groan and then silence. Come the week of his day shift when he would be home nights, my mother would sometimes leave their room and creep into our room at midnight. Finding her by my side in bed in the silence of the night I felt comforted and safe, not only for myself but for my mother as well. That is when he started doing double shifts and talking of 'resources'. I'll say one thing for my father, he never got downhearted, always finding something to replace that which he had to let go. He left home at one o'clock in the afternoon and came back at six in the morning. Other times he left home at five in the morning and returned at midnight. I only saw him on weekends at noon.

On his evenings at home my father would sometimes talk to my mother about back home, of a letter that had arrived or something. On such occasions my mother suddenly came to life, her eyes shining and the colour rising to her cheeks. That was the time when I was most happy, seeing my mother alive and well as tears welled up in her eyes, remembering her people. With great warmth and energy she went on crying even after my father had stopped talking and gone to bed to catch up on his sleep and we, my mother and I, sometimes watched the late programmes on television with the sound turned down, so that from an early age I have this knowledge of a strange sorrow among people that brings up tears of wellbeing, and always it is mixed up with images of naked bodies kissing in large beds. Television held us to itself day and night, though I knew it had nothing to do with us. Only the commercials were real. They were about things that we had in the house. My father would talk about something shown in the ads and say did we want it, to which Hasan said nothing but I said yes, while my mother always said no, that it was not needed or was too dear. After a few days or a week my father would bring the thing home from a sale or it would come by parcel post, and on the Saturday my father would enter the figure of that expenditure in his diary and talk to my mother about it. Commercials became real as nothing else did. Television was the one bright spot in the house and we clung to it. It was years before I couldn't stand it any more. Even today I can watch it in comfort only when I am on my own, never with other people, it's been too long and it is too late. That I was separate from it all came to me shortly after I turned thirteen when I smelled the smell of myself. Living in the house for years, the place, its light and shadows, smell and shape of things, the feel of its air had entered the entrails of my mind, so that I slipped in and out without seeing it because it was there and I didn't have to look for it. Coming back one day, I was not really there but far away, seeing and thinking and feeling and eating somewhere different. I opened the door, and bang! The first thing I knew was the smell. It was like no other smell, not like the smell on the street or in the shops or at school or anywhere. It was fierce and it hit me in the face like a claw. I shifted back to it in an instant, but that instant was a long time. I knew I was different. Afterwards, no matter what I was thinking or whether I was in another world altogether, when I came home I knew that on the other side of my door was a different smell and a separate world.

The smell came from the kitchen. It got into everywhere, the back room and the front room, up through the stairs into the bedrooms, ceilings, roofs. It hung there forever, clinging to the walls and furniture and clothes. It was the smell of onion and garlic being fried in ghee and of other things, turmeric and cumin, coriander and root ginger and the stinging smell of chilli. Of course once I knew that I bore this smell and that it wasn't the smell of our skin or sweat or even the folds of flesh where the hairs grow, I said to them at school that our food was not like the half-boiled cattlefeed that they ate, colourless, tasteless and odourless like themselves. We cook our food, I said, it's an art, we put things in it. But I took all my clothes and put them in the airing cupboard. My mother was puzzled. I couldn't tell her. Most days I came home and my mother would be cooking, producing that wonderful smell which made the saliva gush out from beneath my tongue and fill my mouth with hunger. I came in straight from school and sat in the chair in the back room with the television on while the food cooked. When it was ready I went and sat at the small table pushed against the wall in the kitchen and attacked my food like a hungry beast. My mother stood by the tawa, cooking hot roti one after the other for me to eat as I kept finishing them. When I was full up I drank a whole glass of water, and that was it. I ate no pudding. Once you've had a bellyful of roti and salan you never want to move the taste of it that lingers. I washed my hands afterwards, but not with soap, wanting to keep the smell on them. I brought my hand up to my nose every once in a while, till late at night even when I was in bed, to breathe in the aroma that clung to my fingers. It was lovely. Getting ready for school in the morning I washed my hands four or five times to get rid of the smell, put talcum powder all over them and all over my arms and then on my clothes. 'Rugger, hore rugger!' my mother taunt-admonished me in Punjabi as she saw me scrubbing my cheeks until they were red and black-veined like dead leaves. I understood her and yet I didn't, for already I was in the frame of the school language and out of her range. I stepped out of the house to different sounds and smells. Like a supernatural being, I had walked through a solid wall in an ethereal form without upsetting either the wall or myself, materialising as I emerged into the world of others, crossing from outside to the outside.

Shit, there's a click at the door, hope it's not him. Thank God, it's mum. She comes and hovers about for a few seconds, then sits down. Suddenly, from under her chaddar she produces the thick volume of the Quran, kisses it and lowers her face to touch her forehead with it and then offers it to me.

'What?' I say.

'Quran Majeed,' she says.

'I know what it is.'

'Take,' she says.

'What for?'

'For bahar wallah,' she says.

There are two things our people don't call by their proper name. One is the pig, for fear of soiling the tongue by uttering the haram animal's name, and if somebody does it by mistake they have to rinse their mouth twenty-one times while repeating an ayet from the Quran before it is clean enough for speaking and eating; and the second is a jinn, for the good reason that it's the dweller not of built-up areas but of wild empty places where no-one lives. So each is called bahar wallah, meaning 'one from the outside'.

'What do you mean,' I say to her, 'there's no-one from the outside here.'

'Take,' she says again and keeps looking at me with outstretched hands and eyes.

'What,' I say. I know what she wants me to do, which is to do as she has done, kiss the Quran and touch my forehead with it. Only I am annoyed. 'What?' I say again.

She uses sign language with her hands to tell me to do it. I can't bear her dry-weeping eyes so cover my head in the presence of the holy book with the half of the scarf left to me. I wish she would go away.

'I can't,' I say to her.

'Why?'

'I'm not paak.'

'What? Your blood not finish?'

'It's the piss.'

'What piss?'

'I pissed in my shalwar, for God's sake, what do you expect?'

She withdraws the Quran to her lap. She gets up to go but before she does, she places the holy book on top of the rickety chest of drawers. 'It help,' she says. 'It help all. Word of God.'

'Yes,' I say to her, 'yes.'

Before going up the steps she turns back twice to give me looks full of suspicion as if I had already gone out of my mind. I feel immense relief. The chest of drawers has been bothering me and for a moment I have this compulsion to put the book under the broken leg to stop it from wobbling. Immediately I banish the thought, trembling inwardly with the fear of annoying God and receiving even more punishment. I can't get God out of me ever, or the fear of Him who has an all-seeing eye stuffed into me from the moment I opened my eyes to the world.

Once a month there is a gathering in our house for a prayer meeting. I open the door and the house is full of people. My father takes the evening and the night off work especially for the occasion and he sits in the front room with seven or eight men, Uncle Bashir and Uncle Rashid, my father's colleagues from the post office, Uncle Fazal, an old friend of my father's from when they used to live here together before we came, with whom he has met up again recently, and who is the most horrendous, wearing a scraggly beard of long hairs and weird clothes, white pyjama bottoms that stop short of the ankles and a white loose kurta, a wedge-shaped white cloth cap covering his head and a tasbeeh in his hand with beads that he rolls constantly, reciting something under his breath, moving his lips the whole time. Then there are three or four others, mostly neighbours, drinking coke and lemonade and arguing about politics back home in their country, the price of land in the villages, the state of drought and the floods and the question of shias and sunnis, and disagreeing with each other furiously as if it were all happening just outside the door. Or they have little pieces of paper in front of them on which each has drawn outlines of the land they have already bought back in their villages, showing these to each other, some of them with rough diagrams on slips of paper of houses they're going to build on the land, solemnly asking each other's opinion and inviting sugges-

tions for further improvements in design. Else they are
hatching plots to get their people into this country, legally
or not, whatever. In the back room is my mother, sitting
on the floor with her friends, all of them women from our
neighbourhood, with loose white chaddars wrapped round
their heads and shoulders and enormous boobs and guts
in shalwars as big as parachutes. There's one Auntie Amna
who has such huge ones that Hasan and I have secretly
named them the Hanging Boobs of Babylon. At first they
are usually talking of their relatives back home and what
they say in their letters, or they are fretting over their
children who are of marriageable age and still not married.
I never hear laughter. I have to go straight up and change
out of my skirt or dress and into shalwar kameez. My
mother says that if the word gets back home that I go
round with bare legs no decent family will consider me as
a daughter-in-law. After a while they all start reading from
different parts of the Quran, not looking left or right but
rocking back and forth with heads bowed, making a low
humming noise through their noses while moving their
lips, the idea being to finish the whole book in one sitting
and give the blessing of it over to the souls of saints or
ancestors and other dead relatives. Coming from the
kitchen is the aroma of zarda, the sweet saffron rice cooked
with split almonds and pistachio and cardamom, which
will be eaten by all after the Quran is finished. Looking at
them I always have a feeling that the women lie about how
many suparas they've read. Anxious not to be noticed, I
make for my room upstairs in double quick time and
change into a shalwar and come down, heading for the
kitchen, starving for sweet rice. But I always get stopped.
Shitty me, every time I forget to cover my head in the
presence of guests reading from the holy book. My mother
tells me with a stern gesture to cover my head and my feet
get stuck to the floor in the middle of a room full of people

for what's like ages. I curse myself. It's the same as I curse myself every single time of the month when my mother goes into the bathroom to check whether I'm having my periods. I am eighteen years old, I have four 'O'-levels, I am waiting for an interview for a job I have secretly applied for with the department of social security and all I want to say is 'Fuck'. Nothing to do with fucking, just the word out loud in my mouth and the sound of it in my ears in my house.

It was an ordinary day like this, September, I remember exactly, it was a Thursday. I came home and hopping over the women in the back room I went straight up to my room and shut the door. I opened the window wide and leaned out as far as I could and I said out loud 'Fuck'. I turned back into the room and that was all I wanted to do, say fuck, fuck. Then I put on a shalwar and went downstairs. I couldn't say anything to anyone. I couldn't tell them that when I spoke out of the window, that was a moment when I had a feeling, a fresh and tingling feeling inside me of spilling it all out for everything, for the way they were and what they said to each other and to their friends, women with peasant faces in parachute shalwars and boobs they let loose, and men who talked of nothing that went on anywhere but imaginary worlds and of over-time, of how much they were picking up each week, men in ready-made suits that fitted their size and yet they didn't, as if worn by the wrong species, men with a growth of oily hair, with wide lazy arses in baggy trousers and no sex on them, no sex at all, non-people.

Oh my God, one of them's waiting to come for me from somewhere I have never seen or known, save me dear God . . . Hass, oh Hass, you stupid git, where the hell are you?

11

Mary was a figure of mounting confusion for us: she had caused the set lines of our daily routine to tangle and become uncertain. As for her, once her tummy had settled she slipped into a fixed routine of her own as though she had always been there: cooking English meals for herself morning and evening, drinking cups of milky tea in between and washing up, doing the washing and ironing of her and Hussain Shah's clothes and, as her strength returned, going out to shop. Hussain Shah did his own shopping in the evening on his way back from work and cooked for himself. The two of them always ate in their room. Hussain Shah stopped sitting with us altogether for a time, leaving many questions hovering about our heads, unanswered. In the face of Mary's naturally easy manner which she extended to one and all, our brains became even more addled: we didn't know what to think. The lack of answers created a hole in our lives which gradually filled up with fear. Remembering it now, I can all the more feel the fear of that time and place, as I face another fear of my own in the answerless silence from across this closed door. Ah, fear! I engaged in constant battle with fear, but fear possesses many a visage. In this engagement, from time to time, fear could be made to surrender, as I learned that day when we went out with Mary to the shops. What a blessing it is to be not afraid.

'Aren't you going out shopping?' Mary asked us. She was coming down with the shopping bag as we met her on the stairs. It was still daylight, but we could do nothing. We nodded agreement.

'Come on then, let's go together,' she said.

Sakib and I took our bags and followed her.

We knew of only one way of shopping, and that was to get it over with quickly. Each one of us had a favourite shop where we knew what things were placed on which shelves. We went in, filled up the basket with goods, paid the bill and hurried back. That day it turned out to be nothing like that. Mary first entered a shop and began looking at the prices. She picked things up one at a time and put them back. Then she said in a loud voice, 'This is a bloody dear shop' and walked out. The shopkeeper stared at us all the way to the door. In the next shop, Mary bought two or three things, putting others back after taking a look. Outside, she looked at our empty bags and said, 'Don't you want any stuff?'

Pointing to a shop on the other side of the road, I said to her that we usually bought things over there. She looked shocked.

'Why, that's the dearest shop in the whole street. Even this one is cheaper. Let's get your stuff here.'

We went back into the shop. Mary took hold of our list and selected cheaper brands from the shelves for us. We bought half our things there. Next, Mary got involved in an argument with the shopkeeper woman in another shop. Checking the prices of some items, she remarked that those were sold cheaper in the shop across the road. When the woman answered that cheaper things were of a lower quality, Mary said no, they were of the same brand and exactly the same, upon which the woman said that we were then welcome to go and buy our stuff from elsewhere, adding, 'Who wants customers like you?' Her eyes were fixed on Sakib and me. Mary was already on her way out of the shop, but she heard the woman. She turned at the door.

'All customers are like us here,' she said, 'it's toffee-nosed shopkeepers like you we don't want here,' and walked out.

We were getting nervous. Mary would not change her pace; she kept strolling along, in and out of the shops, as if she had all the time in the world. In the last shop the shopkeeper knew Mary and greeted her as we entered. There we completed our shopping. It was the first time that we picked up things and read the prices, then put them back again and picked up others. We had the choice. Mary stopped at the counter for several minutes chatting to the old shopkeeper. She introduced us to him as 'my friends'. The shopkeeper said 'welcome gentlemen' to us. Outside it had started raining.

We waited at the door for the rain to stop. By this time it had grown dark and we felt safer on the street. After a few minutes we started walking in the light rain; still Mary kept stopping at every shop window, examining goods on display, discussing their prices with us and so on. We were standing in front of a big window showing ladies' clothes when I noticed a policeman on the street walking towards us. Sakib too had seen him. I said to Mary to let us move on, but she said 'hang on a minute' and kept looking at dummies wearing pink frocks. That moment of fear was such that I will always remember the colour of those frocks. I thought of walking to the other side of the street, but how to leave Mary standing there, on what excuse? Sakib and I turned our backs and stood facing the other way. At that moment Mary started off. We could then do nothing but turn back and follow her. We were walking straight towards the policeman, but cautiously in a single file, trying to hide ourselves behind Mary. The constable said 'Hello' to Mary. We stopped, Sakib and I trying urgently to make our bodies shrink behind Mary. I cursed myself and the whole world, for Mary knew the policeman. They chatted for a minute or so, but it seemed like a whole day. The noise of blood in my ears had so blocked off the words from their mouths that I heard them but understood nothing. They were both smiling. Before walking away, the constable joked with Mary. 'What kind of friends are these that won't carry your bags?' he said. Mary looked at us, laughing, and moved on.

Some way down the street, Sakib and I insisted on carrying Mary's bag. Laughing, she finally gave it to me. We slowly walked along, talking, the pressure of the old haste having lifted from our hearts. Opening the door and stepping into the house, we felt for the first time that yes, we really lived here, that it was *our* house.

Things moved swiftly from then on, although they did so over a period of time. In my mind they are all jumbled up, as if they happened in one go, because whilst the household underwent some changes, time inside ourselves had ceased to move. Not having had any choice in the matter, we had got quite used to the idea of Mary living with us as another resident, though we were far from accepting her as one of us. The changes introduced by her in the house were more to our good than bad and pleased us. But every change carried with it also a threat – not of some real danger, for things were getting lighter and brighter, literally so since Mary had bought several sixty-watt light bulbs and fixed them up and down the rooms, the landings and the hall; but rather an anxiety about what might happen – the threat of change. We had felt secure within the bounds of our days and nights in our space, and anything different filled us with foreboding, even though we had no notion of how to reach our ultimate goal, which was to get out of that time and space, get out of the country, and go home. In the beginning we did not know what to think; now we knew not what to feel.

The first time I had the chance to talk to her on my own was on a Sunday morning when Hussain Shah was away doing overtime and Mary and I stood chatting on the landing. Suddenly, she turned and, still talking, walked into her room. I followed her. The appearance of the room had completely altered. There was a table and two chairs. Everything was neat and clean and in its proper place.

'Sit down,' she said, 'I'll make tea.'

This was also the first time I had been inside that room since Mary's arrival. 'Very nice,' I said to her, looking around the room, as she came in with two cups of tea a few minutes later.

'Yes, isn't it?' she said, sitting opposite me in the chair. She had bought a bed, 'from a junk shop' she told me, which was to be delivered the following Saturday. 'Do you like the electric bulbs I put up? It looked like a ghost house in the dark that you lot had left it in. Tell the truth it made me shiver every time I came up the stairs,' she said.

'We didn't mind as long as we could see enough to move about,' I said, laughing.

'Rubbish,' she said, 'you don't need the light just to see, you know, you need it to make room for yourself, for the heart to grow, make contact with the world.'

'It's much better now, of course,' I said quickly.

Encouraged by her open manner, I asked her about herself.

'Nothing to tell,' she said, and briefly told me the story of her life.

She came from the Newcastle area. They lived in a village near the city. Her father was a 'no-good' drunkard who beat up his wife and daughter. One day, Mary's mother stabbed her husband with a knife. He died there on the kitchen floor. Mary's mother was given a light sentence, though she still had to go to prison for a while. Mary and her brother, who was a year older, were sent to foster parents. She was ten or eleven years old then. They lived together at first, then in separate homes and eventually lost contact with one another. When she reached the age of sixteen, Mary ran away from home. For a year or so she stayed around Newcastle and got work, off and on, living in small rooms here and there. Then she joined up with a group of young people who travelled from place to place, with no fixed abode. She found herself in London where, one day, she met a man who came from her village and told her that her mother had been released from prison. Mary then left her friends and went home to live with her mother. By now, Mary's mother had started drinking, and when drunk, abused and beat up her daughter. She had, said Mary, taken the place of her dead father. Mary stuck with her mother for a few months, then left.

She ended up in Manchester. There she found work in a grocery shop owned by an Irishman. After some months there, Mary started living as mistress to the man, who put her up in a room above the shop. After a year's quiet, trouble caught up with her once again. The man's wife, 'a big hefty woman', who lived in another part of the city with her husband and children, 'rolled into' Mary's room one evening and beat her up. Before leaving, she uttered the threat that if she ever saw Mary anywhere in town, let alone in the shop, she would slit her throat. Mary fled. After wandering around for a few weeks, she reached Birmingham. Here she met Jamaica George. George was his name and he came from Jamaica. This man was in the business of running brothels and narcotic stuff such as charas. He was well-off. Jamaica George was in a bad business but he honoured Mary and kept her as his own woman in his house. All the time Mary lived with him, he used to take her out shopping in a car driven by himself or his brother, and on Saturday nights he took her to film shows or to a club in town. But Jamaica George's business was dangerous too, said Mary. One day he was murdered by a rival.

After the death of Jamaica George, his business was taken over by his brother John. John was not an able man, so the business began to slip. John started asking Mary, who was still living in dead George's house, to work for him selling her body. Mary fled once again because of John's threats of violence.

'I will never do business on the streets,' Mary said to me with pride, 'never.' Which struck me as strange, I must admit.

I counted the years in my head from Mary's story and it made her well over twenty years of age, though to look at her I would have said she was not a day over seventeen. I looked at her and wondered, such a hard life and not a sign of it on her face, not a shadow of sadness or anger. And that, instead of clearing my thoughts about her clouded my mind even more. I expected to see some grief on her after her story and found none, not a trace of it, or regret. Her heart seemed utterly cold. It made me make bold to ask her a question I would not otherwise have put to her, not yet anyway.

'Mary,' I said to her, 'what do you think about us?'

'Think about you what?' she said, with the usual ready smile on her lips.

'You know, we are not like your own people, you see the way we live, nobody knows about us, we might as well be dead.'

She thought for a few seconds with a steady stare at my face. 'Amir, I have lived like this before,' she said, 'not once but many times. And then I lived with constant violence. You people stay together, love and help each other. You have left your country once; I felt like I was leaving my country every time I had to run, died each time. This place is alive and warm. Among you I feel free, first time in my life too.'

Her wide-eyed stare, still fixed at my face but now mixed with a small, unsettling smile, somehow prevented me from entirely believing her words. Even if they were true, I thought to myself, did she not perhaps look down upon us a little? Nervously I thanked her and left the room.

Sakib had seen me talking to Mary and was waiting in my room. As I entered, he quickly shut the door and asked me what I'd been talking to her about. I said that we were just chatting. 'Chatting what?' he asked anxiously. 'About this thing and that,' I said. 'What things?' he pressed on. It was like a repetition, only in the opposite direction, of the time that I had questioned him when I first saw him speaking to Mary before any of us had exchanged a word with her.

'Sit down,' I finally said to Sakib and, the two of us sitting on my mattress, I told him Mary's story as she had related it to me.

I got the surprise of my life as I looked up at the end and saw tears in Sakib's eyes. His lips were trembling and he was unable to speak. True, Mary may have been, in the heart of our hearts, something of a fantasy for us, but our uppermost concern had always been to work and earn money. Sakib, with only his old mother back home who had her own house and enough to live on, had no such worries. But on this day my eyes opened to the extent of his feelings for Mary. I became apprehensive about the young boy's state of mind and decided to speak to him at some later time after he had calmed down.

There was a battle going on inside us – our hearts wanting to go out to Mary, our heads holding back with the weight of doubts and suspicions – doubts about her motives, and if not that, then her mere presence amongst us. Why this seesaw? Let me think. It's all bunched up in my head. As much as I am standing in this place facing the door, I am also presently over there, hearing those voices from the past. It has calmed me down. There may be nothing by way of reassurance in all that, but strangely, it has been a source of solace to me as I stand in front of this locked door in this silence. Distance helps. Remembrance too.

One day, we had sight of Mary's stomach and knew why it was that she had worn a loose gown-like dress day and night: she had been with a baby all this time. Whispers of shock flew around the house. We huddled together and tried to match the months that she had been living with us vis-à-vis the size of her belly, eventually coming to the conclusion that Hussain Shah could not possibly have been the father. All our fears from the early days when she first came to live with us, fears which had lain buried because of her harmless and pleasant manner, began to raise their heads again. Hussain Shah's stiff and strange behaviour heightened our apprehension, leaving us utterly confused. Surely Hussain Shah, being more familiar with her body, we reasoned, had known of her condition for some time? Then why his closed face, his avoidance of looking us in the eye and remaining shut in his room most of the time he was home? Although Mary's humour stayed just the same as always, smile on her lips and talk on her tongue as though nothing were the matter, it brought no relief to us. Hussain Shah's down-turned, frowning face held a menace, an anger, a shame that only we the men, not Mary, could understand. With fearful hearts, we waited for something to happen. Something bad.

12

Hasan was missing school when he was still only fifteen and in the fifth year. He was going round with his mate, Ahmed, who drove his father's van. On Sundays they used to go to the markets in town, and on other days out to the suburbs, wherever they could hire a stall for the day. With two suitcases full of jeans and cotton shirts and socks and strings of coloured beads and other trinkets loaded in the van, they put up a stall. Hasan went along as a helper at first, and at the end of the day Ahmed gave him some money to spend. Hasan saved it. After some time, Hasan put his savings into the business and became a one-third partner. Soon they were working three, four stalls each week, selling all kinds of stuff, ballpoint pens and woolly hats and the like, of which they bought job lots at factory auctions as 'seconds'. Hasan read newspapers, every news-paper he could lay his hands on, in the house, at the library, old wrappings from the greengrocers and from the pavement, but never the news, only the ads 'for sale' and 'business opportunities' and the financial pages. Inside of two years they had started going out every day of the week, as far as Walsall and Dudley and all over the Black Country, had bought a van of their own and become full partners. They were shifting a lot more stuff and getting credit terms from the suppliers. I had more dresses and skirts and jumpers and woolly hats and ballpoint pens than I knew what to do with. Hasan sometimes gave me money as well, and he brought my mother material to make her shalwar-kameez with and my mother cried. (My mother cried at every opportunity, as if there were some disease she wanted to shed with the tears.) My father must have known about it for some time, but it was when he saw my mother making herself a suit on her sewing machine from the material he hadn't bought her that he finally confronted Hasan.

I was expecting an explosion. What actually happened was nothing like it. When my brother told him that he wanted nothing more to do with studying, my father, his face a figure not so much of disbelief as of a crumpled hope, couldn't speak for several moments. In a dry, cracked voice, he said 'Why, why,' a couple of times and stopped. My brother just said, 'Don't want to.' All my father did was stand there, dumbly bringing out his little diary from his inside pocket and tapping it with the fingers of his other hand in front of my brother's face, showing it to him, saying not a word. It was ridiculous, there was nothing in that diary but figures of income and expenditure. My brother turned and went out of the house. My father then sat down in the chair. My mother started crying. That day, my father was late going to work for the first time ever. The next two days, my father kept silent; by the third, having come to accept in his heart that his son was not going to get himself an education and become a civil servant, he got his composure back.

'Come and sit here,' he said to Hasan the following Sunday evening. Then, with a calm curiosity, he asked: 'Are you making money?'

'A bit.'

'How much?'

'Some.'

'Tell me the amount. The correct amount.'

'I don't know,' Hasan said. 'We are putting it back into the business.'

'But you are saving some for yourself, are you not?'

'Yes, some.'

'Do you have a bank account?'

'No.'

'Where are you saving then, in your room?'

'No.'

'Where then, in your pocket? Show me. Let me see how much you have saved.'

Hasan wouldn't make a move, so my father thrust his arm into the inner pocket of Hasan's jacket and brought out a wad of banknotes, along with a handful of scraps of paper. He let the bits of paper fall to the floor, keeping a hold on the notes, which he unfolded and began to count. I was surprised to see so much money on Hasan. For the first time in days, my father had a relaxed look on his face.

'Why are you carrying it around with you?' he said. 'It is unsafe to do so. Put it in a bank.'

'We have to buy stuff with cash, dad, can't keep running back and forth to the bank.'

'Put half the money in deposit account and the other half in current account. This way all the money is working for you. Get a chequebook. Are you keeping proper accounts? Show me your account book.'

'Ahmed keeps it,' Hasan said.

'What is your turnover?'

'O, Ahmed keeps track of it.'

'Ahmed, Ahmed! Why do you not keep your own books? You can write, can you not? It is not wise to trust your business partner one hundred per cent. I do not trust this friend of yours.'

'What do you mean?'

'He is a Cypriot, is he not? I tell you, I have experience

of these people. Why do you not have an English partner? They are trustworthy.'

'Rubbish,' Hasan said.

'Don't talk to me like that. Listen, there is a tradition in this country. All big businesses are founded on partnerships, Rolls and Royce, Marks and Spencer. Look,' my father took off his glasses, pushing them in front of Hasan's face. 'What are these?'

Hasan stared at them, confused for a second. 'Your glasses,' he said.

'No, no, no, the question is what is their trademark name and where do they come from?'

'I don't know. Some shop.'

'Then I will tell you. These are Holland & Doland glasses, called after the partnership business which made them.' He tapped the glasses lightly on the tabletop, 'good, strong spectacles, you see. These people know the secret of trade. Outsiders, like your partner, what do they know about trustworthy business? They are only clever at doing underhand transactions. Keep proper company, stay within the law and prosper, that is the motto. You have potential in abundance, I can see that. In abundance, I have no hesitation in saying.'

'We are doing our best, dad,' Hasan said.

'Look, it will profit you to listen to my advice, based on experience. Business acumen, that is the foundation of progress. In the line of work which you have chosen, one thing is of utmost importance: judicious buying. That is it. And proper trading partners will strengthen your hand.'

'Leave off it, dad. We're doing all right.' Hasan swept up the scraps of paper off the floor with his hands, stuffing them in his pocket, and went to his room.

My father said to my mother, 'Did you see the money, Salma, I will bet you that you did not know he had all that money? What he needs now is sound advice. I will see to that.'

Every Sunday evening after that, my father would get Hasan to sit by him on the settee and question him about his progress, offering advice, much the same as before, using phrases like 'judicious buying' and 'business acumen' over and over again, making Hasan squirm. After a few such sessions, Hasan began to stay away on Sunday nights until late when dad, having waited for him to come home, had already gone to bed. That was when Hasan first took up with Janet.

Janet's at least ten years older than me and lives in a flat of her own. But when she paints her face and puts on tight dresses she looks young and flashy. I knew about Hasan and her but I kept quiet a long time, until one day I needed some money and Hasan said he didn't have any. I was furious.

'You've been spending it on that girlfriend of yours, taking her to posh clubs and all, haven't you?'

'She spends her own money,' Hasan said. 'What's it to you, anyway?'

Janet was a whole lot older than my brother and worked as a receptionist at a big hotel in town. I heard rumours that she had been married and divorced once. What I wanted to say to Hasan was, it's wrong. I suppose I was jealous. I wanted to say, Hass, it's wrong. But we never ever said that to one another. Once I was at Samantha's house, my friend from school, and heard her brother say to Samantha about something they'd been discussing, 'It's wrong, Sam, it's immoral.' I was astonished. That was a thing we had never said. It's funny, there's a sticking point somewhere.

'You're dumb, Hass.'

'What do you mean?'

'Just bloody dumb,' I said to him. Hasan just sat there sulking.

Then there was disaster. They had gambled on a huge lot in an auction and it turned out to be a dud lot, containing rejects and out-of-fashion clothes. They couldn't sell them. The factory started pressing for money after two weeks, then threatened them with the courts. They had to sell the van and still couldn't raise the money. Hasan then went to my father and asked to borrow the money, to buy new stock, he said. My father thought about it for a whole day.

'It is in the nature of all businesses, Salma,' my father said to my mother after he let Hasan have the money. 'Investment, that is what it is all about, investment in advance. You reap the benefits afterwards, in the shape of high profits, then invest again, the only way to make progress.'

Now they were left with these seven bales of clothes, neatly wrapped up in rough canvas. First they put these in Ahmed's house. But it's a small house with six people living in it and no back garden, so after a couple of weeks of the stuff dumped in their hall, Ahmed's father told them to clear it. They brought it to our house and put it in the garden shed while the two of them hung about in cafés and parks all day thinking of schemes to get back in business.

One day, a mate of my father's from work saw Hasan and Janet at a pub in the centre of town and told my father. My father took time off his evening shift and came home.

'Your son,' he shouted to my mother, 'is going with prostitutes now.' My mother started crying. My father didn't sit down for a second. He kept going in and out of the rooms, in and out of the house, waiting for my brother. Poor Hasan ran out of luck altogether that evening. In his agitation, my father went into the garden shed and discovered the stuff.

'What is this in the shed?' he shouted. He came through the kitchen door into the back room with a dress hanging rope-like in his hand that he had pulled out of one of the bales. I still remember it was a nylon dress with a ghastly pattern of great big bright red flowers on it. It looked ridiculous in my father's hand, hanging like a limp rag. 'What is this? From where has it come?' demanded my father.

Crying, my mother confessed the whole thing to him. My father was speechless, he didn't even know that the boys had sold the van. Silently, he started tearing up the dress until it flew into small pieces that scattered on the floor. I got up to go.

'Sit down,' my father thundered. 'Where are you going? Where? Sit down here.' He put his hand in his inside pocket and pulled out his little diary. Hurriedly opening it at a page, he pushed it right up to my mother's face. 'You see this?' he put a finger at one spot. 'Three hundred, full lumpsum amount of three hundred. Gone! All gone!' He ran up the stairs, ran down again, went from room to room, got into the garden and stayed in the shed a long time, then he came back and sat in a chair in the kitchen by himself, waiting.

About ten o'clock Hasan walked in. My father jumped up.

'Who is this prostitute?' he asked. Hasan looked quickly at me, utterly confused. 'Who is it? Who is it?' my father kept shouting.

'Who is what?'

'This woman with whom you were fraternising in the pub yesterday.'

'Just a girl. She works in a hotel.'

'Ah!' my father uttered a knowing cry. 'Hotels and cafés,

cafés and hotels, where else? And what is this?' He picked up a handful of pieces of the torn dress and thrust it at my brother's face. 'Lying, lying to me all the time. Going out to business, eh? What business? No education, no nothing, where will you get with this?' he kept pushing the torn dress into my brother's eyes, 'with this, where will you get with this in the world? Liar and scoundrel.'

Hasan looked all around him like a frightened dog, his whole body in a fine quiver. It was as if in an instant he understood the whole thing, torn pieces of dress, the pub, the girl, the rage. He looked to my mother.

'Enough,' my mother said. 'Stop.'

'Shut up you woman,' my father said to her, 'you shut up now.'

'Don't shout at her.'

The words, though uttered flatly, echoed in the room like shots fired from a barrel. This was the first time that Hasan, not yet twenty, had stood and told my father to stop doing something that he was doing in the home. Suddenly, he was standing still, the quiver in his body gone, as if the words out of his mouth had freed him from some vice. My father was simply flabbergasted.

'Why?' he blurted out.

'You are always shouting at her,' Hasan said.

'And why not? Have I no right to shout at her? Who are you to tell me?'

'She hasn't done anything.'

'So you say you are all innocent, right? So you come to her defence because she says so, right?'

'No, she said nothing.'

'So you tell me that she said nothing? What right you have to come to her defence in my face? What have you ever done for her, hunh? This,' he slapped at the arm of the settee he was standing by, 'and this,' he said, walking over to the chair and thumping its back, 'and this, and this,' he kept going round the room, hitting with his open palm all the things, tables, lamps, ironing board, television, pictures on the wall. Then he went into the kitchen. I heard a noise and leaned over to look. Unbelievably, he was trying to drag the fridge over to the back room. It proved too heavy. After a few seconds of wrestling with it, he gave up and returned bearing several things in his arms, the pressure cooker, the food-mixer, the toaster, electric kettle, some cutlery, all of which he let drop on the settee. 'And this, and this, and this,' he said, 'who gave her these? You or me? And this,' he ran over to where my mother was sitting and started touching her clothes, her earrings, the rings on her fingers, the clasp in her hair, finally gripping the gold bangles on her wrists, 'and this, and this. Who provided her with these? Me. Only me. And I have no rights? What have you ever given her? Some no-good material for her shalwar? I tell you what you provided, some material which ripped the very first time she wore it.'

'It didn't rip,' Hasan said.

'It ripped.'

'It didn't.'

'It ripped. And not only from the seams. It ripped in the middle, like this.' He picked up a piece of the torn dress off the floor and rent it to shreds between his fingers. 'Like this.'

'She still has it,' Hasan said forlornly.

'Why does she not wear it then? Ask her. I will tell you why. She keeps it in her trunk because it was the only thing you gave her. You tell him, Salma, tell your son who comes to your defence in front of me, tell him the truth about that no-good material. It ripped the very first time from your – your backside, did it not? Did it not?'

'Stop,' my mother screamed. 'Enough.'

Slowly my father looked all around the room, silently outraged, then sat down on the settee. Hasan went into the kitchen and stopped with his back against the sink, facing the fridge that stood askew like a question mark in the middle of the floor. My mother left her place by the gas fire and began to pick up the things from the settee, returning them one by one to the kitchen. Miraculously, her eyes were dry and her face set, almost at peace. When next my father spoke, his voice was without rage.

'First of all,' he said, addressing Hasan, who was out of his sight though not out of hearing, 'I do not shout at her all the time. That is incorrect. Tell him, Salma, am I shouting at you all the time? No, never. Secondly, you have wasted assets. Depleted your resources. It is proper that you understand this. Thirdly – thirdly—' Here my father ran out of words. He started massaging his temples. 'Come here,' then he said to the unseen Hasan. 'Come.'

Hasan did not move.

'Come, come. Let me talk to you with sense.'

My mother pushed Hasan into the back room. He came and sat in a chair as far away from my father as was possible within the room. My father walked over to him, occupying the chair alongside his.

'One thing, the only thing I said to you by way of advice, you ignored: judicious buying. I have always said that you have good qualities, you will make progress in the future, I can say this with no hesitation. I am prepared to forget what happened, put it down to advance payment in training.'

Within moments, the open, frank look on Hasan's face turned into a furtive one. He didn't move an inch in his place yet seemed to be sinking in the chair, as if slowly dissolving into the seat beneath him. That glinting, rod-like figure that had stood for a moment in the centre of the room when he spoke to my father, was gone.

'You are a good-looking boy,' my father was saying to him, holding on to his arm, 'it helps, I can feel the muscles on your body, good strong bones, you get these from your grandfather. You have all the qualities . . .' The first time he stopped for breath, Hasan quickly got to his feet and went out of the door. My father saw him leave the house and went on speaking, as if to himself, 'all the good qualities, what you need is good guidance . . .' Then he left the chair and came over to sit in the settee, holding his head in his hands.

'Prostitutes,' he mumbled.

13

As Mary's belly grew over the following weeks we got used to the sight of her going about the house, fearful whispers slowly dying on our lips. We saw Hussain Shah's face gradually turning soft, his eyes following the delicately-stepping Mary and his mouth finding the words to address us once again, easing the conflict in our minds about Mary's baby, the source of it, and Hussain Shah.

Then a totally unexpected incident occurred. We had different agents for different people, depending upon which one of us was sent originally by whom from which area back home. All of them were wicked, but Akram Mirpuri's agent was especially so. He had been demanding a sum of money over and above the agreed amount for some time. Akram, having already once paid up the extra amount the week before, refused. We had known from people we met at the film show that this particular agent was extorting. As voices were raised in the hall downstairs, we all came out on our landings to listen. Akram was repeatedly pleading that he simply had no more money to pay while the agent as usual was threatening him with prison and deportation. Mary called out to me from her room to ask what the noise was about. I told her that it was nothing of importance. The voices coming up to us got louder and louder. Mary came out of the room.

'What is the matter?' she asked.

I had to tell her then that it was an agent making trouble. 'What agent?' she said. 'Let's go downstairs.'

Sakib and I tried to stop her, saying it was no use becoming involved in the matter of the agents.

'Why not?' she said. 'Nobody comes into this house and starts messing around with us.'

Mary had been getting weaker by the day. It took her a few minutes to get to the ground floor. She sat down on the bottom step to gain breath. 'What's the matter?' she asked.

The sight of a white woman put the agent back on his heel. He got angrier. 'You stay out of it,' he said to her. 'It's none of your business.'

'It's everybody's business,' Mary said to him calmly. 'Why are you making so much noise?'

'I said it's nothing to do with you, stay out or you'll get it from me. I have dealt with people like you.'

Mary's face flushed with anger. She got up. 'People like me? What people like me? Who are you, what is your name, where have you come from? We are all honest hard-working people living here. What are you yelling about? What – you think someone's trying to rob you? I know your kind. Nobody here has stolen anything from you. Do you think you can threaten us with the police? I know all the police in this area, you will be the first to go, I tell you. No-one who does an honest day's work is illegal in this country. You,' she poked a finger in the agent's chest, 'you are illegal here, do you hear? You and your kind.' Now shouting at the top of her voice, Mary went and opened the front door wide. 'Get out. If ever I see you here again you will go straight to jail, I promise you. Go,' she pushed him, 'get out.'

Startled by the woman's rage, the agent stared at her for just a second before he turned to go out of the house. Mary went and sat down again on the bottom step. Hussain

Shah sat by her side with his arm round her shoulders. After a few minutes, Mary got her strength back.

'There's no need to be afraid of people like him, they are just as illegal as you are. No-one can threaten you—'

This of course was not true. We were more scared after Mary's outburst than we had been before. But her intervention produced immediate results. The agent, who knew Akram worked nights, returned the next afternoon but did not enter the house. He took the regular amount of money off Akram and went away, meek almost to the point of apology. We knew then that we had won a small battle. The news of it quickly spread around the house. The nine of us, including Mary, who were in the house at the time assembled in the Mirpuris' room. We sat on the mattresses and smoked and chatted.

'It's so dark in here,' Mary said, 'pull the curtains aside, it's daylight outside.'

None of the ground-floor rooms had ever had the curtains drawn back. Before Mary got stronger light bulbs and passed them round, all the rooms had sixty watt bulbs. The curtains in the Mirpuris' room were black where even the sixty-watt power bulb was insufficient to banish the darkness of the room. I saw that none of the men got up to go to the window.

'Go on,' Mary said, 'let the light in.'

At last I went and parted the curtains. We all knew every step of the street outside as we walked its length each day back and forth from the factories. This was the first time that I had a view of it from inside that room. It looked different. Then, as I stood in the window looking out, men in the room started getting up one by one to come and stand beside me, until all but Mary had gathered there. An elderly couple was walking down the street, side by side, the woman with her hand under the man's arm. They stopped opposite our house and looked up at the window in surprise. They stood looking for a long time, maybe a whole minute. Inside the room, no-one moved a hair, the lot of us staring out at the street as lifeless dummies. Then just as suddenly, the old couple outside turned their heads and walked slowly away. I thought that I vaguely recognised the man.

'Are they not your friends from the other house?' I asked Roshan with a smile.

Roshan's face turned red.

The elderly man, who had stopped to look at the window from which the curtains had suddenly disappeared for the first time, was the very same one who had come to our door and spoken to me through the letterbox some months previously on the day that Roshan, miscounting his fingers, ended up at the house belonging to this man further up the street. Anyone in the old man's place would be taken by surprise to see eight faces staring back at him, still as statues, after being told that no-one lived here.

That day was some kind of a turning point in our exchange not only with the street but with this country and the world beyond, and indeed with Mary.

The Mirpuris went crazy over Mary. They made her sit down in their room each time she went to the shops, made her cups of tea, gave her cigarettes to smoke and carried her shopping up to her room. Every now and then, either the Mirpuris or the Hafizabadis sent up a plate of salan from their night's meal for Mary to eat. One of them brought it up while the others stood around the bottom of the stairs and called out, 'We put very small chilli in it, Mary, will do no burning to you.'

'Promise?' Mary would ask.

'Promise,' they all shouted back.

Mary would dip her finger in it and suck it for taste.

'Oh, it's lovely. Ooooh – it's delicccious! Thank you,' she would say, 'thank you.'

On the day of her weekly visit to the hospital, Akram Mirpuri would specially wake up in the afternoon and go with her in a taxi for which he paid from his own pocket. Except that when the time came for Mary every one of us happened to be either working or doing overtime, so she rang up for the ambulance and went to the hospital on her own, from where she returned three days later with a baby boy. That evening, Sher Baz held a majlis to welcome the mother and the baby and to bless them.

Everyone who was in the house took quick ablutions, put on clean clothes and assembled in my room. Hussain Shah could have taken the night off but he didn't. We understood his position and made no mention of it. We all sat on mattresses along the four walls, with Mary reclining in a corner, holding the baby in her lap. Each one of us recited an ayeh or two from the Quran, while Sher Baz and the other two namazis recited several. After they had finished, we raised our hands for du'aa. Upon seeing us do this, Mary too raised her hands in front of her. As we wiped our hands on our faces at the end of du'aa, saying Amen, so did she, looking at us and smiling shyly. After-wards, sweetmeats were distributed round from the basket of laddoos and samosas. Everyone ate, including Mary, and we joked and laughed. Then each one of us stood up in turn and gave a pound from his pocket to Mary. Mary accepted the gift of money with a smile and a thank-you to everyone. Hussain Shah remained absent from our company for three days, going to work and staying in his room on his return. He emerged finally on the fourth day, holding the baby. He was stiff with shyness and unduly harsh in manner with others. But he held the baby gently in his arms. It was a lovely baby with slightly off-white skin, the hair and eyes black, lips and nose naturally a bit fat considering its paternity. It never cried except when hungry. Mary consulted with everyone and named it

Michael George, said she might one day change his name by deed poll to Michael George Shah. Such a day remained far off. Ah, but that was the best time of all of the two years that I spent in that house. There were sounds of living in the house. Over and above the thin layer of the hard residue of our doubts and fears, which was merely the dread of someone – an another – who was not like us, we were calmed by the thought that things were working out to our advantage. We even had a faint hope that one day, Mary might prove to be of help to us in escaping from here with money in our pockets to go back home. Soon after the birth, Sher Baz announced to us that the visit of the prostitute had to stop because irreligious acts such as these should not be allowed to go on in a house that had received a new-born soul from God's limitless treasures. We all agreed to this, except for the two Bengalis and a Hafiza-badi, who were told to go and get their pleasure outside. 'Sons of sparrows,' muttered Sher Baz, 'cannot eat till they ride a woman.'

'All right, all right,' said the Bengalis, 'we will stop.' But they continued to go out on Sunday evenings to do business.

14

'Who that?' my mother asked me late one evening.

'Where?'

'That,' she said, pointing to the figure sitting on the wall of our front garden in the dark.

'I don't know.'

I was standing in the window of the dark front room as my mother came up behind me. There was suspicion on her face. She went and put the light on and saw my face turning red. She was the first to see Martin out there but never said a word after that.

'If you sit on my wall again I'll never speak to you,' I told Martin the next day during the break at school. 'I won't walk home with you or anything.'

'Why?'

'Because I'm telling you, if my father sees you he'll kill you.'

'Why?'

'Stop saying why why, dumbhead.'

So that night he shifted. Instead of our wall, he was sitting on Mrs Perkins's two houses down from us. Mrs Perkins would never notice, she's eighty-five years old and goes to bed at four in the afternoon.

Martin had been transfered to our school in the final year.

Three weeks after joining my class he started following me everywhere. Wherever I turned, he was there, big and awkward with a baby's face. Martin is not backward, just a bit slow. He attended a special school some years ago but was supposed to be catching up. At my school they made fun of him and I was embarrassed. I didn't want a dope for a boyfriend, but he wouldn't leave off. He wasn't interested in girls, wasn't interested in other boys or books or school. He just wasn't interested, the way he was. He picked me I suppose because I could look after myself and there were boys after me but I wouldn't let them lay a hand on me. I began to like him. I fought other girls for taunting me because of him, and other boys for pestering him and taking the mickey. Martin offered no resistance. He would sit and wait for me on the steps of the school, regardless of whether it was raining or blowing. I told him he couldn't come to the house or see me any other time because that was the way we lived. He would linger at my door, but once I had said Martin, go, he would go quietly.

A time came that wherever I turned, I expected him to be there. Gradually, everyone at school knew about him and me. After I had said goodbye to him, I would find him sitting quietly on our wall till late. At first I didn't even know it was him, took it to be some kid who didn't know what to do with himself. One evening he moved his head a little to one side and I saw it was him. I turned off the light in the front room and went up to my bedroom. The next evening and then the next after that I couldn't move away from the dark window of my room, looking at him sitting outside. The third evening I could bear it no longer and went out to speak to him. He smiled, with no surprise on his face, as if he'd been expecting me, though he'd sat there for God knows how many evenings and hadn't got to see me.

'What are you doing here?' I asked him.

'Nothing,' he said.

'What do you mean nothing? It's freezing out here. Look, I don't want you to come and sit on my wall at night.'

He got down from the wall and went away.

The next evening he was there again, not even looking at the house but at the road, with his back to the house as if without a care or need. It went on for several more days. That was when my mother saw him. After that he went to Mrs Perkins's wall. I could just about see him from my window. Evening after evening, he sat there, as always looking at the passing cars and the people on the pavement. For three days I stopped speaking to him at school. He sat there while I stood at the window in my dark room until it made my sight blur and my back ache. On the fourth day, just as my mother had started the night namaz, which is the longest one, taking a half hour or more, I went out of the door and sat alongside him on Mrs Perkins's wall. I was furious. Martin didn't say a word, only offered me his ready, silly smile. I looked straight ahead. After a few minutes of silence, I came back to the house and ran upstairs to look out of the window. He was gone. That made me more angry. Next day in school I didn't even look at him.

Not long after that I began coming out of the house in the evenings when my mother was busy cooking or praying in the back room, to sit by him and talk. Martin gave me things. Each day he would bring something out of his pocket, a small shiny metal carton of some foreign chocolate, an almost new golf ball, a discarded ballpoint pen, one time a man's wristwatch that had stopped at half-past five. 'Where did you get it?' I asked him each time, and he said, 'I found it.' He didn't get much pocket money, though his father was rich, owned a factory that made plastic buckets and things, he told me. 'Martin, don't bring me this junk,' I used to say to him, and threw away the things in front of him. That made him miserable, the sod, I couldn't bear that, so then I began to take the rubbish from him and say, 'oh, isn't it lovely,' and throw it away afterwards. I went out for walks with him in the afternoons, began to tell more and more long-winded elaborate lies to my mother and went out with him in the evenings. Once in a while we went to a pub on the other side of town. With little money between us, we managed on half pints.

I remember the day Martin kissed me for the first time. It was a Tuesday, funny how I remember exactly what day it was, remember it as I remember nothing else, a hot day during the time we were finished with school after sitting 'O'-levels. We entered a large park and walked right through it from one end to the other, then walked all the way round it in a circle. A strange mood had taken me. I wanted something, something to do with my limbs, my body, my skin jumping with the thump of blood underneath, my temples hissing like train engines. There wasn't a patch of cloud on the whole blue sky and the sun was straight up there shining hot above my head. Finally, I jumped over a low hedge and sat down, exhausted, on a separate piece of lawn. The place was safe and secret and bright bluish-green and it looked etched into the ground and in the air. I lay on the grass and looked at the sky. Nothing stirred, not a bird or a leaf of the tree, all things were like stone, the sky, the tree, the air, yet were plump and juicy. I moved my face over the ground and gazed at a blade of grass. It was warm and dry but moist at the root and very, very green. Then I saw Martin lying on his back not two feet away from me, half in the shade and half in sunlight, his eyes closed and his body at perfect rest. I let my hand stretch out, to rest against the side of his leg. He squirmed. I stayed with my eyes shut, appearing to be asleep. He became still once again. After a few minutes, I effected another sleep-motion, of having my hand lift and fall lightly on top of his thigh. A brief shiver ran through his body. We kept our positions still. I let my hand lay there, feeling on the inside of my fingers the fine texture of the cloth and beneath it the warm skin within which tiny muscles jumped like small fishes. After some time, I moved my head very slowly, a fraction of an inch at a time, and opened the corner of an eye to look. He was lying there, his eyes open, with a faint grimace on his face and a quiver in his jaw. Next to my hand, I saw his groin swell and swell, becoming big, taking tight little leaps and crossing over to my fingers. There was a power in my limp hand that I felt flow to his body and turn it into an area of hot rising flesh. I felt full, and whole, and strong. Long slow seconds passed. All of a sudden, under my tightening grip on him, he let out a sharp moan. I slid back my hand on to the grass and opened my eyes. Martin was sitting up, looking at me with a slight frown. A moment later, he turned over on his knees. Teetering on his hands, he lowered his head on top of mine and kissed me on the lips. Then he lifted his head back to look in my eyes. I sat up. Martin fell back on to his haunches, then with a violent jerk to his body, stood up. He was standing there by my feet, his round head of short curly hair and tall body outlined against the sky, shoulder muscles showing in the tight T-shirt with arms loose by his side and on his face a great consternation, offence, pity, as if he would begin to laugh or cry any moment. He turned and walked away a few steps, then stopped. I panicked. I jumped up and ran, leaving Martin behind in the park. He did not follow me home.

My first kiss from a man. In my room, hours later, I could still feel the wetness on the edges of my lips. I don't know where the heart lies, underneath my left nipple or where, but it was in my ears and eyes, my lower belly and hips, seeping down to my thighs, the back of my calves and into the heels where I still felt the quiver of flesh that had made me panic and run.

Despite the freshness of it, I could not recall it. It made me cry. Only a feeling remained, some pride and some shame, some threat, some hum in the body, some warmth of breath, the swelling of tears. But no smell. The touch, the touch of the skin, was gone. The moment was ever-present, yet I could not recall it. No matter what I did, I could not bring it back with clarity.

Martin became sillier. He kept laughing, not chuckling but laughing in his own kind of soundless way the whole time the next day. 'Do you love me?' he asked me over and over and then laughed with happiness until I had to tell him, 'Martin shut up, shut your face Martin, please,' I was so embarrassed. After a while, he became silent. The day after that, Martin began to be another man. His face changed, it became, how shall I say, more set, as if the features began ever so slightly to be composed, or recomposed, in their frame, or the frame that was supposed to be there but wasn't before. The laxness of jaw, the wildness of stare, all went. He looked around with intent, sat upright, stepped forth as if taking the earth for his playground with his feet. Was it my imagination? I began to test it. Sitting or standing, moving or still, near or far, I would suddenly turn my head, and Martin's head would turn the same way, as if tethered to mine with unseen strings. Walking in step with him, I would take an unexpected turn, negotiate the wrong corner, even do an about-turn and start walking back on myself, and Martin, without question, would follow my footsteps wherever they went. If I said to him, 'Martin wait here a sec,' he'd wait there an hour until I pretended to forget all about it, and still Martin would be waiting at the spot with his face raised, open to the rain and snow, in the direction that I had taken. It wasn't my imagination; it had happened. One sunny day that year when I was nearly eighteen, I discovered that I had absolute power over another human being. That was when I began to be cruel to him. I wanted the feeling to return again, and again, and to exercise my power over him to the limit the only way I knew. Martin had got a raise in pocket money. One day, with three weeks' savings, he went into a shop and bought a new scarf for me. We were standing on the bridge of the canal when he gave it to me the next day. It was a lovely scarf of pure silk, light as a feather, with a green polka-dot pattern on it. It was the first ever present Martin had bought for me. 'Thanks, Martin,' I said, off-hand, 'You shouldn't have.' Leaning over the railings, I extended my arm over the bridge, holding the scarf in my hand above the surface of the water, and let go of it. It flew about in the light breeze for a second or two, making wavy patterns in the air, before alighting on the water. 'Oops! Go get it, Martin,' I said to him.

'What did you do that for?' he said, and ran.

Round the bridge he went, sliding dangerously down the canal bank, running along by the water while keeping an eye on the scarf floating lazily downstream. He started removing his shoes and socks on the run, hopping along on one leg and then the other. Within moments he had stripped down to his underpants, scattering his jeans, shirt and vest on the sloping bank as he went. Coming up level with the scarf, he made a running dive into the canal. It was an almost deserted Sunday morning. A middle-aged couple, with stacks of newspapers under their arms, and a little boy with his dog, were the only people on the bridge. They had stopped by the railing to watch Martin in the water. The man struck his hands together soundlessly a few times in an imitation of clapping as Martin emerged from the canal. The dog uttered a single bark. On his way back Martin kept picking up his things piece by piece from where he had discarded them. Holding his clothes underarm and his shoes and the wet scarf in his hand, he clambered up the bank. The scarf had changed into the shape of a thin rope, losing all its shine and loveliness. Martin stood beside me, rubbing the seat of his jeans on his head to dry his dripping hair, then on his chest and arms, beginning to shiver in the wind. 'Thanks, Martin,' I said, feeling strong and happy inside myself. In all my days since, I have not crossed that bridge without a sense of pride and a great deal of shame. It was the night of the fight in the pub a little while later that finally stopped me, when Martin, hearing me scream, rose from the ground, oblivious of the blows falling upon his bleeding face.

I was to rue the day I suddenly came across Jenny after all these years.

I hadn't been there before. It was in part of the city where Martin and I strayed one early evening on our aimless, determined walk: severely run-down, dirty old newspaper-strewn streets with tall black houses on both sides falling apart, little patches of front gardens squeezed dust-dry by neglect, full of empty beer cans and other household rubbish under broken windows. It looked like some foreign land almost entirely populated with our people and blacks, mostly men, standing around motionless, their smileless faces splashed with growths of beard and deep suspicion, in tight shabby knots outside small cafés with faded wooden signs above their doors. There were only five or six visible women, hanging about in pairs and on their own here and there. I felt scared.

'Martin, I don't know this place.'

'I know it,' Martin said.

'We're lost,' I insisted.

'No we are not, you see that road, it goes straight to your house.'

'I don't recognise it.'

'It's a long road,' Martin said, 'weaves and winds, ends up near where you live.'

'Let's get out of here,' I said.

'Let's.'

A few paces on, I thought I saw something and stopped. It was a woman's back. She was standing on the pavement with her face away from us, talking to a light-skinned coloured man.

'Hang on a minute,' I said to Martin, 'stay here, I'll be back.'

'OK,' he said, following me all the same across the road.

The woman turned as I approached her from behind.

'Jenny!' I said.

It took her a few seconds to recognise me. I had never imagined her like this. She had very high-heeled shoes on and black stockings that went way up beyond her knees with no sign of the hem of her skirt, hidden under an equally short coat of cheap black fur. She drew a sharp breath and put her hand to her mouth. Her eyes widened.

'Parvin! Is it you?'

'It's me.'

'Fuck me! I can't believe it. What are you doing here?'

'Just out walking.'

'Oh my God, Parvin, it *is* you. How many years it's been? How are you?'

'I'm fine. How are you?'

'Great.' She eyed Martin. 'Friend of yours?'

'Yes. Martin.'

Taking a quick look at him from head to foot, she said hello to Martin with a toothful smile. The man who was with her had moved away and was now talking to another a few feet from us.

'Let's get out of the way,' she said and taking my arm, led me to the side of a shop door. 'Are you still living with your mum or—'

'I am still there.'

'What are you doing dese days?'

'Just finished school. I got four "O"-levels,' I told her.

'Get away, is dat true Parvi,' she screamed, 'you got four "O"-levels? Dat is outa dis world, girl, I'm so glad for you.'

Only dimly aware of my answers, I kept looking at her, nearly out of my wits to come across her suddenly in a place like this. Always a big girl, she was now large, almost a foot taller than me, though she still had her old stick legs which spread out suddenly half-way up the thighs into a huge bum. Her voice, thicker, almost hoarse, had completely changed, seeming to fade away at the end of each word she spoke. Clearly pleased to see me, she nonetheless had an odd stillness in her eyes, a lack of recognition of things, as if they were objects separate from her face, failing to respond to the rest of her quick features.

'Where did you disappear, Jen?' I asked her.

'Back den? We went to live in London.'

'You never said a word.'

'George kicked us out, didn't he, the bastard, didn't give us a day.'

'So what are you doing here now?'

'Oh, my mudder's new boyfriend didn't treat us right and my fadder didn't want to take us in, so my brudder and I came back here.'

'Roy?'

'You remember him?'

'Of course I do.'

'He remembers you too. He's on de buses, good boy he is, earns good money, overtime an'all.'

The man was beginning to look impatiently back to Jenny. He came away from the man he was talking to and headed toward us.

'Get rid of her,' he said without bothering to hide his voice as he passed us and went into the shop.

'Len!' Jenny said. 'What's the matter, it's not time yet.'

Jenny and I stared at each other for a startled, speechless moment. 'I'm working in a club,' she said, glancing nervously at the man's back and at her wristwatch. 'It's time I was dere. Never mind, Len's a partner in the club. It's not every day I meet you.' She laughed, a bit embarrassed but her usual full, easy laugh, though her eyes were unchanged, beady. 'I don't live with Len, not my boyfriend or anyfing, only work in his club. Look Parvi, why don't we make a foursome, me, Roy and you two and go some place nice, what you say? Roy'll be happy to see you, does nuffin' but work all hours poor boy. Yeah?' I hesitated. 'For old time sakes, Par, yeah?'

I'm not a child any more, I had twigged by now what Jenny was all about. And it wasn't that I felt indebted to her for something that happened years ago either. It was just that despite her heavy presence, her weird eyes, rough voice and the way she was dressed, there was a deep vulnerability in the way that she had asked me. Our roles had changed. I was the safer, stronger one. It had startled and also pleased me that she had spoken to Len without her typical hard D but with me she'd slipped back into the speech she used when we were at school together. It sent me back to those far off days and when she said, 'for old time sakes', I couldn't say no to her.

'Great,' she said, 'so it's on den. I'm working through this weekend, how 'bout the next one?'

'Yeah. OK,' I said.

'Right. Meet me by John Lewis's at seven Saturday week, yeah? I gotta run now. Bye.'

15

One day Hussain Shah began making mention of his nephew. We thought nothing of it, only that he probably had a nephew like everybody had a nephew back home. It was not long after that I heard Mary's voice coming from the room. The door was shut and she was saying something to Hussain Shah of which I could not make head or tail, except for the angry tone. A few minutes later she emerged from the room. I was standing there and she did not even look at me. She had unhappiness written all over her face. Holding the baby in her arms, she went straight out of the house. Ever since Mary had come to live with us, she had not been out of the house without some purpose. This was the first time she had stepped out at that time of the night when she had no business. I turned out my light and lay on the mattress, waiting, sleep having fled my limbs. There was no sound from Hussain Shah's room, but I knew that he too was awake. Two hours passed before Mary returned. Still holding the sleeping baby to her chest, she went directly into the toilet. There she remained for a long time, sitting and smoking, as I could smell cigarette smoke coming out of the door. It made me feel uneasy to think of a baby in a small room full of smoke. Finally she came out of there and went into her room. She did not even turn on the light but quietly closed the door behind her. From that night on, Mary was a changed woman. The features of her face became pinched, as if she had been walking in a snowstorm, the skin around them creased like a soft fruit that had withered on the branch. Often she finished her cooking before we returned from work and went back into her room, or spoke only briefly to us, like 'Hello' in passing and that's all, avoided looking at us and even went shopping on her own. Hussain Shah too stayed at work or back in his room most of the time. We the others still mixed, but we sat on the floors below. We chatted among ourselves about Mary and Hussain Shah but had no notion whatsoever of what was going on. The air in the house was like a piece of muslin being stretched taught across the atmosphere. Then one evening, Sakib came into my room and sat down. This is what he told me:

He had come back early from work and found Mary cooking on the landing. Sakib stood around. Finally Mary raised her eyes and gave him a long hard look.

'What is it?' Sakib asked her.

'Hussain Shah wants me to marry his nephew,' she said to him, 'says his nephew is poor, cannot pay the agents, and if I marry him, he can come here legally.'

Sakib did not know what to say. Mary spoke to him with irritation, 'Is this the way to carry on?'

After Sakib told me this, we went down and told the others. Such a thing had never been seen or heard of, everyone said. Sher Baz said that it was against the laws of God and our religion that two blood relatives have carnal relations with one and the same woman at one and the same time. Tobah astaghfar was uttered by all and forgiveness sought. We were all on Mary's side in this matter. Something had to be done. But what? The truth had to be known from Hussain Shah's own mouth first of all, everyone agreed. Except that Hussain Shah was keeping himself away from us. So what was to be done? Whispers and rumours circled the house like trapped birds.

The day Hussain Shah at last appeared among us we heard the story from his lips: 'Who is talking of real marriage? Am I fool that I hand over my woman to him? No sir, I told Mary all, made clear to her it is only a paper marriage, just to go by the law so the poor boy can come in here, that is all. He will do nothing with the woman, position will not change, stays same as now. But Mary has no sense, no brain, does not understand, is very stubborn.'

Some men nodded in agreement.

'You get woman from outside and pay her money to do this or put your own woman forward, what is the difference? Saves money,' Hussain Shah continued. 'You go to office, fill forms and job is done, no?'

More men nodded in the affirmative while others just looked on.

'Look,' Hussain Shah said, 'we are all brothers, and all in trouble. Agents, police, foreman, everybody trouble for us. Hiding, hiding from this, hiding from that, everybody our guvner. This here is chance that one of our own can come in freedom and live in the open, so why not? I was left with no father. My brother, God rest his soul, looked after me. Now his son, poor boy, has no money, cannot pay agents, will borrow from here and from there to pay even aeroplane fare, so what has Mary to lose just to sign a paper when nobody can say no to her in her own country? The boy comes in freedom, is trained electrician, will earn good money. We help him, he will help us. Tomorrow one of us is sacked, then what? Then the boy can help us, no? I have some rights over Mary, brought her in from street and made her queen of my house, have given her respect, food, clothing, all from my pocket. Have I no rights? You are my brothers, nothing hidden from you, her bastard I am bringing up as my own, no? His milk, clothes, many nappies, all is expense from my pocket, what more she wants? Can she not sign a paper? Our first duty is to help our own, our life tied with them, only they treat us good in the end. You tell me, if you are in my place, what you do?'

Most men agreed. Sher Baz said it was true, to give to our kith and kin was our first worldly and religious duty. But what could we do about Mary? Hussain Shah said that she did not answer him nor speak to him any more.

Mary's condition grew worse. Hussain Shah was right, she had stopped speaking altogether, as if struck dumb, her face becoming more and more deserted, her eyes forever fixed on the baby in her arms. Though she continued to cook for Hussain Shah besides warming up the baby's milk two or three times a day, she began neglecting other work. Dirty dishes stayed in the sink for days at a time, clothes piled up which Hussain Shah put in a plastic bag and took to the launderette on Sundays. She used to take good care of her hair, which now hung about her face unwashed in thick strings. She seemed to be walking backwards into herself, the sight in her eyes withdrawn. Sakib told me one night that he had tried to speak to her in the day. He said hello to her and said something like why did she not do as Hussain Shah had asked her? And she looked at him as if she did not believe him. He had the feeling, Sakib said to me, that with that look in her eyes she was saying that she expected other men to say this to her but not Sakib, that she was disappointed in him.

The next time I heard her voice was as I returned from work one evening and found her shouting loudly in her room. Sakib was already out on the landing. The two of us stood there listening. Mary appeared to be speaking another language. In between we heard Hussain Shah's voice, but only yells of 'Shut up – shut up.' In the house, people were coming back from work and stopping on the stairs, on the landings, in the doorways, to listen. Voices in the room kept rising. Suddenly, there were sounds of dull thumps, as if someone was dusting a thick carpet or mattress. There was a brief silence, followed by a heavy thud on the floor. Then we heard the sound of Mary's weeping. We have all, at one time or another, heard our women weeping, with cries and screams, but this was different. It was like someone was trying to catch their life at the throat to stop it from escaping the body – a long and low howl, reminding me of wolves and jackals in the night back in my village. We stood listening to that terrible sound. Slowly, it died down. Only once or twice we heard Hussain Shah's very low voice saying 'sorry', then the light in the room went off. We moved from our places and started cooking and finishing other chores of the night. Sounds of utensils and smells of food arose from each floor. But no voices of men. Just once the light in Hussain Shah's room came on. He appeared with a milk pan in his hand, warmed up some milk for the baby and went back in. We went to our beds with the silence of the house sounding in our ears like that of a graveyard.

Ah, I'm forgetting Sakib. We were all distressed, but what gave me the surprise of my life was the condition of Sakib. As I went to the stove to cook my food, Sakib, instead of joining me, moved to his attic. Attempting to climb up, he slipped on the step ladder. Trying again, he got up to the third step and fell. I hadn't looked at him until then. He was shivering like a bamboo shoot in a storm. I had to virtually pick him up off the floor and take him into my room. Settling him on my mattress, I asked him, 'Are you ill?'

He could only stammer out, 'N-no.'

'What is the matter, Sakib?' I asked him quietly.

He looked at me dumbly with his eyes full of a strange terror.

'What is it, Sakib?' I asked again.

'Shhhe's an – angel,' he said in a trembling whisper.

'Lie down here,' I said to him, 'I will get you a glass of water.'

'No, no,' he said, recovering a little but still choking on his words, 'I want – to go to my room.'

I supported him up the step ladder. Climbing into the attic, he put the trapdoor back in place. After I had cooked a meal, I called out to him to come and have something to eat. He did not answer. A young boy like Sakib, I thought, away from his mother's love and cooking, had no business to be here. He should have been back home and married to a nice girl instead of in a confusing situation like this. And confusing it had surely become: we did not know who to blame any more. Blaming Hussain Shah was like marking all of us as guilty. It was two days before Mary came out of the room, looking weak with dark rings round her eyes, although we noticed a change in her from the very first: she looked straight up at our faces now with unfamiliar but determined eyes. Fortunately for us, she began to recover quickly, her natural behaviour slipping back to what it had been – standing with us on the landing, cooking and talking and the smile returning to her lips as she gained strength. The shock we had received also began to wear off. What we found in the coming days was that Mary had come out with a will of her own. If she was cheerful and nice before, she was now free and frank. Even to Hussain Shah, in front of everyone, she said, 'Hussain do this, Hussain don't do that, Hussain don't you under- stand, how many times do I have to tell you?' She objected to our ways, openly criticising our actions, our habits. She went through the house during the day and instead of sitting and smoking and talking with us, picked out small things, a patch of dirt on the stairs, a bit of food dropped on the floor, and screwed up her nose. 'Come, lazy thing,' she said to anyone who was around, 'clean this up. Remember, if you don't clean where you live, you make the place a pigsty, and you know who lives in pigsties, don't you?' And if there was nothing to clean and the mood came upon her, she just said, 'Why are you sitting doing nothing? Come and help me.'

The odd thing was that we all liked her to be like this. She gave out a feeling of strength and we felt sheltered by it. Hussain Shah went around cheerfully following Mary's instructions, Sakib got increasingly anxious and did what Mary said and very often even that which she didn't. I had determined to find a quiet moment to speak to him, that he should not hang his heart on something that was not his and might wound it, at times wishing that he had taken part with the rest of us in the business with the prostitute so that he could have seen another face of love between men and women besides the one he found in books and in his imaginings. But our lives were such that it was some time before I got the chance. Meanwhile, Mary had been going out often on her own, wearing nice dresses and make-up on her face. Her new self, added to the dark circles around her eyes, which had stayed but were now partly covered with creams and powders, made her look a bit older and, I must admit, more attractive. She was entering into her own independence. One fine day she came in and got us all together.

'There will be some people coming to see me,' she said to us, 'nothing to worry about, they don't want to know about you, are only coming to have a chat with me. So don't do anything silly when they come, just go about as normal. All right?'

True enough, two men came in the afternoon the next day. Sakib, who was at home, off sick, saw them. On hearing the doorbell ring, he immediately climbed into his attic and put the trapdoor down, leaving a slit open through which, he told me later, he kept looking. They wore no uniforms but he could guess that they were policemen. Mary quickly put the baby on the mattress in my room and shut the door. Mary's room was the best of all the rooms, with the only proper bed in the whole house on one side and on the other a table and two chairs. In the second corner was another slightly larger table on which were placed cooking pots and pans, three plates and cups and saucers and tins of food. By the bed she had a dressing table with a mirror fixed on it, and a tall table lamp near the head of the bed. It was also the only room with thin lace curtains at the window behind thick cloth ones. The two men sat in the chairs and talked with Mary, drinking cups of tea which she had made for them. After fifteen minutes they left. Mary went down to the front door to say goodbye to them.

'No problem,' she said as she came up to Sakib, who had jumped down from the attic. We the men sat together later that day, without Hussain Shah or Mary, and talked among ourselves. We knew what was going on but were not upset by it. Our spirits in fact were up on account of the fact that policemen had visited the house and none of them had paid attention to any of us. Within days, a telegram arrived and Hussain Shah and Mary went off by coach to London. Late in the evening, they came back with Irshad, Hussain Shah's nephew. Mary was talking with Irshad in the same way that she did with everyone else, free and easy. Irshad kept staring at Mary and nodding his head, only speaking two words of English, 'yes' and 'no'. We had already cooked a meal for them. The three of them took their food with them into their room. After they had finished, Mary washed up and then they shut the door of their room and talked in low voices for a long while. Sakib sat with me in my room and we talked, I more than him, off and on, Sakib keeping all his attention fixed on Hussain

Shah's door. Mary had arranged for Irshad's mattress to be laid in my room. It was after midnight that they finished talking and Irshad, a well-built young man with a thin moustache, came into my room. 'This is like home,' he said, 'own food, no difference.' He wrapped himself in blankets and went to sleep.

The marriage took place a week later on the following Saturday. Scared stiff as Hussain Shah and Sher Baz were of accompanying the bride and the groom to the marriage office, they had no choice before Mary, who had insisted upon it. It took three hours before the four of them returned in a taxi. Mary had bought a white silk dress for the ceremony and had made up her face and brushed her hair. We had all stood there in the morning just staring at her, so struck were we by her beauty. Mary was carrying a bunch of flowers on her return and talking to all the three men with her and laughing. She handed Sakib – the first one she saw as she entered the house – the flowers and, leaning over, quickly kissed him on the cheek. 'Hey,' she said to him, 'it's me who is the bride, why are you blushing?'

She took the baby off me, kissed him on the face and head and went upstairs, Hussain Shah and Irshad following her. All the men – except for Sakib, who had gone straight up to the attic – were excited and wanted to do something to celebrate the occasion. Sher Baz got us all into a room and told us off. 'Celebrate what? Hunh, what, what? Are you crazies? Just be quiet and go to your own business.'

Mary had changed into an old dress and was busy doing things for the baby. She wore the gold ring that Hussain Shah had bought for this day. Sher Baz was right, there was no occasion and nothing had changed. Irshad slept in my room and Hussain Shah and Mary in theirs. Irshad proved a good boy. Not only did he go to the employment office the very next day to arrange for his insurance and medical cards and, a few days later, to an interview to secure a job as an electrician's mate, but he also continued to sleep in my room, never bothering Hussain Shah and Mary in their time of rest and giving some money out of his wages each week to his uncle. No-one asked him, but we guessed that he was probably paying back the aeroplane fare that Hussain Shah had sent him.

I had one chance, a brief one, to speak to Sakib. We were now living under what we saw as Mary's beneficial umbrella. I aimed to bring this point to Sakib's attention so that he would feel responsible for the wellbeing of all of us. Our exchange went something like this:

'You are not reading books like you used to before.'

'I do,' he said, adding, 'sometimes.'

'This is the point. You came here to become a writer, did you not?'

'Yes,' he said eagerly, 'yes.'

'Then you have to keep your attention on your books. This you are not doing. You take many days off sick and are always circling around Mary. Do you not think this is improper?'

'She speaks to me sweetly,' Sakib said.

'She speaks to everybody sweetly. Look, there's no use denying that you are too much taken up with Mary. But it is not right.'

'Why not?'

'Because she is Hussain Shah's woman. If he takes notice of it, he will throw you out of the house. In jealousy he may even turn Mary out. Where will we be then? In trouble, I tell you. We will not only lose protection but she may go to the police.'

'She will not,' Sakib said.

'How can you say that? Listen, it is good and also very useful to learn to speak the language they speak, which is what you are doing, I am all for it. But you cannot depend on these people to be always on your side in everything.

They may be good to you for a time. But in the end you can only put your faith in your own people. If you do not take care we could all land in jail and then be deported. We are like your father and uncle and older brothers, you do not want to bring trouble down on our heads.'

Sakib looked at me blankly for many seconds with a stare that hinted at tears swelling up behind it. 'I have no father or uncle or brother,' he said.

To calm him down, I said, 'Sakib, I have a firm belief that you can make progress with your books.'

'I have,' Sakib blurted out, choking on words, 'no-one. She is – very nice—'

'Sakib, Sakib,' I put my arm round him. 'Do not talk like this. You have us. All of us. Just stick to us and books and you will gain success.'

Sakib finally nodded his head slowly in agreement. Looking at the wilderness on his face at the time I was struck with grief. I felt that if I had left it to my heart I would not have said to him what I did – this young and innocent boy with a good brain, who took the step to come here attracted only by the English Travelling Libraries and nothing else, ending up in a mixed-up situation like this, all alone.

16

The day after my unexpected meeting with Jenny I bumped into Janet in town and she invited me to the party celebrating their birthday in her twin sister's flat on Saturday. I had no intention of going at the time, though by the time Janet sent a message through Hasan confirming the date I thought it'd be no big hassle, the flat being two streets away, and I hadn't been out to a proper party anywhere in a while.

I took a whole day over what to wear, deciding in the end upon a tight shalwar-kameez. Martin met me outside the flat. It was a nice, one-bedroomed flat, simply furnished. She got it, Hasan said, on easy terms through the estate agents with whom she had worked for years. 'Got a good head for business, Pat has,' he said. On one side in the sitting room there was a large table laden with food and drink. The rest of the space, cleared by pushing the few chairs back against the wall, was taken up by fifteen people, more men than women, many of Janet's age, mostly standing, with drinks in their hands. A huge rubber plant, growing in a pot, occupied one corner of the room, while in the other stood a radio recorder on the floor playing tapes. The little light there was came from a sole low-powered red bulb in a table lamp placed high up on a shelf. Janet took me by the hand and introduced me – 'My sister Pat,' she said. 'Short for Patricia,' Pat said cheerfully, 'do help yourselves,' pointing to the large table.

Wrapped in the beat of the music were other sounds – the clink of bottles and glasses, Irish voices, laughter, the loud chat of a lone couple standing face to face in the middle of the room, their feet moving in the pretence of a dance. Martin opened a can of lager and started taking mouthfuls from it, tipping his head back. Someone poured white wine in my glass. Nervously, I drank the wine in three gulps. Martin had moved away. A man came up to where I was standing by the table and said 'Hello, my name is Michael.' I said 'hello' without giving my name. The man picked up a bottle of Guinness and edged slowly along the table, looking for a bottle-opener. Janet was talking to Martin. A minute later, Hasan joined them. Then Janet left them and went into the kitchen. Hasan and Martin stood alongside one another, looking around, both drinking from cans of lager. They seemed to be standing miles away from me. I was already feeling a bit heady. Pat emerged from the kitchen and clapped her hands together several times, creating a partial hush in the room. 'Come on people, this isn't a wake. Let's have a party. Dance.' There was laughter, and a few more people started dancing. The man named Michael asked me for a dance. Opposite him, I moved my feet with the music, not touching or making eye contact. Janet was moving her body slowly with the rhythm, talking with both Hasan and Martin. The music stopped. I moved away from Michael. I don't know what it was, the wine, the too-loud music, or the way Janet was looking at Hasan and Martin and laughing; but instead of loosening up, I was becoming tense inside. Michael followed me to the table, trying to start up a chat. I answered him briefly, looking away. Janet went to change the tape and fiddled with it for a few minutes, swearing at it. On her way back, she passed by me. 'Are you enjoying yourself, Parvin?' she asked. I heard my own voice, at a remove, saying, 'You're not really twenty-five, are you?' Janet looked at me, becoming absolutely still, her face assuming several expressions in a few seconds. 'What do you mean? How do you know how old I am? What's that got to do with you, what's that got to do with anything anyway? You're at my party, in my sister's flat for God's sake, what bloody cheek!' She turned and went into the kitchen. A minute later, Hasan appeared from the kitchen door.

'What did you say to Jan?' he asked me.

'Nothing,' I replied.

'She's upset.'

'I just asked her a question.'

'What question?'

'I said she was not twenty-five, was she?'

'What kind of a question is that?'

'Well, she isn't, is she?'

'What's that got to do with it? It's a daft thing to say, you've no business saying that to her. What're you steamed up for?'

'I'm not steamed up.'

'You're out of your head, Par, you're out of order,' Hasan said and went back into the kitchen.

Three feet away from me, Martin was dancing. Martin has no sense of rhythm. Arms and legs flying in all directions out of step with the music, he was supposed to be dancing with me, but he wasn't really. Every now and then he would look at me and smile his silly smile, then his eyes would go back to some point over the dancers' heads and concentration return to his face. Around him on all four sides a space had opened up, and within the orbit of his furious, disjointed movements, he looked completely happy. Everyone knew he had come with me. They were looking at him with amusement, smiling good-naturedly, then looking at me. My head was clearing up. Out of embarrassment, I moved forward and started dancing with Martin. Janet had come back into the room. She seemed to have calmed down, though she avoided looking at me and stayed on the other side of the room with her back towards me. She and another girl with a large can of Guinness between them, from which they took turns drinking, stood facing one another and laughed with their heads thrown back. The music stopped and started and stopped again, during which several of the men approached me to start a conversation, staring at my long uncut, untied hair and at the kohl around my eyes which I had taken some trouble putting on. I went and sat down in a chair.

'Can somebody open the window?' a girl asked.

'The window's open,' Janet said.

'I can't breathe. I wish people wouldn't smoke so much. I loathe the smell.'

Stepping over some low tables, Janet came up to the other window next to where I was sitting and opened it a crack. I looked up, hoping to catch her eye. Janet didn't look back. Nor did she move away. She stayed at the window, looking out.

'Hasan,' she called out, 'come here a minute.'

Hasan came and stood by her, placing an arm over her shoulders.

'That man,' Janet said, pointing to the street, 'has been standing there.'

'A neighbour?' Hasan said. 'Do you think we should keep it down a bit in here?'

'He was there when I looked out the other window,' Janet said.

Hasan craned his neck, frowning, trying to focus his eyes in the dark. Suddenly, he drew back, screening himself behind the curtain.

'Par,' he said to me quickly, 'come here.' He had gone quite pale.

The flat was on the first floor. Through the window, I saw him standing on the pavement below, right opposite us, looking up.

'He hasn't moved from there in twenty minutes,' Janet said.

Clutching a side of the curtain, hiding most of my face behind it, I looked through a chink, desperately hoping for it not to be him. Standing in pyjamas and slippers under the dim street light, wearing his old tatty dressing-gown, he was unmistakable. Hasan and I looked at each other, our eyes vacantly confused. Hasan turned and bounded across the room to turn the volume of the music down. In his panic, he did the opposite. A burst of sound momentarily shook the walls before Hasan moved the knob the other way, turning it right down. Everyone looked at him.

'What's the matter?' asked someone. 'Are the neighbours complaining?'

'Yeah,' Hasan said.

'There's going to be an announcement,' someone else said.

'Announcement of an engagement? Hurray!'

'Come on man, it's not even midnight yet.'

'Don't say a word,' whispered Hasan to Janet.

'Is it your dad?'

'Just shut the window, please.'

Shutting the window and drawing the curtain in front, Janet clapped her hands. 'All right, everybody, back to the party. Anyone want more drink? There's plenty.'

Someone had put the music back up. Helplessly, I looked around the room – fifteen or more people, dressed up for the party, drinking, laughing, telling jokes, dancing, enjoying themselves. I wished I wasn't there. As Hasan and I headed for the kitchen, a girl called Siobhan came out, bearing the birthday cake on a platter with candles stuck on it. Walking precariously round moving bodies with the cake in her hand, she approached the table, in the centre of which a space had been quickly cleared. Oohs and aahs rose from the crowd at the sight of the cake.

Hasan and I huddled in the kitchen.

'He will probably go away,' Hasan said uncertainly.

'He won't.'

'He was supposed to be at work, for Christ's sake.'

'He's been standing here for God knows how long, Hass, he won't go away.'

'How did he know we were here?'

'What are you going to do?'

'Don't ask me,' he said.

'You have to go out.'

'What for?'

'To take him home.'

'You must be joking.'

'What do you mean?'

'I'm not going anywhere. You go if you want to.'

'Are you kidding? You know how he behaves with me. At least he won't go crazy if he sees you.'

'No way, Par. Look, let's stay put. He can't stay out there all night.'

'What if he comes up to the door and rings the bell?'

'Christ, we're in shits.'

Pat poked her head in the door. 'What are you two doing in here? Come on out.'

We followed her back into the room. I came face to face with Janet in the crowd. Hesitating just a moment, I went up and kissed her on the cheek. 'I'm sorry, Jan,' I said to her. She looked at me for a second, surprised, then she put her arm around me and led me to the table.

They crowded round the table, talking of the beauty and size of the cake, raising a huge roar, followed by prolonged clapping as both Pat and Janet had three gos together at blowing out the candles. In the back of the crowd, I lifted a corner of the curtain and looked through the window. It had started to drizzle outside. He was still there, standing in the same place, getting wet. I dropped the curtain-end.

In the room, the singing of 'Happy Birthday' over, couples were beginning to step out on to the floor, food and half-eaten pieces of layered cake suspended delicately in their fingers like butterflies, waiting for the slow dance music, the last gaiety, to start. Somewhere inside me, a decision had been made.

I borrowed a shawl from Pat and told Hasan that I was going out. 'Here,' he said, handing me a polo, 'better chew on it before you speak to him.' Next, I spent several severe minutes persuading Martin not to follow me out.

Walking unsteadily up the path, I said, 'Dad, what are you doing here?'

'You ask me the question? May I ask you the question that it is midnight and what are you doing here?'

'I came to a birthday party.'

'Do you stay out all night for birthday parties when I am working?'

'What are you talking about, it's not midnight yet. I asked mum, I have permission from her to stay until twelve on special occasions. I was about to leave anyway.'

'Whose birthday?'

'A girl friend of mine.'

'I know who you are calling your girl friend. Where is your brother?'

'I don't know.'

'Are you purposely telling a lie to me?'

'No, dad.'

'I saw him with my own eyes. There,' he pointed his finger up at the window of the flat. The sound of music was coming distantly from above. Someone had opened both the windows.

'Must be someone else you saw,' I said.

'Are you saying I do not see properly?'

'There are twenty people in there, dad.'

'Are you saying I cannot tell the difference between the other nineteen people and my own son? Go and bring him out.'

'Look, dad, if he is in there he won't come out. Let's go home.' I tried to slip my hand under his arm.

He pulled his arm violently away from me. 'In that case I will personally go and get him,' he said.

'You can't go in there, dad.'

'Why not?'

'Look at the way you are dressed.'

'Dressed? What is the way I am dressed? These are my own clothes, I wore them when they were new, bought them with my own money.'

'Look, you are wet all over.' I passed my hand over his dressing-gown sleeve. 'You can see Hasan tomorrow.'

The two of us standing in the rain, he glared at me for what seemed a long time. Impulsively, I leaned out to him and kissed him on the cheek. He turned abruptly and started walking, heading for home.

17

What we suffered were the ills of freedom – the freedom of one man. What is freedom, I ask myself? It is nothing, I say, but more problems. When you are not free, all you fear is the outdoors; you can come in and be in a place of safety. When you are free, you can go to the outdoors and fall victim to your desires. And desires are no places of safety. Irshad was a free man; this was his problem. He made friends outside the house, bought bottles of after-shave lotion which he put in large quantities all over his face and neck, covered with hair grown long. Finally, one day, he went to the pub. He came back late, knocked at Hussain Shah's door and gave him the money, it being the pay-packet day, a Friday. Then he came into our room and talked to Sakib and me. Just the usual things, but it was the way he spoke. He looked different. Hussain Shah had a word with Sher Baz the next day and Sher Baz began telling Irshad of the tenets of our religion, as to how it forbade the drinking of beer and of what happened to those who defied it. Irshad got scared, especially when he heard of the punishment meted out to drinkers, garlands of cobra snakes and scorpions slung round the neck and suchlike in the next world. He promised, in our presence, never to drink beer again.

The following Friday, Irshad was back in the pub; he had forgotten it all. As before, he returned late and knocked at Hussain Shah's door to give him the money. Hussain Shah, who was then doing round-the-clock shifts instead of permanent nights, opened the door in a rage. 'Be off, drinker,' he shouted, 'be off with your drinker face, go spend money on sharab, spend, throw it away, die a poor man. Be off.' Irshad just stood there and grinned. Then, from inside the room came Mary's voice. 'Leave him alone, he only goes once a week, does no harm to anyone, does he, what's the matter with you? Leave him be.' Hussain Shah looked back into the darkness of his room and said nothing. He banged the door shut and went back to bed. He took the money off Irshad the next morning. Every Friday from then on became for Irshad the pub-going night. He would return from there to a sleeping house and attack whatever food was left over for him from our hearth, not even bothering to bring the food into the room but eating it standing up by the stove. Afterwards, he came in and woke me up to talk. Irshad was a strong young man and did not lose his senses, but his tongue loosened, even when he talked about his uncle, often jokingly, but at other times as if from the heart. 'Sleeps on a real bed himself and has us thrown here on the floor.' In a short while he went to sleep and snored loudly. I did not look forward to Friday nights in those days. Irshad did not get into the habit of drinking, like going to the pub every night and so on, but he got into the habit of freedom. Which one was worse than the other, I did not know.

What followed made it definitely worse: Sakib got pulled into it. The early part of his story I heard from him afterwards, while the rest of it happened in my presence. Although Sakib was one of us and not a free man like Irshad, his position was half-free, as he didn't have to send money back home or do overtime or save to buy land or a house. For this reason, I think, after Irshad had been pressing him over a couple of weeks, as Sakib told me later,

he agreed to accompany Irshad to the pub. At first he did
not like the taste of beer. But as it went to his head, Sakib
said, he drank more and more, for Irshad kept buying it
for him. On the way home, he began to feel sick. Leaning
against the wall at one place, he vomited. Then coming up
the stairs inside the house, Sakib felt really sick. He bent
over the sink on our landing and vomited. And vomited
again. Each time we thought it had finished, it came up
all over again, until there was nothing left in him but the
sick wind, which came up and choked him. I thought he
was dying. His legs were trembling and he kept falling
down to his knees. Hussain Shah and I were in a panic,
running in and out of rooms, not knowing what to do,
just wishing he would stop. Only Mary was standing there
with her arms round Sakib's waist, holding him up, and
laughing. 'Don't worry,' she was saying to him, 'you'll be
all right in a minute,' while Sakib was groaning with pain
and crying out, 'don't let me die, please don't let me die,
let me live, I will never touch it again God I promise,
tobah astaghfar, tobah tobah tobah.' Mary was looking at
Irshad with a smile as if she thought it was all a game.
Hussain Shah kept swearing at Irshad, 'Don't you have
shame you damned drinker soul, taking this child with you
to the house of evil? May God drown you in the sea. If
God gave me this knowledge beforehand I never never get
you here—' Gradually, Sakib came back from the dead. He
fell to the floor flat on his back, shivering with no control.
Tears were flowing down the side of his face and he was
uttering tobah astaghfar to himself, unable to raise his voice
above a whisper. Then he passed out. We put him in my
room for the night. Some time during the night, he got
up and climbed into his attic. Not three days had passed
before Sakib was feeling fine and, I could see from his eager
face, looking forward to his pay-packet day. The first-time
sickness never returned to Sakib after that as the pair

became a fixture on Friday nights, coming home late and, on some nights, singing in the street with their arms round one another, attracting attention and alarming us out of our minds. Irshad and Mary, being free people, did not care, but we the others had to protect our freedom to stay unknown.

I remember a Friday night that I heaved a sigh of relief upon seeing Sakib waiting in my room for Irshad hour after hour, getting more and more anxious, as Irshad did not appear. Once or twice he contemplated aloud going out on his own, but stayed back; with Irshad he felt safe. I had stopped advising Sakib against his actions after having tried more than once to no avail, though I still felt a deep sympathy for him in my heart, only hoping now that things would work themselves out to the best for all of us. There was still no sign of Irshad when Hussain Shah returned from work at eleven o'clock. He immediately emerged from his room asking where Mary was. Until then we had thought that Mary was there, resting. Hussain Shah went downstairs and found that Mary had left the baby with the Hafizabadis to look after and gone out. Where to, they did not know. Hussain Shah picked up the baby and came back upstairs. With his eyes and ears watchful for any sign of sound or movement from the front door of the house, Hussain Shah walked about the house holding the baby in his arms, talking to everyone, while Sakib, who had given up on Irshad by now, and I cooked our food and got over with the meal. Hussain Shah did not touch the food that Mary had cooked and left inside the stove to keep warm for him before she went. He just sat in his room, coming out every few minutes on to the landing, standing on top of the stairs looking below, going into the toilet, coming out and standing some more, leaning over the banisters and going back into the room. He took ablutions and stood facing Makkah to offer namaz but finished it in half the usual time. After that he stayed in his room.

It was near midnight when Mary appeared with Irshad. Hussain Shah shot out of the room and stood at the top of the stairs, his face pale with anger. Irshad was quiet but Mary was talking with the usual laughter in her voice. Coming up to the landing, she said to Hussain Shah, 'Hello!'. Hussain Shah stood there looking at her as if he did not believe that Mary was speaking to him and smiling.

'Still up?' Mary said, standing very close to Hussain Shah. I was awake and from the dark of my room I saw this: Hussain Shah's face changed, the colour returned to it. Mary reached up and kissed him on the cheek lightly. Then she put her arm around Hussain Shah and led him to their room. Losing his direction in the room a little, Irshad tripped over me in the dark and eventually found his mattress. Out on the landing, Mary was warming up the food. They ate in silence, then the door of their room shut, though the light inside stayed on. I heard Hussain Shah's voice speaking to Mary for the first time during the evening, speaking in a low, flat voice, bereft of the usual tone, and speaking for a long time thus, not angry but heavy, as if telling her off but with sorrow. I heard Mary's voice only once, and that was at the end. It was a totally different voice, harsh and loud and angry, and short. I could not make out what she said, but the sound of it stayed in my ears for a long time. The light inside their room went off. Irshad was snoring loudly and I could not sleep. I was happy on the one hand that a storm had passed over our heads without causing damage, on the other I felt a strange emptiness appear in my chest, a void through which waves of weakness were passing down my limbs. Things were taking on a bad shape. Some while later I got up to release pressure in my bladder and as I passed across to the lavatory, I saw the trapdoor of the attic slid back several inches and framed in it Sakib's face. He was lying on his stomach, his eyes wide open and fixed on Mary's closed door. I whispered to him to go to sleep but his concentration was such that he stayed completely unmindful of my presence. The shape of things to come became clear very shortly after when I witnessed Mary with Irshad's name on her lips all day long: 'Irshad come here, Irshad do this, Irshad do that.' Irshad was now a nightshifter and stayed home all day with Mary.

What happened next was a merry-go-round of the two men's work shifts; I could not figure out how they did it. Hussain Shah managed to have himself transferred once again to permanent night shift, so Irshad got himself back to day shift. Hussain Shah moved on to the day shift as well, whereupon Irshad was back on the night shift. I knew that Hussain Shah had good relations with the foreman, having made a gift of a bottle of whisky to him at Christmas time and on the occasion of Eid a basket of sweetmeats from our sweet shop. But it is an accepted fact that the white people have a regard for the skill of a worker and Irshad, being a good electrician, held a fair position. After racing each other thus for several weeks, Irshad eventually came out the winner of the two, with Hussain Shah getting stuck in the day shift. Irshad spent hours in Mary's room, talking to her, running errands for her up and down and in and out of the house. The door of Mary's room, with Irshad inside, began to shut.

A regime had been set: Hussain Shah worked days and slept at home at night, while Irshad went to work at night and returned in the morning. Mary went about making breakfast for the two of them and the baby, after which they waited for the baby to go to sleep. Once the baby was asleep, they shut their door and then there was no sound until the afternoon, when once again the door opened and Irshad appeared, yawning. I learnt of the said routine one

day when I was off sick with this hollow in the chest and
stayed home all day. Irshad, after coming out of Mary's
room, wandered about. About six o'clock, Mary called out
to Sakib, who joined them in Mary's room. The three of
them sat around chatting for some time. If Mary spent
more time with Irshad and Hussain Shah, she still liked to
talk to Sakib a lot as he was the only one in the house who
could speak to her in proper English, almost as well as she
herself did. In between sitting and chatting in her room,
Mary got up and made sandwiches for Irshad to eat during
his shift. Hussain Shah arrived about ten at night. This
routine did not last long though, because Hussain Shah
suddenly stopped doing overtime. Most days he was back
home shortly after six o'clock, which forced Irshad to leave
Mary's room at five. He lay about on his mattress for a bit
to make the blankets look like they had been slept in until
Hussain Shah arrived back from work. Mary called out to
Irshad and Sakib, who went and joined Hussain Shah and
Mary in their room, to sit and chat until it was time for
Irshad to leave for work. Mary, who had by that time
learned to cook our food, having had instruction from
Hussain Shah, Sher Baz and me over months, then began
to cook a meal for Hussain Shah, though she still cooked
separately for herself and the baby, who had started eating
soft food. Although they sat with each other in their room
almost on a daily basis, Hussain Shah had stopped speaking
to his nephew altogether; he took the money off Irshad on
Saturdays and turned away. The visits to the pub, however,
continued, though shifted to Saturdays since Irshad had
started working overtime on Friday nights. Mary would
leave baby Michael with Hussain Shah and go – saying
that she needed to get out of the house after 'slaving over
the stove' and being 'pickled' in there the whole week and,
she said, as Hussain Shah would not in spite of her best
efforts go with them to the pub, she had to go with Irshad.

Hussain Shah, for his part, readily agreed to give over the care of the baby to others in the house, as on Saturday nights he was not quite himself in Mary's absence after she left for the pub. He would get his night namaz over with in double-quick time and then wander in and out of his room and through the house. He would not touch his meal until Mary and Irshad came back to the house, however late. All the rest of the week he took his time to perform his prayers of the day and night, sometimes three or four together after he came back from work. There was a discipline in Hussain Shah's life. Looking at him, I saw a great and dense tree. There is a natural discipline in such trees. We always felt that in some way the whole balance of our home depended on Hussain Shah. But many forces were now beginning to act against him.

And act they did – with a vengeance! Ah, the worms of memory, waking up, bringing to me the terrible twins, fear and trouble . . . If fear is like a cunning fox, hiding in the bushes, always behind you, then trouble is like an obstinate mule, always ahead of you, but refusing to go. It arrived on the day that Hussain Shah came back from work at midday and stood in front of the closed door of his room, carrying in him weeks and months of half-doused fires and a silenced heart beyond sorrow.

18

'Your daughter,' my father said to my mother on the morning after the night of the birthday party, as Hasan and I sat on the settee while my father stood, pacing within a small circle, in the centre of the room. 'Your daughter, Salma,' he repeated, pointing to me, 'was ashamed of my clothes.'

'I never . . .' I said, exasperated.

'And your son,' pointing to Hasan but still speaking to my mother, 'did not come out in case his white woman catches sight of me.'

'I don't know what you are talking about,' Hasan said.

'Ask your sister. You were in that flat, were you not?'

'All right, I was there. I didn't come out because you'd have made a fuss.'

'In a suit and tie, I would be all right. Right?'

'Rubbish,' Hasan said. He left the settee and went to stand by the window, looking out to the back garden.

'Don't say rubbish to me. This is what happens,' he turned to my mother again, 'I tell you, Salma, this is what happens when your son gets a white woman for himself. She is the source of all trouble.'

'What trouble?'

'The trouble of unholy women.'

'Don't call her that,' Hasan said, turning round and taking a step towards my father.

Trembling inside, I said to Hasan quietly, 'Don't be stupid, Hass, come and sit down.'

'You see that?' my father said.

'Sit,' my mother said in a strangled voice. 'Sit.'

'You see that, Salma? Do you witness that? He stands up before me, ready to attack me, all on her behalf. Has it happened before? Never. And why? All on her behalf. The white woman will be trouble, nothing but trouble, I tell you. I know, I have spent a good part of my life here, I know.'

'*You* are making trouble, not her,' Hasan said. 'Who told you to come there anyway? You were supposed to be at work.'

'Listen to that. Do you hear that? Now I have to explain my presence. I can come and go as I please, where I want. I have the choice. Do I have to explain my existence to you? To my own son?'

'You treat us like children,' Hasan said.

'And what else are you, taking up with people like that?'

'People like what? You yourself have been asking me for years to take up an English partner, have you forgotten?'

'That is *business* partnership. Altogether different matter. Listen, come, I will explain to you, since you do not understand.' He walked up to Hasan, taking him by the arm.

'Listen to your father,' my mother said to Hasan.

The two of them sat down alongside one another on the settee. I moved to the next chair.

'Taking a good partner is the road to profit, but also a road to learning. In business these people have set standards. I have read history. Get this into your thick head, when you take them as business partner, you are not trying to be English, you are only learning standards. That is unlike when you get yourself a white woman. Then you are trying to be like them.'

'I am not trying to be like anybody, what are you talking about? She's not even English, for Christ's sake.'

'You hear that, Salma? Says he is not trying to be like them and then says Christ's sake. Already he has forgotten who his God is.'

'What difference does it make, it's only words. You wouldn't let us speak anything but English in the beginning, remember?'

'That was to put you on the road to success only in the beginning, not to become like them.'

'Come off it, we're not going to become like them.'

'Very true. You cannot become like them. But you can become better than them. *This* is what I mean. From their experience of trading with the world you learn the standards, then you use your own qualities. Look all round, what do you see? From these trading people we have taken all profitable shops. This is only the ground floor of trade, in a way of speaking. Right? In twenty years, we will go to the next floor, banks, friendly mutual societies, building societies in other words, and no more little so-called supermarkets on the corners of streets but real ones, big department stores. After that the top floor, high civil servants, ministers in government, controllers of the telly, etcetera and so on. You have the successful future ahead of you.' Unheeded, he lovingly stroked both Hasan's arms with his hands. Hasan tried gently to extricate himself. 'You know why you have a shining future? I will tell you: you have the choice. For example, if business is not good for you, you can take a job. I can help you. I have given good service here.'

'Leave it off, dad. I did go with you last month, didn't I? What happened, have you forgotten?'

'There was no vacancy, I took you along to show your face, that is all. Such things are taken into consideration, faces are remembered. Now there is vacancy. I keep an eye on these things. Maybe not a big job to start with. You know our head Postmaster? He made progress from the position of a trolley pusher. If once you do not succeed, no need to lose heart.'

'I didn't even want to go. You and mum pushed me.'

'What is wrong with that? All for the good of you.'

'What is wrong is the way the man treated you.'

'How do you say he treated me?'

'You know what I mean. I don't want to talk about it, what's the point?'

'No, tell me,' my father insisted, 'speak your mind.'

'He treated you like dirt.'

'Did you hear that, Salma?'

'No talk like that,' my mother said to Hasan.

'It's true, though, isn't it?'

'No, false.'

'He won't even speak to you properly. We sat outside his poky little office for fifty minutes . . .'

'Ten minutes,' my father interrupted.

Hasan tapped the glass face of his wristwatch. 'Fifty minutes, and then he gave you two minutes, just two minutes. I don't think he even knew who you were.'

'That is a lie. It is not true, Salma, everybody knows me. I have a respect there, rendered service for many years. With the Unions as well, I was the first man to volunteer for the picket line when they called us out. You do not know about these things, Salma, I will tell you, there are two sides, management and the Unions, they are like this,' he made a sign of crossed swords using a finger from each hand. 'It is not easy to be on good terms with both sides. I have good standing with one as well as the other. Ten months after I started I got promotion. People wait for years. I have got on. That is the main thing. Do you think,' he turned to Hasan, 'that it is easy?'

'What are you talking about, there are thousands who have *got on*, as you say.'

'Oh no, not just got on, my boy, but got on well. That is the main thing. You do not understand the difference.'

'Hunh!' Hasan uttered a grunt with a dismissive toss of the head.

'Do you see, Salma, he cannot understand the difference because he has not got on in his life. This is what I am trying to explain. Do you not say that I have got on well?'

My mother gave a slight nod.

'Say it. Let him hear it. Anyone can get on, but to get on well is the main thing. Do you not think that I have gotten on well?'

'Yes,' my mother said sadly, 'well.'

'You are not going to be the head Postmaster, are you?'

'Who wants that?' my father said to him. 'All a man wants is respect. That is the main thing. Esteem. Didn't the gaffer say to you to come back when there is a vacancy?'

'We all know what that means, dad, stop deceiving yourself. Who was this man you call gaffer anyway, some little man just above your head, and he didn't even look at you straight, kept fiddling with papers on his table and in two minutes we were out of there. You know what you said to him after that? Sorry to have bothered you, that's what you said, sorry to have bothered you. What for? That's when I was really ashamed of you.'

'Saying sorry is no bad thing. You have never learned that, picking up wrong notions. Makes me feel aggrieved for you.'

'Look at the way you speak. Aggrieved for you. Wrong notions. Diligent. What's all that mean?'

'You do not know what that means?'

'Nobody says things like that. It's absurd.'

I wished Hasan would stop, he was getting out of order.

'You tell me it is absurd? You do not know the meaning of the word. I will tell you what is absurd. It is when you ask me how I speak, how I dress, why I am at this place and not at that place, that is absurd. One other thing, when you do not know the meaning of the words I speak, that is absurd. Do you hear what he says, Salma? He has no vocabulary. Let me teach something to this no-education boy who says saying sorry is no good. Now listen to me, young man. Saying sorry is a clever thing. I will tell you how. These white people went to our country and treated us like children, tried to break the esteem of our own selves making out they were doing us favours by being there and sitting on our heads, so that we would become useless for ever. So what did we do? Did we answer back like you do in front of me? No, sir. We shut down our faces on them and only smiled false smiles and only when we wanted something. We said sorry and thank you and got benefits, schools, railways, English, and so on, and kept our esteem. And not only that, but when we saw they had nothing more to give, we told them to go. And furthermore, not only that, but we came here to live among them as equals. Now listen carefully what I am telling you, which is this: these people are still doing that, trying to make us live like them and attack our own esteem. But they will have no victory. You know why? Because for two hundred years we said sorry and thank you but kept living in our own way, so how can we not do that now and betray our forefathers when we are in equal position? And now the main thing, the very main thing I will tell you, which is this: we do not lose sight of the target, which is to make progress, so we say sorry and thank you and get on with it. That is how saying sorry is clever.'

'Are you joking? You didn't even see their so-called Raj, you were too young. Two hundred years indeed.'

'Ah, but I have read history, unlike you. Let me enlighten you about this. The second best after the English master was my history teacher, Master Dost Muhammad sahib. No, not second best but nearly equal, when I was in class ten. Another thing, the system in our schools, of which you know nothing, back in my country – *your* ancestral country, is proper teaching. Spellings, times tables, grammar, everything. Here they let you play around until you are sixteen and then kick battalions of no-education people like you out on the streets to dig ditches. Do you know that this is all arranged in advance? Because if they do not do it then who will dig the ditches? Hunh?'

'I am not digging ditches,' Hasan said.

'This is because you have special qualities, as I have already conceded. But what about the others? Well, not so in our schools, no sir. Very learned man was Master Dost Muhammad sahib. You laugh at my mention of two hundred years? I tell you, in class nine and ten he taught us *two thousand* years of history and more, dates, years, places, wars, from Mahatma Budh right up to the British invasion. He knew history backwards and forwards, all from memory. And not just history alone but also how we lived in that history, and so on. So that is how I know. All by virtue of a first-class history and geography master. Do you remember Master Dost Muhammad sahib, Salma? He lived down your street, small kutcha house on the left-hand side? Do you not remember?'

My mother nodded sadly. 'Master saab,' she said, 'he dead.'

'Dead? When? How do you know?'

'From letter,' my mother said.

'You got a letter from home? Why did you not tell me?'

'You forget. I told. His house fall down in rain. Master saab try for pukka house, but dead before. Poor man.'

'Poor yes, but not ignorant. History lived on his tongue.'

'So much for history,' Hasan said with a sneer.

'Do not laugh at a poor dead man and his history,' my father said angrily, 'it will punish you. I lost my country and home to learn many things in the world.'

'I didn't lose a country, so how was I to learn?' said Hasan with a smile.

'Because you were provided with a home by the labour of my hands.'

'Well, it's neither here nor there,' Hasan shrugged.

'It is here, right here where you grew up. You have the wrong notions.'

Hasan said under his breath, 'Bollocks!'

'What? What do you say? Speak up. You never speak up, only mumble, mumble, all the time mumble. Do not think that I am deaf. Only I want you to say it loud.'

In his rage, my father pushed Hasan. Hasan staggered a step backwards, steadying himself against the wall.

'You say bollocks to how I live? Say it again.'

'Don't push me,' Hasan said.

'You say bollocks to me, to my life, to my way of life?'

'What way of life,' Hasan said. 'I've seen you wandering about in those streets looking for . . .'

My father slapped my brother on the face. I felt my heart jump up to my throat and choke me. My mother uttered a cry. I saw a glistening film of tears leap to Hasan's eyeballs. He stood looking at my father and blinking. Suddenly, my father took a step forward and tried to clasp Hasan to himself, wrapping his arms around Hasan's body.

'My boy, my son.'

Ducking and twisting himself out of his grasp, Hasan ran out of the house. Stumbling, staggering, my father ran after him. 'I do not mean bad for you, son, forget all this . . .'

But Hasan was gone. I went to Janet's flat several times and found it permanently locked. At the hotel where she works they say she's on holiday. My father has cut his overtime and goes from work all over the city every night to look for him – for his beloved history that has abandoned him.

19

On the day of Hussain Shah's unexpected return, Ali Zaman the nightshifter followed him up the stairs to ask after his wellbeing. He later told me what he saw. Hussain Shah stood in front of the closed door of his room and made no effort to open it, just touched it lightly, then turned and walked into my room.

Sitting here today with no-one but myself after all these years, it is only now that I understand why Hussain Shah had come: he had a question in his heart and was lost without an answer.

My room was empty. Hussain Shah lay down on my mattress straight on his back and shut his eyes. Seeing him laid out like this, Ali Zaman did not dare speak to him and went back. Some minutes passed. The door of Mary's room was still shut. Silently, Hussain Shah walked out of the house.

Later, I had just returned from work and was sitting in my room, giving my feet a rest, when Hussain Shah came up the stairs. He seemed to be in deep thought and did not, as was his habit, say assalam alaikam to me or to anyone else. The door of his room was open and inside were Mary and Irshad, Irshad sitting in the chair, Mary reclining on the bed, talking. Hussain stopped in the door. Mary said 'Hello' to him lightly and went on talking to Irshad. Then all at once, the two of then stopped speaking, becoming fixed in their positions, heads turned, eyes staring at Hussain Shah's face. God knows what they saw there, but Mary and Irshad began to rise slowly from where they sat. Hussain Shah's eyes were set on Irshad. He walked right up to Irshad and caught him by the hair with one hand. With the other, he slapped Irshad hard on the face, then brought down the hand in reverse and slapped with the back of it on the other side of his face. The third time the open palm of his hand fell flat on Irshad's eyes. Under the slaps, Irshad uttered a single squeal: 'Chacha!'

Men were running up the stairs to look. Hussain Shah raised his fist and thrust it in Irshad's face. It fell on Irshad's mouth with the force of a hammer. With the blow, Irshad's hair snapped out of Hussain Shah's other hand. Irshad stumbled and fell, hitting the wall with his back. There, very slowly, he slumped to his feet, finally sitting on his haunches, looking up. Mary ran out in front of Hussain Shah. 'Hussain,' she cried, 'what are you doing?' Hussain Shah pushed her with the violence of both his hands. Mary reeled and fell back on the bed. From there she cried again, 'You'll kill him, you'll kill him, your own brother's son!'

Hussain Shah stood in the middle of the room, absolutely still, his arms hanging by his side and his thick legs, like stumps of dwarf trees, planted firmly into the ground. He looked like a statue. Only his chest heaved. His narrowed eyes were fixed on Irshad, as if peering through the dark in search of something quite different from what was in front of him. The lights had not been switched on yet, but outside the day was already ending. In the half darkness, it looked as if Hussain Shah's shoulders had expanded and were touching the walls, occupying the whole width of the room. Irshad was a strong man with young limbs, his body lean and long and light, appearing to float in the air as he walked the ground and bounded up flights of stairs. But at this moment he was like a calf reared on mother's milk in front of Hussain Shah's grown bull. He was sitting now with his knees on the floor, his hands spread wide as a child's. Hussain Shah's forty years of hard labour was spun into ropes of steel round his short, thick limbs and from his old bones seemed to leap a fire of terrible anger. Irshad's face was broken and bleeding. A tooth lay on his open palm and blood poured down to his chest, wetting his shirt. As Hussain Shah advanced towards him once more, the expression of a cornered animal spread over Irshad's face. Without moving from his place or trying to protect himself, Irshad yelled, 'Chacha, I will send you to jail, you are illegal, I will tell them, I will send you all to prison—'

Hussain Shah did not seem to hear a word of it. He bent down and picked Irshad up in his hands as if he were a ball of cotton. Mary screamed. Hussain Shah raised Irshad above his head and tossed him out of the room. Irshad fell on the landing right in the middle of us with a thud that caused the whole house to shudder.

In the room, Hussain had turned and now stood, with his arms loose by his side, confronting Mary just as he had Irshad a moment ago. Mary screamed again. Hussain Shah's chest heaved. We thought he was going to pick up Mary too and fling her out of the room. Within seconds, even as we looked on, Hussain Shah's heaving slowed, and the anger inside him seemed to evaporate. He turned and banged the door shut. He did not even look at us.

There was silence in the house, broken only by the cry of the baby who had been woken up by the noise. After a moment or two, Sakib and I put our hands under Irshad's arms and stood him up on his feet. Irshad rinsed his mouth under the tap a few times, splashed water over his face and came and sat down on his mattress. Everyone else followed him one by one and sat down. Nobody talked. After some minutes, Irshad took off his bloody and torn shirt, made a ball of it in his hands and pressed it against his mouth, which was still bleeding. Then he threw it in a corner, put on a clean shirt and left for work.

Gradually, we began to talk. We talked of other things, not once mentioning the fight, only looking at each other every few minutes and shaking our heads as if merely to remind one another of our fear and grief. Underneath all our talk was a single thought: were Irshad to make good his threat, there would be no hiding place for us any more, the earth would throw us up. All our unspoken hopes now rested with Mary. Although in our hearts we held her responsible as the origin of all our troubles, we also knew that no-one but she could save the situation. God at that dangerous time listened to our prayers. Presently, the door opened and Mary came out to prepare Hussain Shah's food. She was standing by the stove when Hussain Shah too emerged to go to the lavatory. He was on his way back to his room when Sher Baz went to the door and put his hand on Hussain Shah's arm. Hussain Shah quietly came with him into my room.

'Irshad is young,' Sher Baz said to him, 'cannot judge things, but is your flesh and blood. You are man of years, can judge things. We must stay united. Had there been no unity, tell me, would one man be there in the world today to utter the name of our holy prophet, peace be upon him? In unity alone is our safety.'

His head bowed, Hussain Shah listened in silence. As Mary spoke to him a few minutes later in her usual urgent voice, 'Come on Hussain, food is ready,' we breathed easy. Afterwards, Mary washed up. We cooked our meal. The meal over, Sakib went to his attic and shut himself behind the trapdoor. Standing in her own doorway, Mary chatted to me for a few minutes about the baby's gripes and such things, turning her head several times to look back at

Hussain Shah who sat on a chair inside the room. Then she said goodnight and closed the door of her room behind her.

Although Mary told me the very next day that Irshad had begged forgiveness of his uncle and Hussain Shah had taken the money off his nephew, yet our hearts did not settle; in the following days we saw that nothing much had changed. There was a gap of three or four weeks during which Irshad went out on his own before Mary began quietly to step out as well on Saturday nights, though they took care not to start off or return in each other's company but met outside and came back separately.

Mary had asked Sakib why he was wasting his time with his boring books when there were very good stories to be read in magazines, and gave him one called *True Stories*. Sakib read the whole of it in one night and said to Mary the next day that he liked it very much and wanted to read more. Mary said that he could buy a new one from the shops, which Sakib did straightaway. Mary leafed through it, reading the titles of stories and other things in large writing and looking at the pictures. She said she would borrow it after Sakib had finished reading it. Then she said that she had an idea, why didn't they read it together? Together how, asked Sakib? Why, she said, he could sit there and read it to her. Like this, Mary said – as Sakib later told me – they could both enjoy the stories at the same time. Sakib sat in her room and read the first story all the way through there and then. Mary sat in the chair opposite him, getting up in between to attend to the baby and do other things, in and out of the room, listening all the while to the story. Sakib never got so much interested and involved in a story any time before, he told me, saying that he enjoyed it much more than if he had read it on his own. He read very well too, Mary said to him, 'just like listening to the radio'.

Every day from that time on, between five o'clock when he got back and six, the time of Hussain Shah's arrival, Sakib went into Mary's room and read a new story to her. Once or twice during the first week when the story was especially good and at an exciting stage, Mary had handed the baby to Irshad and told him to go and leave them alone until the end of the story. Irshad, using the baby as an excuse, kept coming back. Then, even when Mary had the baby with her in the room, Irshad walked in, trying to talk to Mary when he knew she was listening to the story. In the end, Mary had to shut the door. The first time, Irshad immediately opened the door and went in while Sakib was reading. Mary paid no attention to him, just waved a hand, bidding him to go away. Irshad went out, only to go back in a few minutes later. This went on for three days – Sakib giving me all this day by day – until the last time when Irshad opened the door and started to say something but was cut short. 'Shut up, you idiot,' Mary shouted at him. Irshad backed off in surprise, but he stopped bothering them after that.

That one hour each day Mary and Sakib had all to themselves. Sakib worked from six a.m. to four. From his factory he had to take two buses. Instead of waiting for the bus, he set off from the factory at four o'clock and caught the bus wherever he found it. At times, in his impatience he started running and did not care to stop until he reached home. By so doing, especially in the rush hour when buses moved very slowly, he saved himself some time, so that he and Mary had up to an hour and a half together. Some days, after he had finished the story and there was still time before the hour of six, Mary did not open the door straightaway but sat there talking to him. Nothing special, said Sakib, only the usual things about herself and the baby and Hussain Shah and Irshad. She had told him that Irshad kept complaining about Hussain

Shah regarding one thing or the other. Sometimes, before opening the door, said Sakib to me with a blush, Mary kissed him quickly on the cheek.

Once or twice Sher Baz spoke to Sakib. 'This is matter between uncle and nephew, family matter, no problem. You are outsider, should stay outside.'

Sakib said he told Sher Baz the truth, that there was nothing to it, he only read her stories from magazines.

'It is matter of where you are standing,' Sher Baz said to Sakib. 'Standing where?' Sakib asked.

'Like on the bank of river, very close to water. Water rubs the wet bank and earth can give way under feet any time.'

Sakib said Sher Baz was an old fool.

The routines of the household had changed. The prostitutes' visits had started once again on the quiet, carried out on the ground floor without much ceremony and, in the absence of Hussain Shah now administered by Sher Baz. I woke up to Sakib's situation the day he walked into my room straight from his story-reading session and said, 'Mary is going to London with me.'

'When? What for?' I asked in some consternation.

Sakib's face was flushed and he had a strange shine to his eyes as if he had fever. He just repeated, 'We are going to London.'

'Sakib,' I said to him, 'sit down. What do you mean Mary and you are going?'

'She will go with me to London and we will live there.'

'Are you joking? What will you do, how will you live?'

'I will support her with my writing,' Sakib said.

'But you are not writing anything yet. You don't even know if anyone will give you money for it.'

'I have a copybook full of stories in the attic. I will sell them to magazines. We can live easily on that money.'

I was dumbfounded. 'I don't believe it,' I said to him.

'No, no. She just said so.'

'Then *she* must be joking.'

'No, no, no,' Sakib almost shouted, 'it is true.'

Considering the state he was in, I said, 'All right then, it is true.'

'Do you believe it?' Sakib said, his face as eager and sharp as a small rodent's.

'Yes,' I said.

But I had decided to speak to Mary; if what Sakib said was true, the sky would fall on all our heads. I got the chance late that night when Mary came out to warm some milk for the baby. It was a good moment as Irshad was away at work and Hussain Shah was probably asleep with the door of his room half shut. I went out and whispered, 'Mary, can you come with me, I want to talk to you about something.'

She nodded. 'I'll be a minute,' she said, and took the milk pan back into the room. After a few minutes she came into my room.

'What did you say to Sakib?' I asked her.

'What did I say what to Sakib?'

'He says the two of you are going to go to London.'

'Oh, that,' she said with a little laugh, sitting down on my mattress. 'Did he say this to you?'

'Yes,' I said.

'Foolish boy. It was only from a story he was reading.'

'What was?'

'You see, there was these two young lovers who were going to elope to London from their homes up north. It was a good story, mind, and I just remarked "Oh, that's nice", meaning the couple in the story. He completely misunderstood me. Right out he asks will I go to London with him? Honestly, I didn't know what to say. I just laughed and said yes. That's all.'

'He is very worked up about it,' I said.

'Oh he'll be all right,' Mary said with a toss of the head.

'Mary,' I said to her, 'he is like a child, lives entirely in his dreams, not like us grown-up men, we can take anything as it comes, not him, he takes it to heart.'

There was a hint of anger in Mary's eyes. 'I didn't lead him on, you know. First he took me by complete surprise, then the way he was looking at me, like begging, I mean, I just sort of went along with what he said.'

'I am sorry, Mary,' I said, 'I did not mean it like that.'

Mary was quiet for a minute, not looking at me but at the wall with a far-off look in her eyes. 'You know, Amir,' she said, 'it's not just the boy, it's everyone, I don't want to upset anyone. I like it here. You must have wondered why I put up with all that went on here. You've never asked me, but I've seen it in your eyes sometimes. I will give you the answer. This here is the nearest I've ever had as a home anywhere. All my life I've run from one place to the other, from one thing or the other. The day I walked in here I felt like I had found my own space. I looked at you people and saw that you were not committing a crime or doing bad business, only earning a living in peace. I had a good feeling. Well, that is why . . .' her voice trailed off. After a few seconds, she said, 'Yeah, I can never say no, you know.'

'It is very nice of you,' I said to her, 'we like you too very much.'

Mary sat silently beside me on the mattress with her knees up and arms wound round them. After a few minutes she said, 'Don't worry, I can handle Sakib.' Then she leaned over and kissed me on the cheek, said goodnight and went to her room.

Not long after that came the night when I saw Hussain Shah standing in the middle of the room with this shiny red dress in his hands. The dress was spread between his two hands which were raised towards Mary who was sitting on the bed. As I came up the stairs I heard him say, 'When he gave you?'

'A few days ago,' Mary replied.

'Why? Why he gave?' Hussain Shah said.

'I don't know, he just gave it to me. Maybe he got it cheap somewhere.'

'Not cheap, it is very dear. Why he gave you?'

'Don't keep saying why, why?' Mary said. 'How do I know? Ask him.'

'He spend money on this,' Hussain Shah said, 'and pay no money to me.'

'What are you talking about? He gives money to you, doesn't he?'

'Less. Every week less, not full. Why he gave you this? He has nothing to do with you.'

'What do you mean nothing to do with me?' Mary said to him in a voice suddenly grown heated and firm. 'I have some rights over him, haven't I?'

'No. Nothing,' Hussain Shah said angrily. 'Nothing.'

At this point Mary got up and shut the door of their room. I got so scared of what I thought might happen next that I went back downstairs. Everyone present in the house at the time had heard the voices from upstairs. We sat together with our tongues tied, waiting as if for the roof to fall on our heads. When nearly an hour passed and no more sounds came from the top, we relaxed a little and began playing some of our songs on the tape-player at very low volume. We had played and enjoyed these songs a hundred times before, but on that night it seemed that they had lost their spirit, that the tone was right and words were the same but the rhythm was out, that somehow they were the wrong songs.

One more storm had passed over our heads and we were still safe; but we also knew that within this protection we were trapped. We did not know what we should and would do and did not think about it. We had no idea of tomorrow or of yesterday but only of the hours of the day in which we lived and all we could do was to earn money and take our pleasure where we found it. Time had broken and fallen inwards.

20

'Not come late,' my mother said.

'Be back soon, mum,' I said to her at the door as I left for an invented girlfriend's birthday party on Saturday evening. I had been dreading going out with Jenny for the way she had looked the other day but was glad to see her in a decent dress and with less aggressive make-up on her face. Roy seemed to have grown no more than a couple of inches since I last saw him. He was small and gentle and pleasant, the exact opposite of his sister. We took a bus from the city-centre that took us to the Deerhorn club on the other side of town where Jenny said a band was playing. In the bus, Jenny said to me suddenly, 'I saw your dad.'

'Did you? When?'

'Some time back.'

'Where?'

'I was down de street when a man at my back said "Hello." I turned round and it was your dad. He recognise me too and said how was I and then bye bye and was away quick. I think he was trying to pick me up before he recognise me,' Jenny said, laughing as if it was no matter.

'Don't be silly,' I said, my face reddening with embarrassment.

'Don't get me wrong, Par, I like your people. Your men are gentle wid little potbellies and soft eyes. Look at our men, nothing on dem but sexual organs, big tight arses and bulges in front wid kilos of meat and rum going down to make dem bigger, trousers not big enough to fit dem. And whities, mealy-mouthed who can't even get it up half de time, dey make me sick.'

All this your men and our men and everything was getting me down. 'Leave it off, Jen,' I said to her. She took the point and started straightaway to talk about her and Len who was not, she insisted, her boyfriend but a 'work partner' and anyway was a half-caste of 'no deep colour'.

Inside the club, the room was so full we were lucky to find somewhere to sit. There was a group of four men at the table next to ours who kept looking at us with eyes full of mischief, making me nervous. None of the others with me noticed the men at first. Jenny had got a round of pints of lager for Martin and Roy, a sherry for me and double rum and coke for herself with Roy helping her carry the drinks. We had only taken a sip from our drinks when one of the men at the next table got up and went up to the bar. On his way back he stumbled and spilt some of his drink on Jenny. Jenny jumped in her seat.

'Hey, look where you're going,' she said.

'You're blocking the way,' the man said with a crooked smile on his lips.

'I'm bloody not, are you out of your head?'

'If you didn't spread your legs so much you wouldn't be in trouble, would you?' the man leered. The others at his table started laughing. One of them shouted something I couldn't catch, which made Jenny scowl. The band had started up again.

'You bastard,' Jenny stood up threateningly with her glass in her half-raised hand. The man laughed in her face and turned away. I pulled Jenny down to her seat. She kept taking tissues from her bag and pressing them on the wet spots on her dress and throwing them on the floor. 'Don't

look at them,' I said to her, 'ignore them, they're louts.'
Jenny calmed down a little and turned her back to them.
She sat leaning forward with her elbows on the table, still
pulling tissues from her bag and blowing into them. We
tried to concentrate on the music. The men on the table
didn't let up, they kept taunting us and laughing and
drinking and shouting. It was our turn to get the drinks
and the only way to go to the bar was to pass in front of
them between our two tables. The man who had spoken
to Jenny put his leg out just as Martin reached him. I had
seen it coming and held Martin with both hands as he
stumbled. On the way back I led with two pint glasses of
lager full to the brim, looking straight at the man, making
as though I was going to empty both glasses over his head.
He pulled back his leg. Our evening had been ruined
anyway. I was beginning to be scared. Jenny was just angry.
Martin has little expression on his face as it is, unless you
know him and can see that there are all kind of feelings
underneath. Towards the end of the evening, Martin's face
began to change. Martin is big and slow and he was beginning to move as if from slumber. I told him not to keep
looking at the men. For the first time in his life, he ignored
me. He kept his eyes on them, answering all their taunts
and bad language with a steady, slow-heating gaze. I said
to Jenny we might leave a little bit early, considering. She
said yes. A few minutes before the last number, we got up
and left.

We were waiting at the stop opposite the pub but the
bus was taking ages. I said to Jenny to let's walk to the next
stop and she said the bus would pass us half-way up and
it was the last direct bus, we'd never get home. They were
pouring out of the pub. I saw the four of them coming
out and making straight for us. They had spotted us. As
they came near they started pushing each other and one of
them knocked into Jenny. Jenny swore at him. Then their

pretence was over. The man stood and swore back obscenely and pushed her. He looked drunk and angry. He kept pushing Jenny all round the bus stop, yelling things at her like 'fucking black cunt' and staggering all over the place. Jenny cowered in the doorway of a shop to avoid him. One of the men who didn't join in was standing on the side and saying over and over, 'Come on John, come on, leave it, not worth it.' The third man, without uttering a word, pushed Roy roughly. Roy fell on me. I ran to where Jenny was and stood beside her, both sheltering her and taking her shelter. Roy followed me. I stood with the two of them in the narrow doorway foolishly hoping that a shutter or something would drop and screen us from the attackers. Only Martin was out in the open. There were people all around us looking on, but nobody even tried to stop the two men from shoving us. I screamed. Martin jerked round to look at me. In a flash, he leapt at the man facing him. I couldn't see whether Martin butted him in the chest or what, but the man was kneeling on the ground holding his stomach, making small gasping motions with his head as if vomiting, and Martin was running awkwardly and falling on the two men in front of us, trying to clasp them in his grip. The men pushed him to the ground and started kicking him, shouting 'nigger lover son of a bitch' and other things. Martin jumped up, not protecting his face, leaving it exposed to the men's feet, and in that moment or two when he was coming up I felt as if the blows were falling on my own face and my heart wrenched. I began to shout and cry with the actual pain of it. Martin picked one man up by his waist and threw him over. The man fell against the wall near our feet, just missing the big glass window of the shop. Martin lunged at the other man. He was fighting like an animal. His arms and legs were flying in all directions and falling with great big thuds on the man, who was now trying to protect himself. Martin seemed to have increased in size several times over and was all about the place. Suddenly, I felt strong. I put my hand lightly on Roy's shoulder. He looked back at me for an instant and there was boldness in his eyes. He broke away from us and straddled the man who had fallen near us. I beat the man on the head with my fists while Roy held him down. Jenny went to the one still gasping on the pavement and started kicking him in the ribs with her pointed shoes and using her bag to hit him on the head, screaming terrible obscenities, 'Fuck you, son of a cunt, fuckin' white trash', scaring the man out of his wits. The whole thing lasted no more than a minute or two. The two men on the ground managed to scrape themselves up and run to join the third grappling with Martin. The fourth was still standing on the side and saying parrot fashion 'Come on John, come on, leave it, not worth it.' They started to back off. One moment we were all fighting, the next we were gripping Martin's arms, trying to hold him back. Then the crowd came between us. The last I saw was one of the men crooking his arm vulgarly to us, walking backwards. Roy had hit his head against the wall and was cut. Jenny was wiping Martin's face, bleeding from several places, with her tissues while I tied my scarf around Roy's head. The bus came just as I heard a siren in the distance.

'Jenny, wait,' I said, 'it's the police, don't you want to report it?'

'Fuck de cops,' Jenny said to me, 'come on.'

I begged Martin to take his bus home but once he had decided he was going to see me to my door there was no changing his mind. I sat nestled against him in the bus. He had an arm round my shoulders and brought the other arm across my chest to link his hands. I spread my free arm and twined it with his. He looked down on my arm and said, 'It's like a baby.'

'What?'

'Your arm.'

'It's bigger than a baby,' I said.

'No,' he said, 'your arm is *like* a baby.'

'That's daft, Martin.'

Silently, he freed his hands and began rolling up my sleeve, first the jumper, then the shirt, until my arm was bare up to the elbow. He took it in both hands and lowered his face over it. I thought he was going to kiss my arm. But he was passing his nose back and forth along the length of of my forearm, sniffing at it.

'Martin,' I said to him, 'there are people looking,' and pulled away the goose-pimpled arm.

'It smells like a baby,' he said.

'Martin, you *are* crazy.'

I wanted to take Martin into a room and shut the door behind us and tend to his wounds and then take him in my arms. But there was no such place. At the top of my street, finally I said to him, 'Martin, go,' knowing that he would have to wait maybe an hour for the night service bus from here and an hour again for a second bus to his home. He walked backsteps for as long as he could see me. Back in my room, he had left something with me, something of his own, an arm, a leg, his eyes, which I could feel next to me just as there was the bed, the chair, the table. My chest bled for him.

I was still in bed at eleven the next morning when Mr Stanley rang my doorbell. As I opened the door I saw Martin sitting in his father's car parked right opposite the house. Mr Stanley said he wished to speak to me and asked if he could come in. I said what about, and he said it was about a personal matter, could he please come in. Thankfully my mother was not in the house. She had put her head in my bedroom door earlier and said she would be next door at Auntie Shirin's house where she went virtually every day to sit and chat and drink cups of tea, after my father had had his breakfast after the night shift and gone to bed. I let Mr Stanley into the front room. He had a grim mouth, had a dark suit on and a grey hat. He kept touching his hat, not taking it off but shifting it a little bit each time he touched it. He stood in the room and looked all round, taking in everything, the flowery wallpaper I'd always hated and the rumpled blankets still on the settee where my father had sat the evening before with his shoes and socks scattered over the floor. I hadn't even washed or changed or anything, just thrown my quilt dressing-gown over my shoulders on top of my nightie and the thing was dirty. Mr Stanley made me feel small the way he looked at me. He moved from the centre of the room to one side but did not sit down.

'I know your father,' he said finally. 'He has lived in this town for many years. Nice man, I must say, and a conscientious worker. I know virtually everyone in this city. You see, we people have lived here for generations.'

I didn't know what to say or do but go and start picking up shoes and socks off the floor and folding the blankets that made little hills on the settee.

'You know my son,' Mr Stanley said.

Knowing full well he was Martin's father, I said, 'Who?'

'Martin.'

'Oh, yes.'

'You have been seeing him.'

It was the way he put it. It made me cross. 'He's been coming to see me, off and on,' I said.

'Look, young lady,' Mr Stanley said in the same mild voice, 'he's been seeing you every single day, so let's stop playing games. Suppose you tell me what happened last night?'

'Nothing happened,' I said, feeling silly.

'There was a fight. He got beaten up. How did that happen?'

'We went to hear a band, four of us. There were some drunk louts there.'

'So you went to hear a band and there were some drunken louts there. Who were they?'

'Some men, never seen them. They were bent upon making trouble.'

'Why?' Mr Stanley said.

'I don't know. They were drunk and they were louts. Haven't you seen people like that who are looking for trouble?'

'There is a reason,' he said, 'there is always a reason.'

'How do I know? They didn't like us, I suppose, they picked on us.'

'You should have thought twice before taking Martin into a situation like that.'

'Situation like what? It was a pub where a band was playing. And I didn't take him anywhere, he came on his own, he's old enough.'

'He's nineteen,' Mr Stanley said.

'So?'

'How old are you?' Mr Stanley asked suddenly, 'twenty-one, twenty-two? I know you people are a couple of years behind, having come here not knowing the language and so on.'

'I am not behind,' I said stupidly.

'I know for a fact you were born in your own country and came here when some years old.'

'Five,' I said. 'What's how old I am got to do with it anyway? We were at school together, you know that.'

'He is a simple lad, easily led,' Mr Stanley said.

'Well, nobody led him to anything,' I said.

Mr Stanley took a packet of cigarettes from his pocket. He lit a cigarette without asking me if he could smoke. I offered him no ashtray nor did I invite him to sit down.

'I want you to stop seeing him,' he said.

I was so surprised I said, 'Who?'

'My son, Martin.'

'Why?' I said. I realised at once that I had done wrong. I should have refused to talk to him at that moment, shown him the door. I am angry enough at what he did, but nothing like how I feel about not having told him to piss off there and then.

'Because I don't want him to get mixed up in this sort of thing.'

'What sort of thing?' I said to him. 'I can't stop him coming to see me. Why should I anyway?'

'Because he is a simple lad. He can't think for himself.'

'He can think all right, if you treat him properly.'

'He is not clever,' Mr Stanley said with emphasis, 'can't you see?'

I couldn't believe he was saying this about his own son.

'He is simple,' Mr Stanley repeated. 'He's easily led.'

I burst out then. 'Who is leading him on? You barge in here trying to hustle me in my own house. How can you tell me to stop seeing anyone? Is there a law against it?'

'What has he said to you?' Mr Stanley asked, still in a mild, enquiring tone.

'What has he said to me what?'

'Has he talked to you about it?'

'About *what?*' I nearly screamed.

'He's got it in his head that he's going to marry you.'

I just stood there staring at him without a thing in my head. I went and sat down on the edge of the settee. My hands shook.

'Look, Parvin,' Mr Stanley said, calling me by my name for the first time, 'I see that you are probably as ignorant of this thing as I and his mother were until today. I have a feeling that if it were put to your parents they would be equally against it. But that is the way Martin is. He gets something into his head and then it is difficult to budge him. I fully sympathise with you because you may not even have dreamt of it. Martin is our only child. Academically speaking he is not clever, but he is not a total loss to us, thank God. I have built up a business from scratch, I am trying to train him for it, train him from the shop floor up. He cannot stand on his own, he needs help. It will take years, but with patience – I'm afraid I am not always patient with him – but with luck and a little patience, I hope that one day he will pick up the routine, it's only a matter of routine, this business. He is in no position at the moment to get into anything like he's suggesting, I'm sure you will see my point of view. I am on the council. I have always helped your people in my capacity, housing, jobs, etc., sometimes in the face of opposition, stiff opposition I can tell you. I can help you. I know people of position in this town, I have contacts. I am sure you will understand.'

Mr Stanley was smart, but not smart enough. He was making me really cross. Had he stopped going on about your people and my people at the time that he sprung the marrying bit on me, I would have gone along with him. But Mr Stanley was making me ashamed of myself, trying to bribe me and all, putting me in the wrong position.

'If Martin feels like that then it is his own idea,' I said to him. 'It's your problem, there's nothing I can do.'

'Stop seeing him,' Mr Stanley said abruptly, 'that is the only way he will listen.'

'No. You stop him if you want to.'

Mr Stanley suddenly lost his patience. His voice changed, became hard, his mild manner gone. He had been standing sideways, looking at the things in the room and then at me. Now he moved and stood facing me, his hands in his trouser pockets.

'So that is my reward, is it? This is what I get in return for all my help to your community? I have made enemies in this city, enemies, I tell you, for my humanitarianism, for taking the side of your people. I expect it's too much to ask for understanding. If he could look after himself it would be a quite different matter, we'd know he would not get into this kind of mess—'

Mess! I looked down at myself, the dirty quilt gown, my hair standing on my head, my father's soiled socks on the floor. He had jumped me and was accusing me of being the cause of all this mess. Now I think of it, that was the word which freaked me out. I lost control. The awful thing is that I was bursting to say something, something hard and pointed, something that I could hit him with. And I could think of nothing. It was terrible. I could find nothing to say. So all I had was my voice to hit him with.

'Get out,' I let out a huge scream, 'get out!' Mr Stanley stepped back, pulled his hands out of his pockets and looked at me from head to foot for a second. Then I saw Martin. He came running out of the car.

'What have you done?' he said to his father.

'Get back in the car,' Mr Stanley ordered him.

'What have you done?' he repeated. He was trying to shield me with his funny long coat. He has other coats but why he is always wearing this stupid coat that comes down to his ankles and shuffling about in it, looking shabby, God knows. His face was all swollen, covered with blue and purple bruises, his left eye nearly shut. He kept mumbling something I couldn't hear for the noise of my own two words that hung in my ears.

'You get back to the car straightaway,' his father shouted again, trying to push him away. Martin pulled himself back violently. For a moment I thought he was going to hit his father. Instead he turned and spat out his words to his father.

'You are a Jew,' he said.

It was so odd, it made no sense hearing him say it at a time like this, funny too, like me finding no hard and sharp words to say but only screaming 'get out'. I saw Mr Stanley go pale with rage.

'Shut up,' he said.

'You are a Jew,' Martin said to him again, 'grandma told me. You changed your name.'

Mr Stanley took a step towards Martin. He was shaking. Now I thought he was definitely going to strike Martin. But he didn't.

'I'll deal with you later,' he said to Martin. Then he shook a finger at me, 'and you will be hearing from me.' He ran out of the house, jumped into his car and drove away.

My shitty luck! I wouldn't have made so much noise or at least would have shut the back room door had I remembered my father being in bed upstairs. Just as Mr Stanley was driving away, my father appeared behind me.

'What,' he said, 'what?'

Woken suddenly, he blinked his sleep-filled eyes. 'About what is so much noise?'

'Nothing,' I said, startled and afraid.

'Why nothing?' Then he saw Martin at the door. 'Who is this boy?'

And daft Martin just said, 'She's old enough.' This totally confused my father.

'Old enough? Who is old enough? And who might you be, young man, I ask again?'

'I am Martin.'

'That is your name, but I am enquiring about your person.'

Maddeningly, Martin repeated, 'She's old enough.'

Wide awake by now, my father came to a half-realisation what Martin was on about and said, 'Off you go,' shutting the door on him. Immediately, he ran back into the house. Simultaneous sounds of the flushing of the toilet and a knock on the door came from two ends of the house. I opened the door.

'You're old enough,' Martin said.

'Don't keep *saying* that Martin, please, go now.'

Martin didn't move. A thunderous sound arose behind me.

'You,' said my father, stabbing a finger in the air at Martin, 'I said to you to be off. Off!'

'You can't force her,' said Martin to him, 'she's old enough.'

'Old enough. Nobody old enough. This is my house. Get out of my house. Old enough, old enough,' my father mimicked him, 'who are you to say? Who? Who are you?'

'I am Martin.'

He said it so simply that my father was stunned into silence. He merely looked at Martin's bruised open-eyed gaze without saying a word, the expression on his face a mixture of wonder, puzzlement, outrage. He just shut the door and stood staring at it. There was another knock, followed by an insistent second knock. My father opened the door again to see Martin standing there and looking at him the same way, as if silently asserting his name again to explain everything. I had the feeling of a magical moment in the air.

'I am manager of my factory,' Martin said. 'I work.'

I didn't know whether to laugh or cry. I knew it wasn't true. Standing there in his long coat flapping around his ankles, his hands stuffed into its pockets and hair all ruffled by the wind above a disfigured face, he looked ridiculous saying this. My father came back to life, his body seeming to take little jumps without leaving the ground. 'What manager? What factory? What is the purpose of your presence here? Leave us alone. If I see you again, I will teach you a lesson. I will call the police. I know the police here,

and they know me. I am a householder. Be off. And you,'
he turned to me, 'have you friendship with this boy?'

'We were at school together,' I said.

'You will not see him again.'

'Why?' I said to him. 'He has done nothing.'

'Is this nothing? Him standing at my door saying
nothing about his person or purpose of presence but only
his name and old enough, old enough, all this is nothing?'

'Look, dad, *we* have done nothing. Nothing has happened. Why don't you believe me? Nothing's been going
on, nothing at all.'

I think my father sensed at that time that I was lying
and how I felt about Martin. 'He will not come here again,'
he said to me.

'All right, he will not come here again.' I turned to
Martin. 'Go away, Martin.'

Martin still wouldn't move, making me furious. My
father glared at him for a moment. 'This is my house,' he
said to Martin. 'No place for your person here. This,'
he said, 'is my land.' He was standing in the middle of the
room, stamping his foot on the floor and pointing down
with his finger as if showing us something on the ground.
'My land,' he said again. 'Freehold land.'

I nearly laughed, before realising that there was no boast
in his voice, only the simple pride of a long labour. At that
moment, when we locked and held our gaze, I realised
that I carried in me the weight of both his pride and of
his old shame, knowing too that I could never free myself
from it.

'Oh, dad,' I said and closed the door on Martin.

My father stood there for another few seconds, shifting
his weight from one foot to the other, his finger still pointed
to the floor. Then as if he was reminded of something, he
rushed to the telephone and picked it up. I went into the
back room and sat down on the carpet against the wall and

overheard him ordering my mother back home over the phone from next door. My mother came in by the back door.

'What is matter?' she asked.

'This,' my father said, pointing to me with his finger, 'your daughter,' and stopped.

'What matter with you?' my mother asked me. I did not answer.

'She is fraternising with English boys,' my father said to her.

'Is right?' my mother asked me.

'No, mum,' I said, 'just a boy from school.'

'Liar,' my father said. 'This boy is present in person outside the front door.'

My mother moved towards the door. But instead of going to the front door, she went and closed the middle door that separated the two rooms, as if putting a buffer of the front room between her and this person at the front door.

'And he is telling me that she is old,' my father said to her.

'Old?' she asked.

'Yes, old enough, he says.'

'What that mean?'

'Only God knows. You,' my father stabbed a finger towards me, 'go up to your room at once.' I jumped up and ran upstairs. He stuck his head around the bottom of the stairs and shouted, 'And you will not take one step out of this house until my next order.'

I shut my bedroom door behind me and got straight into bed, covering myself from head to foot with the sheets. I couldn't stop shaking. It was like malaria. I remember malaria, I was four years old when I had it. It brought with it the kind of cold that entered the bones. It didn't make the flesh feel cold, only the insides, so that the guts shivered like live wires over which you had no control. After a while the pain of it started in the pit of the stomach and spread out to cover the whole body, from ribs to legs to arms and the small bones of fingers and toes, until it seemed it would never stop. But suddenly the sweat broke, and the shivering gradually died, leaving the body broken in bits. Then the fever came. In high fever you felt good, as if you had spread your wings and flew the heights.

21

I had already been living in Glasgow for a year before I learnt what happened after we were blown out of that house. All the while in the last few days of that time we had half expected something to happen. But it was on the lines of being caught and deported, or caught and not deported, or something in between, we were not sure what. What actually did happen on that day was something totally unexpected.

I still cannot believe it, my room was only next door and I did not even know, it happened so quickly. I had just come back from work and was sitting down on the mattress, stretching my legs, trying to settle myself before I got up to cook when I heard some voices coming from Hussain Shah and Mary's room. At first, I paid no attention. Suddenly, somebody shouted in anger. My ears stood to the sound. It was Hussain Shah, swearing in rage. Then the voice stopped. Someone uttered an oath, followed by a long groan, 'Aaahhh'! There was a knocking of furniture, a thud on the floor, then another, making the walls shudder. I quickly got to my feet. Some voices rose and fell. A moment's silence. Then it was as if the storm broke. Mary screamed, and screamed.

Everyone came running upstairs. We pushed each other out of our way to have a look in. Inside the room, Hussain Shah was spread out on his back on the floor and looked dead. Half of his shirt, from the left shoulder to the trouser belt, was wet with blood. Irshad had his back flat against the wall and was sitting up, his knees raised to his chest and feet wide apart, pointing in different directions. One of his hands rested, palm up, on the floor beside him, the other half-covering, half-holding the left side of his chest, absolutely still. Looking at the quick movement of blood gushing through his fingers, I remember thinking at that moment 'Why is he so still?' so unnatural did it seem in the presence of living blood. Sakib was standing by the two bodies with Mary's kitchen knife in his hand. On the sharp end of the knife hung a drop of blood which looked like it had begun to fall, but had hung on. That one drop of blood, in my mind's eye, occupies the whole room, covering everything. Memory is a strange sight. Sakib was looking with great attention at Hussain Shah and Irshad, but there was no recognition in his eyes, as if looking at newly-met strangers. Mary had the baby pressed to her chest and, half turned away, she was standing there screaming with a twisted face as if she was never going to stop. We all stood at the door, pushing and pressing and at the same time hanging on to each other and to the walls, looking but not crossing the doorway or taking the knife from Sakib's hand or covering Mary's face. We felt as if we were suspended in a long tunnel of silence, though Mary's screams pierced our ears. It was like being on the edge of a dream. All of a sudden, we started breaking up. One of us turned and bounded down the stairs two at a time. Someone else shouted,

'Run. Run from here. We will be caught.'

All I remember then was the heavy drubbing of many feet running up and down the stairs, collecting things. We who were in the house had time to stuff our belongings in suitcases and plastic bags before we fled, while those who were out at the time did not dare come in but went from outside to the outside. I put my clothes and a pair of shoes in a bag, felt for money in my inside pocket and was out of the house within three minutes.

It was evening. The front door of the house was opening and closing time after time. One by one, we were all fleeing. I was only in the third street from the house when a police car passed me with its siren on. Quietly I thanked God. I have not been back to that street, but I shall never forget the sight of our leaving that evening. The front door would open and the light from the hall would make a shaft in the night to the pavement. Someone would emerge and quickly shut the door. The darkness would return. In the dim street, that someone would scurry along a few steps this way or that, and then disappear. I kept looking back until I got to the end of the street and turned the corner. From where I saw them leave, I could not tell who was who, but that was my last goodbye to my mates of two years. In the end, we became only digits in the dark, which was just as well. It was that kind of time.

How I reached Glasgow is another story, the memory of which makes me shiver to this very day. Do they know what I have seen and suffered? One day when all this is over I will tell them, tell them how I lived and made progress. I was running for two whole months.

In those two months I exhausted, one after the other, all means of transport, from buses and trains to, finally, my own legs when I walked, from one point to the next, through the countryside, abandoning direct routes in order to mix up my tracks. I exhausted all modes of lodging too, from parks and railway stations to graveyards and grown fields. It was summer and I enjoyed some nights sleeping among the standing crops, the only time I have slept under an open sky in this country, remembering the nights in my village. After I reached Glasgow I had only enough money left to stay – for another seven weeks – in uncomfortable accommodation; some attics, some tiny box rooms always covered in dust. One time it was a room so small that a boy's bed laid in it was sufficient to prevent the door from opening, which in turn necessitated some manoeuvring in order to gain entry. I had to force myself through the narrow opening into the room and then, for want of a foothold, take a small jump to land on the bed, usually hitting some part of my body against the wall. It is true that I did not live in a palace back in Birmingham, but there I had my comrades around me, the nearness of bodies and souls that I missed.

My luck changed when, by mere chance, I found reasonable living space in Mrs McTaggart's house, for which she made no demand for money in advance. It was a small room, but clean, furnished with a chair, a table and, best of all, a bed. I could not remember when last I had slept in a proper bed. The only dirty part was the windowpanes which, said Mrs McTaggart, she had cleaned only once a year, since that was all she could afford. This bothered me little. After having spent many nights without sleep and with no hiding place, this room was like paradise to me. The first day, I slept for twenty hours at a stretch. Soon, however, I was out and about, looking for work. Avoiding straying into the main streets and the open outskirts, I found employment in small factories and workshops situated in the narrow back alleys of the city, where I felt safe. The work was of a temporary nature, but no questions were asked and cash was in hand on Fridays. Economising on food, clothing and other requirements, I was able to pay the rent and save a few pounds on top each week. Mrs McTaggart took a liking to me from the start. In my search for work, I encountered a problem I had not met before – that of providing a reference. Mrs McTaggart readily agreed to give me one, putting it in writing, thus equipping me with a piece of paper that exhibited proof of my permanent address, good character and so on. It was the first document of credentials that had come into my possession, and as I stepped out of the house with it in my pocket, I felt rich and confident of my existence.

Mrs McTaggart was forty-six years old and had had more than one husband. Some died, while others, as I figured from her conversation, absconded. She had inherited the house from her first husband, one Mr McTaggart, a foreman in the factory where she worked as general help, who had died on account of drinking two bottles of whiskey one New Year's Eve shortly after marrying her, his insurance money paying for the house. Mrs McTaggart was of good bodily size, though quite active, and possessed a sweet nature. Gradually, as time passed, I settled down to a comfortable life, eating an evening meal cooked by her, for which I gave a pound on top of my rent. After some time, Mrs McTaggart started coming into my room every now and then for a visit and a chat, and then, occasionally, staying the night.

One day, quite unexpectedly, I met a man I used to know. While shopping for some small things in the city, I caught sight of him sitting in a café. I stopped and looked through the window. It was a cold day, and inside men huddled around bare tables, drinking cups of tea. I remembered then that this was a man who used to live two streets away from us in Birmingham. He had arrived in this country about three years before us when there were no prohibitive rules of entry and anyone who had the money to buy an aeroplane ticket could come here without being apprehended for wrongdoing. I went in and sat in the vacant seat beside him. His name was Badar, a well-educated man who had left his country in order to better himself. In Birmingham, he used to be night watchman in a big office block in the city. At first he did not recognise me, as I had grown a beard to disguise my true identity while I was on the run. When I told him who I was, he remembered me well. He had come to this city recently after securing – being a free man – from a newspaper advertisement a good job in an office. We talked of our time in Birmingham. From Badar, I learnt what happened after I left.

First, he told me about what happened to Hussain Shah and Irshad. They were both dead, he said. He was actually at home, he told me, at the time that it all happened and had seen the police arriving. Everyone, except the Bengalis, was gone. The Bengalis too were almost out of the house when the police came and caught them. All the people in the street were gathered outside the house. Sakib was taken into custody, the owner of the house was called out, and the ambulances came with their lights on and sirens going. Police cars came and went while photographers and news reporters jostled with the crowd.

They brought the covered dead bodies out on stretchers and put them into one ambulance, which quickly left. The other ambulance took Mary and the baby away. Sakib and the two Bengalis were put in two separate police cars and driven away. The house was locked up. A policeman stood guard over the house for a day or two, during which time the police came and entered the house once again, then the guard was taken off. For as long as Badar lived in the street after that, the house remained empty. Children broke its windowpanes by throwing footballs and stones at them, birds flew in and out to nest in the rooms, cats of the street made it their hunting ground, the house became a ruin. After a time the owner sold it to the council. The council boarded it up. That was the end.

While he was in Birmingham, Badar followed the whole case in local newspapers as it came up in the courts. It was the first thing he read every day, he said. The two Bengalis had turned witnesses for the crown and gave the authorities the names of all the residents of the house and whatever they knew of their home addresses as well as names and addresses of their friends and relatives in this country. In addition they supplied the names of all the agents they knew. In return they got freedom from prosecution, and the rumour was that they also got work visas for six months with the promise of temporary extension after that. God knows what happened to them in the end. Some white men, it was said, were also arrested in this connection. Mary appeared in court as a witness. In the eyes of the police the evidence against Sakib was solid and complete. He was sent for medical examination and was eventually sentenced to be detained in a prison for a period of time to be set at Her Majesty's pleasure, upon the expiry of which he was to be deported to his own country. Later Badar came to know from someone that Sakib was locked up in one such prison near Wolverhampton.

Badar invited me to come with him to his home. Normally I would have run a mile rather than go to the home of people not known to me. On Badar's insistence, I went. It was a house of medium size in which eight men lived. It was arranged in a way similar to our old house – number twenty-six, Mathews Street – with two kitchens, each shared by four men, on two floors, the only difference being the presence of chairs and tables and beds in the rooms instead of mattresses on the floor. We sat in the chairs and played cards, listened to our songs, exchanged news from back home. It being a Sunday, they were all home and had time to spare. One of the men brought out some bottles of beer and I had a glass of it. Nobody asked me questions. I enjoyed the evening. I could not help feeling, however, that I was with eight free men who could do what they liked, drive cars, attend public places, join the labour Unions, go to their doctors. Sitting among them, drinking beer, I almost longed for the company of men that I had in Birmingham, where everyone knew everyone else's situation, each one relying on the other. It was a community. This here was a group where everybody was proud of his rights and was for himself alone, sitting down with others only to pass the time.

Then one day, like a bolt of lightning from a clear sky, I was arrested. It was four a.m. and Mrs McTaggart and I were in bed, fast asleep. They made a lot of noise, thumping at the door in the night. I was taken to the local police station and locked up in a cell. About ten o'clock, I was led into a small room in the same building where questions were put to me about this thing and that, my name, address and occupation, but mostly about my existence in this place, to which I had no reasonable answer. The questions were civil, more or less, and free of abuse. Afterwards, I was returned to the cell. From then onwards, things began to go very wrong.

A mix-up, for a start: a man, whom I assumed to be a detective wearing a suit, entered the cell carrying some papers in his hands in which he seemed to be engrossed. He did not care to look at me as he came in but walked over to the middle of the cell and stood there, his head down and the lower part of his body thrust forward, still turning the sheets of paper back and forth, biting his lips and frowning. When he was finished with them he did not raise his head but merely rolled up his eyes to look at me from a lowered brow, as if peering beneath a low object, fixing me in his gaze.

'Are you the bloke who pressed up against a woman in a supermarket?' he asked.

'No, sir,' I answered.

I said it without thinking. My brain had adopted a totally negative position, resolving, independently of me, that my only defence was to deny everything. Later on, when I regained some control over my thinking, I realised that this was perhaps a mistake. Unfortunately at the time, the decision had been already made through fear, which dictated that I refuse, refute, rebut, negate everything and anything, thus leading myself, hopefully, into a form of non-existence. In the state of such fear one also begins to rely on fantastical happenings. Taken up with thoughts of disappearance, I am sure that at some point I willed myself into believing that the old jinn from back in my village would come and spirit me away, thus bringing the proceedings to an end. The next day, after gaining a night's sleep and familiarity with my surroundings, it came to me that I could more profitably have done one of several things, like stayed mum, played dumb in other words, or else pretended that I did not understand what was being said, even made myself incomprehensible by saying things rapidly in my own language. That, however, was wisdom gained after the event.

The detective's two subsequent questions, which were only variations of the first, I answered in denial. Then I slipped. The next question was, 'Do you deny it?', to which I repeated, 'No, sir.'

He advanced towards me. 'Do you admit it, or do you deny it?'

'No, sir,' I said, 'I deny it.'

Glancing at the sheet of paper in front of him, he said wearily, 'It says the lady complained.'

'No, sir,' I said.

'Are you saying the lady is lying?'

'No, sir.'

'No sir what?'

'The lady is not lying.'

'You admit it then.'

'No, sir.'

With no word of warning, his right leg appeared below me as if from nowhere and the knee crashed into my testicles. 'This is just to make you forget your wily ways,' he said. 'Now listen to this carefully. It says the coloured man followed this woman all round the supermarket, and when she joined the queue at the check-out he pressed up against her from behind. What do you say to this?'

'No, sir,' I said through my pain.

'How many times have you done this before you were caught? Do you people come here to press up against decent women?'

'No, sir,' I said to him, 'to work.'

'What?'

'I came here to work.'

'And is it part of your work to assault defenceless women in the street?'

'Supermarket,' I said without thinking.

'What?'

'You said supermarket,' I babbled.

'Ah, so you admit you committed the offence in the supermarket and not in the street.'

'No, sir.'

'Look, you randy bastard, you'll get two years for this.'

I was talking too much. I was at the centre of great panic and it was pushing me more and more into the wrong. Even as I answered his questions I was becoming aware that sooner or later I would have to stop denying things without thinking about them, it was burying me deeper and deeper under my own words. I had kept his right leg in my sights in case he decided to attack me again. He kept questioning me in the same vein for one or two more minutes, becoming more abusive. Just when I was at the point of saying something very foolish in desperation, aid arrived, as if from God, in the shape of a man who looked exactly like the man questioning me. This angel of rescue poked his head round the door and said, 'Malcolm, can I speak to you for a minute?' The officer left me and I never saw him again.

I did not know what it was all about until Mrs McTaggart came to see me four days later. At first they would not let her see me, she later told me. But Mrs McTaggart was with a solicitor and they made so much fuss that the authorities had to give way. This was when I came to know from Mrs McTaggart that there had been a mix-up. Presumably, the wrong man had picked up the wrong papers from the wrong pile, or something. That cleared up the first mystery. What about the second, namely my arrest? Mrs McTaggart said that obviously it was a case of someone having informed on me. The solicitor was a Scottish man. I had by this time acquired a state of mind that made me take alarm at the sight of a white man's face. I asked to speak to Mrs McTaggart alone. I told her that I did not trust the solicitor. 'He is a fine man, an experienced man,' she said, 'and wants to help you.' Although I half believed that he was on my side, I approached the solicitor with caution, positioning myself at a lateral angle to him and not looking straight at his face. At the end of that meeting, of which I remember little, I again took Mrs McTaggart aside and gave her Baba Rehman's number in Birmingham, begging her to ring him. This was a man, I told her, who knew ways of getting our people out of trouble. Mrs McTaggart came back three days later, furious with anger. The man, she said, 'went ape' over the telephone, abused and threatened her, and put the telephone down. 'What kind of people are these?' she asked.

I had lost faith in everything. I would most probably be traced back to Birmingham and implicated in the events that occurred there, and be put away for a long time, with no future.

On the day of my appearance in court, I sat beside the solicitor and answered his questions, took his instructions, etc. I was sent back on remand. On my second appearance in court, I was charged with illegal entry into the country. I was relieved of worries and thanked God for it, as the punishment for this was only some time in jail and then deportation. I was saved from having had connections with the fearful events in Birmingham.

Then something happened which had a good and a bad side. The good: my sentence did not include imprisonment but only deportation. And the bad: on the nineteenth day of living in police cells and appearances in court, I was taken out of remand and sent to this detention centre near Liverpool. In this prison, for a prison it was, I sat, along with several others in a similar situation, awaiting the result of an appeal already lodged by my solicitor against the decision of the court. I will say this for Mrs McTaggart, that despite her weak financial position, her bodily weight, her asthma and swollen knees on account of rheumatism, she came to see me, all the way from Glasgow, once every two weeks on average, besides arranging for a local solicitor, Mr Kelly, an Irish gentleman, to visit me regularly. In actual fact, I was not unduly upset about the prospect of deportation, being more than happy to escape the charge of involvement in the Birmingham events. But again it was Mrs McTaggart who persuaded me with her argument – 'What do you have to lose?' – into the lodging of an appeal for permission to stay in this land, supported by Mr Kelly, who said that there was hope.

During the unending period of my stay at the detention centre, I settled down to a silent and simple life from one day to the next, entering into no conversation with the others nor engaging myself mentally with them, just answering questions directly and asking none. I had so much time at my disposal that for the first time in eighteen months or so, I found myself pondering over many things, but chiefly the future – is it not a fact that thoughts of

tomorrows always ail our souls? The toughest periods
of time were those when I had to sit in the room and look
at the walls, because there was nothing on the walls to
look at. Those walls looked more bare than other bare walls
that I had seen. The walls of this room were bare in a
way that transferred to me directly their bareness,
reminding me constantly that I possessed nothing, sometimes reminding me of death. I could cope with not having
good future prospects, but I could not do with being dead.
As long as I was alive I could do the usual things, like sit,
stand, eat, sleep, think. That was sufficient; it was possible
to be happy. Wading through these thoughts, I lived on
until the seventy-second day of my detention, when Mr
Kelly came in, beaming. A law had been passed, he said,
by the Parliament, which granted amnesty to people who
had entered the country without legality before a certain
date. There was some more work to be done, however,
because I had been caught before the law came into effect.
'But we have a good case, so not to worry,' he said to me.
He had known about the law being put through, had crafty
Kelly, but hadn't mentioned it in case it proved a false
hope. Now a very bad thing happened – with hope came
thoughts of all the things that had been taken away from
me: my own room, a picture of scenery on the wall, Mrs
McTaggart, my clothes, food. The food in that prison was
so bad that I had been experiencing difficulty swallowing
it, although I did not become overly aware of it until the
day Mr Kelly gave me the good news and I began enter-
taining hopes of eating good food once again. I also began
having thoughts of the things that I had done wrong, ruing
all my mistakes, wishing I had done differently. Prospects
of better times to come caused me unhappiness. Finally,
after such remorse I became aware of the nature of hope
and made a big effort to dismiss these things from my
mind. Just then, twenty-eight days after Mr Kelly gave me

the good news of amnesty, making up a sum total of one
hundred days in detention, I was freed. My things were
returned to me: the clothes, my cancelled, false passport,
all my payslips, letters, money and all the other items that
were taken away from my room during the police raid.
Directly, I was off to Glasgow.

I arrived in the city in the late afternoon. Mrs McTaggart
clasped me in her heavy arms, hugged and kissed me.
'Lovely to see you, lovely, lovely. Sit yourself down, let
me see you. You're a bag of bones. I'll have to feed you
properly, fatten you up.' My room was kept vacant for me.
All my effects that were not taken away were in their place.
We spent a good night in bed. In the morning, I ate a
good breakfast fried in butter – eggs and everything, cooked
and brought in by Mrs McTaggart while I was still in bed.
I was already beginning to think of the future. All the
time I had spent in Glasgow, I had done nothing but work
and hide in the terrible cold of Scotland which had frozen
my bones. I knew neither the city nor other men. I knew
the city of Birmingham and my way around it and had
worked with foremen whom I had given gifts, earning their
goodwill; I wanted to go back there as a free man. On the
fourth morning of my arrival in Glasgow, just before daylight broke through the night, I packed my things in the
suitcase and left the city for good.

Having worked in Glasgow over a period of a year and
a half, I had accumulated some savings over and above the
money I sent back home every month. This amount I had
kept hidden inside my bed through a tear in the mattress,
which is where the police found them during the raid.
Upon my release, it had come back into my possession. I
counted out a sum of money sufficient to cover three
months' rent, adding a generous sum over. This I placed
on top of the pillow before I left. I only stopped for a
moment out in the street to have a last look at the house.

The light of the day was coming up. The street was empty except for a milkman going around on his float. 'Good morning,' he called out to me. 'Good morning,' I replied. Then I walked away.

This is the one thing in all my life of which I am ashamed. Mrs McTaggart had shown kindness to me and I had not responded with kindness. I left without saying goodbye to her. To pay such bigness of heart with a sum of money and no last words of thanks is a misdeed, which cannot be forgiven. The only time I will not respect myself is when I will think of Elizabeth McTaggart.

Birmingham – home from my home, so to speak. As I entered the old city I felt as though I bore on my head an eagle, and knew why I had wished to come here: I wanted to regain my pride in the very city where I had once lost it. I would have my papers in hand bearing legality and could go, as and when I wished, through passport and immigration control and by regular airline to any place without fear. I could have myself treated by a GP whenever the need arose, earn money and put it in a proper bank. These things I proceeded to obtain in rapid succession: documents of residence from the Home Office, National Insurance number without which no money in the pocket is proper tender, my medical card and registration at the Labour Exchange as a person seeking employment in his own right. I had no wish to go near Mathews Street, which still held the threat of criminal involvement to me, so I went across to the other end of town and acquired temporary lodgings. There I lived for the first nine months. I was able quickly to secure employment at the post office. At first it was a labouring job on the trolleys. After three months, in view of my literacy in English, hard work and regular attendance, I was invited to take an examination, which I passed with ease. I was then promoted to a position in the sorting office. Living in rented accommodation, I no longer sent money back home but saved every penny, economising on all things, with the sole purpose of buying my own house. Before long I was in a position to apply for a mortgage and put a deposit on a house. Since I knew that a queue system operated for the families back home to come and join us here, and that it took some time for their turn to come, I put through the necessary papers required for this purpose soon after taking employment. Overtime here was available from the very beginning to those who wanted it, and I worked, as I still do, ten and sometimes twelve hours a day, six days a week on the regular. Outside of working hours, I had little to do. Life during those months was not nearly as quick as it had been prior to that. In the free world, after my needs were met and worries settled, I was left with only a space that was populated by people who had neither the need nor a care for me. It was for me an empty space. I felt this more acutely when I had a day off, like on Sundays, when I sat looking out of the window. At times like these I could not help but remember my mates of old in this city, Hussain Shah and Irshad, now dead, Sher Baz and Roshan. But most of all Sakib. It was on one of my days such as this that I accidentally found a small scrap of paper buried in a corner of the inside pocket of my jacket on which Badar had written for me the name of the place near Wolver-hampton in which Sakib was supposed to be shut up. I read it with difficulty on that dirty and crushed piece of paper and decided there and then to go and visit Sakib on my next day off.

It is not easy, as I learned, to go and visit somebody just like that in these places. There was a procedure. I had to see official persons, fill up forms and answer questions, such as who I was, my name and address, means of livelihood, what was my business with this person, how did I know him and did I know of his condition? And so on and so forth. I duly answered, as and when and where required, all the questions, producing all the papers which proved that I was a legal resident of this country, paid my taxes, had a job and was of good character, and all the rest. Then I was told to go and wait. After five weeks I received a letter directing me to go to such and such a place and secure an appointment at my convenience. After following the instructions, I waited some more. Finally the day arrived when I set out to meet Sakib. Although the fear of being implicated in the old murders had by now largely gone from me, it was still with a trembling heart that I arrived there.

To judge from the security arrangements, it was very like a prison, though of a different kind, as it turned out. I waited in a small room for a while. There were three office chairs and a table in the room and an old and thin carpet on the floor. The door opened and Sakib entered with another man. The man spoke to Sakib as soon as they came into the room.

'This is your friend Amir, come to see you, Sakib,' he said.

Sakib nodded in response and offered me his hand. We shook hands. 'OK Sakib?' the man said to him, and repeated, 'OK Sakib?'

Sakib nodded again. 'Yes,' he said.

'All right then,' the man said, 'you sit down here and talk to your friend.'

'OK,' Sakib said and sat down in a chair opposite me. The man went across the room and stood at a window looking out, facing away from us with hands clasped behind his back.

Sakib had changed in appearance. He was wearing a suit and tie. With his shoes polished and hair cut and combed neatly, it looked as if he had got ready to go out for the day. He had put on weight. He still looked innocent, but in a matter of just two years had grown old. He was a young man with an aged face, as if the expression on his face had frozen at some stage whilst the flesh went on forming.

'Do you recognise me?' I said to him.

'Yes,' Sakib nodded.

'How are you?' I asked.

'I am all right now,' he said happily. He spoke only English.

'What were you doing when I came?' I asked.

'Watching football,' he said.

'Were you watching a match?'

'Yes,' he said.

'Do you still read magazines?' I asked him.

'Yes,' he said. 'I work in the carpenter shop.'

'What do you make there?'

'Desks. Chairs. Everything.'

Our conversation came to a stop. Sakib kept looking at me expectantly, though he had nothing to say. I had an urge to talk to him of our old times.

'Sakib,' I said to him firmly, 'do you remember Birmingham?'

'Yes,' he nodded vigorously, and fell silent.

I had a strange feeling. On the one hand I did not want to remind Sakib of the past, on the other I had this desire to say something that would break his stare, make him recognise the world.

'Sakib,' I said to him, 'do you remember Mary?'

'Yes,' he said. He looked round the room aimlessly, his eyes stopping for a moment at a picture on the wall of some bare-bodied men working in a field.

'Have you had your lunch, Sakib?' I asked.

'We had fish,' Sakib replied. 'There is a film at three o'clock.'

'What film?'

'On television.'

We sat in silence for long minutes. To be honest, I had always thought of Sakib as serving his sentence of a few years for his crime in a regular prison and, given his education and interests, working somewhere like the prison library, reading books and magazines and practising his writing. The actual figure of Sakib that I faced in this special prison-like hospital had unsettled me. After only a few minutes, I had nothing left to say to him. I was feeling restless. I got up to go. Sakib rose immediately. The man at the window came and joined us.

'We went to town in a bus yesterday,' Sakib said to me.

'Very good,' I said. 'Nice.'

'Yes,' Sakib said and put his hand out to me. 'You will come tomorrow?' he asked, shaking my hand.

'Not tomorrow,' I said to him, 'but I will come.'

'OK,' Sakib said, nodding his head. 'OK.'

On the bus coming back, I sat by the window. It was a clear afternoon. The sky was blue and the sun shone on the green fields on both sides of the road. I am not one for a soft head or a heavy heart, but there was something in that sunlight, so brilliant and tense, that looking at it from the moving bus my heart suddenly began to sink. I wept a little. Sakib's world was closed from every side and there was no opening. I remember the time when we used to live together in Mathews Street and Sakib was so young, so clever, never wasted his time like us in idle gossip but read his books and magazines in his attic. In that house, Sakib's world was not ours, but looking at him we forgot our own world and joined his for a moment. This was not the Sakib I had seen today who had been the companion of our old days. There was one question that kept coming back to my mind: what was Sakib's fault? God only knows what the actual situation was regarding the murders, but what had he done to deserve this life? In the end, it was a question with no point to it. What is anyone's fault? Nobody deserves their life. I decided that I had to put Sakib behind me, he was not the same man I had once known but someone else who had no name or memory or history, just a place where he lived.

22

Whispers, whispers was all I heard the whole week that I stayed shut in my room, whispers rising from the kitchen, the back room, the front room, flying about the house flapping their batwings, clinging to the walls, the ceiling, making silent mocking faces at me, attacking my brain. I covered my eyes with the sheets to block them, then the whole of myself, to hide, to go away from them, to cease to exist, but couldn't stop their penetrating gaze, just couldn't. My mother kept coming up with food, calling out for me but I wouldn't unlock the door. All I had for three days was glasses of water from the trays left outside. I quietly unlatched the door after she had gone, to pick up the water and withdraw, locking it behind me, hiding under the sheets again with the noise of whispers rising in my ears like approaching traffic. For the first time in memory my father took a whole week off. It must have broken his heart to get a sick note from his friend Dr Shamim, our GP, to whom he sends baskets of fruit, the only time he buys it from a proper shop and not the street market. He does it every few months, because the GP helped my mother through three miscarriages and an operation to sling out her uterus, which I found out about years later. So he was at home walking through the house, he and my mother following one another all day long and half the night from one end of the house to the other, talking constantly in low voices. Bug-eyed whispers homed in on me, seeing the filth on my body that I never could wash off, until that day when Martin put his nose to my arm and said it was like a baby. I said it's daft Martin, and he said, no, you smell nice, and with that he lifted the weight of the earth from me, as when the black cloud splits a hole in itself and the light comes in through the window. Thank God the loo was upstairs so I could go without knocking into them. Each time I came back to my room my mother ran up on the dot to check whether I was having my period and thank God I was, starting early by a whole week the very second day I was ordered to my room. What with this and no food I was actually dying on the fourth day when on the way back from the loo I heard my father on the phone asking for the international operator and stopped at the top of the stairs to listen. After a few minutes the ring from the operator came with the connection and my father talked to someone in Punjabi for some time in a way that made me think it wasn't his first conversation with whoever was at the other end. It gave me the creeps. I went straight down on trembling legs for the first time in four days and stood in front of my father.

'What's going on, dad?'

'About what going on?' he said innocently.

'I overheard you on the phone.'

'Ah, that,' he said. Then with a sweet smile he turned to my mother. 'Have you cooked our baby her favourite food? You are so unmindful of her tastes, I have told you so many times to properly look after her, look, how pale she has become in the face. Give her food to eat. Go, leave me and my daughter alone. Now, you sit down here my child.'

'Dad, I am not hungry and I don't want to sit down. I

want to know what it was that you were talking about on the phone.'

'Only to my friend, beti.'

'It was an international call, you were talking in Punjabi, I heard everything. What was it about?'

My father was stumped for an answer for a second. Then with a happy grin, he said, 'We are making arrangements.'

'Arrangements for what?'

'For the marriage of our dear and lovely daughter, what else?'

'What marriage,' I said to him, 'when, how, where?'

'Among our own very respectable people, my sweet, people who will give you respect.'

'I don't want it, dad, whatever it is or whoever.'

'Not whoever, not unknown, I know the boy's father. Very high position he has in society over there. Much property he owns.'

'Look, I've told you, dad, I don't want it.'

He pretended not to have heard me. 'A young and good-looking boy.'

'You haven't been back since you came here years ago. How do you know?'

'I know his father and his mother, very beautiful both of them, the boy looks exactly like him, pure Kashmiri, just like white people here. Educated too, BA pass. You know what that is? It is high education, more than "A"-levels. Very good. He has a position in government office but he will be prepared immediately to leave all these good things and come here. Because you know why? Because of only you, only for my lovely daughter.'

'That's a lie, dad, he doesn't even know me. He will come because he wants to get out of there and come here.'

'No, no, no,' my father said, 'for only you, I am telling you. It will be good life. If you want to live with him alone in freedom, I will provide you home, new house for the two of you only when the marriage takes place. I am able to do so, you know, can afford it, I am picking up approximately three hundred pounds a week all told – net, mind you, not gross, take home money.'

For a moment I thought he was going to pull out his diary from his pocket and show me. It would make me laugh. He didn't, thank God for that.

'I have been paying for this house over the top,' he went on, 'so it is nearly paid off. I can now secure one other mortgage with no problem, I tell you, it is nothing for me to do this for my dear beti—'

'Dad, dad,' I interrupted him, 'I don't want another house or marriage or anything, I'm not ready—'

'You do not have to do anything to become ready, it will be all our job, necessary papers, visa, travelling, all expenses and arrangements.'

'What about me, dad?'

'You don't understand, beti,' he said, 'every girl is ready at your age, and it is not easy to secure a good boy, a boy with education just like you. He will be not only your husband but also a son to me. Our family will be complete. I know his father and mother—'

'No,' I shouted. It stopped him in his tracks. 'I've told you, I don't want a house or husband or marriage. No. I won't have it.'

Suddenly, my father lost all his sweetness. 'You are nothing but foolish. Very foolish. Go back at once to your room. I will decide what to do.'

I ran off upstairs. My mother followed me but by the time she got to my door I had already locked it. I heard her calling out for me and crying. Later, when she came up again to leave the tray of food and knocked at the door to let me know, I said what the fuck, I've told him what I think, I'm not starving to death, so I opened the door and couldn't even look at roti and salan but took an apple and ate it and drank the cup of milk, which caused the wind to rise and roam inside me. From then on I started taking little bits of food from the trays she would leave out twice a day though I didn't open the door to her until . . .

Oh, she's coming down, I can hear the loose slippers she wears at home falling thrup thrup thrup on the brick steps. I shrink into a corner trying to disappear into the lit-blackness of this hole in the ground. I can't make myself unseen in front of her wordless cow-gaze, nor stay quiet.

'What,' I say finally.

'Why not you say yes?' she says.

'You know I won't. Why are you doing this to me? I hear people coming and going up there. Who are they?'

'No, no, not true yes. False yes.'

'False yes?'

'Lie. Only say yes.'

'You mean I say yes just like that and not mean it?'

'Yes,' she says. 'Then your father forget.'

'Are you joking? He will never forget.'

'Only say yes.'

'I won't. Don't try to trick me. Leave me alone.'

She keeps looking at me with her dry-weeping eyes for a whole minute, then gives up and goes away, taking her sinned-against eyes with her. This eases my stomach. I have been listening to the footsteps above me that I don't recognise, unknown feet, men's feet, they put the death in my heart and make my mind up that I won't give in.

23

I had already selected this house, and as soon as my mortgage came up, I moved in. From that day on I had my
hands full, with more than enough to do by way of
obtaining essentials such as pots and pans, beds, tables,
chairs and so on. I never had an occasion to meet the
previous owners since the whole business was carried out
via solicitors and house agents, but they had not left a
straw in the whole house, except for a single chest of
drawers with three and a half legs. I did try to mend it but
found that it had permanently lost its balance, so I put it
away as a relic of the house. Every Sunday early in the
morning I went to the street market looking into junk
shops to pick up items of household use in good condition
at cheap prices. Who would think that on one of these
outings I would come across a figure suddenly emerging
out of the past! I was walking down the market looking at
each and every thing, stopping and touching and examining
and moving on among hundreds of people on the pavement
when I came face to face with this woman with a child
toddling along beside her.

'Mary!' I shouted to her.

Mary recognised me immediately and remembered my
name. She shouted back in astonishment. We walked away
from the crowd and stood in front of a closed shop, where
Mary greeted me with warmth and love. I knew at first

glance the boy Michael, now just over three years old but looking bigger than his years, a beautiful child. I extended my hand to him, which he shook solemnly. 'I saw you when you were a baby,' I said to him. He smiled shyly and looked away.

'Small world,' Mary kept saying, 'small world.' She lived just down the road, she told me, and had come to the market to see if she could find some clothes for the boy. Then she asked me, hesitantly, whether I would like to come with her to her house, perhaps she could make me a cup of tea? I said I did not want to trouble her in any way.

'No trouble,' she said, 'no trouble at all.'

Mary lived in a council house with two bedrooms. She had very little by way of possessions, just beds, tables and chairs, and some plastic toys which were scattered on the lino-covered floors. There were alcoves in the walls with green-painted shelves fixed in them. On the shelves were placed some things: an alarm clock that had stopped, a small clay statue of the Virgin Mary, a framed poster of green fields on the surface of which, in the absence of glass at the front, dust had settled; an empty bottle of Dimple whiskey. Michael picked up a toy elephant and started twisting it in his hands. Mary led me into the kitchen.

I sat in a chair in one corner of the very small kitchen and looked at the dirty dishes all around. In Mathews Street Mary couldn't rest until every last dish was washed and put in its proper place. Mary had changed in appearance, she had not become fat or old, but her features had fallen round the edges, like wet clay left too long in one place. The black rings around her eyes had become permanent marks which she no longer tried to hide. There was a bad blue bruise mark above her left eyebrow which she kept touching while talking to me. She dragged her feet, walking as if tired to the very bones. I wanted nothing more than to talk to Mary of the time we lived in Mathews Street, when she had bounce in her walk. But Mary was talking of other things. There was one thing about Mary that had not changed – her cheerful chat.

She was living with an Irishman who worked on buildings. The man was a good worker and wage earner, Mary said. There was just one thing, she said, he drank. And when he drank, he sometimes changed. But that was his nature, said Mary, at heart he was a good man.

'He's gone to the pub right now,' she said to me. 'If he was at home, I wouldn't dare bring you here. He has a jealous nature. But don't worry,' she said with a smile, 'he won't be back for an hour yet. They have to throw him out first.'

Mary brought two mugs of tea and put them on the table. She sat opposite me and lit a cigarette. 'You used to take two spoons,' she said, handling the sugar bowl.

'You remember?'

'Oh, yes, I remember,' she said. 'I have a good memory. Right, enough of me, now tell me about yourself. What have you been up to all this time?'

I told Mary briefly the story of the past two years. She was pleased to know that I was now a free man, had a good job and my own house.

'Like me, you've had a bumpy ride,' she said, laughing a little, 'thank God you have found peace at last.'

'I hope that you find peace and comfort too one day,' I said to her.

She uttered a small laugh again. 'Oh, I don't worry about that. My life will go on, one way or the other.'

'I still hope and pray to God that you will be happy in the end, Mary,' I said.

'Thank you,' she said, 'thank you very much,' and became silent. She sat there quietly thinking for a moment. Then she said, 'Tell you something . . . you may not know, I have a brother, a year older, lost track of him now, but when we were small and lived at home, we played together. If we had a visitor sometimes, a friend of my father's or a neighbour, my father would say to my brother, come on lad, show us how far you can kick the ball. My brother would take the football out of the house and give it a kick. The ball would go up in the air and fall on the other side of the road. Our visitor would hoot with laughter and he would slap my brother on the back and they would all be proud. Then it was my turn. My mother would already have put me in a pretty dress. She would take me by the hand and present me to the guest. This is my daughter, she would say proudly. Oh, how lovely, our visitor would say, how very, very lovely. He would pick me up and sit me upon his knee and admire my dress, my hair, my hands. He would pass his hands over my shoulders, my back, and be very pleased to look at me.' Mary stopped and gave me an open-eyed look. 'So this is what it is, Amir,' she said, 'this is how we grow up. We develop a natural cunning inside us. I know that I do not have to do anything, kick a ball or show a trick, I just have to be there, and please people. I have always known this, like it's in the blood, so I never worry about tomorrow. I know that wherever I am, I'll get along, my life will pass, one way or the other.' Mary stopped for a moment again. 'Though one thing you said is true . . . we had a great time in Mathews Street. I was happy there, happier than ever in my life. You people were all digging in to make a life here, all without a country. I joined in. I was one of you.'

Child Michael came in. Mary put him in her lap and continued talking to me. I remembered Sakib. I mentioned Sakib to Mary and told her where and how Sakib was and that I had been to see him. Mary became very quiet. With her head bent over the empty teacup, she moved a spoon in it round and round. Then she looked up and said, 'It wasn't Sakib, those two had already done one another in. It was my fault.'

'What do you mean?' I asked her.

'My fault, all my fault,' she repeated, with signs of some distress appearing on her face.

'What happened, Mary, tell me,' I said.

Mary rested her chin on her hand and gazed at me for many seconds, as if looking into her mind to bring it back to her, or trying to find the right words. 'All them three were in the room when the fight started,' she said. 'Irshad had been missing payments. He accused Hussain Shah of using his money to buy land back in their village for himself and not, as Hussain Shah had promised, for Irshad. Irshad accused him of charging money in return for me. The dispute between them had been simmering. That day finally Irshad lost his temper. "No more woman money" he shouted. Hussain Shah slapped him on the face. Irshad picked up my kitchen knife from the table and put it in Hussain Shah's chest. Hussain Shah snatched it out of Irshad's hand and stabbed him back. They both fell to the ground. Sakib tried to run out of the room but I grabbed his arm and clung to him, I was out of my wits. The knife was stuck in Irshad's chest. I shouted to Sakib to get it out, hoping maybe Irshad could be saved. Sakib pulled the knife out and just stood there with it in his hand. I told him to throw it away but he wouldn't move, looking like someone who had done his nut.'

I sat there stunned. 'Do you mean he never killed anybody?'

'No,' she almost whispered, shaking her head. 'He wouldn't even have been found there if it wasn't for me. I'm sorry.'

'Did you tell this to the police?' I asked her.

'I told the whole thing truthfully in court,' Mary said.

I don't know whether I was blaming Mary for all that

had happened, but I wanted at that time to turn away from her. When she went to put our teacups on top of heaps of dirty plates and other empty cups in the sink, I got up.

Underneath, Mary remained the same as ever, always making a joke about something or other. Saying goodbye to me, she was cheerful, staying at the door waving to me until I'd walked down the whole length of the street and turned the corner. I didn't know what to think. She may have had a warm human heart in her, but truth to tell, she had no honesty in her heart. In my eyes she was no better than a woman of loose character, not to be trusted. All the way back, I was bothered by thoughts of Sakib. All the rest of us had kept the prime purpose of our life in view, which was to make and save money. Sakib got diverted from it and had paid the price. It made me feel sad for him all over again, the thought of him gnawing like a rat inside my skull, until I decided that I had to put it out of my head one way or the other for I had much work to do yet, to complete the furnishing of the house and make it ready to receive my wife and my dear little son and daughter. They were to be the light of my eyes. I especially chose this house on account of its nearness to the infant and primary school, beside the fact that it is a good strong house, made of old brick, not wood, and even has a cellar underneath it, dry, not dirty or flooded, with proper electrical connection. Ever since then I have stayed here and looked after the house, attending forthwith to the smallest thing that needed mending, never putting it off till later. With the labour of my hands I made it a palace for my wife and daughter, plucked them from their village and made them queens of my house.

24

'I'll run away,' I said to my father.

I had been eating a little bit each day and felt strong enough to go downstairs. There had been comings and goings and voices of strange men in the house. My mother had come up in the night and knocked at my door.

'Parvi – Parveee – open,' she cried, 'I want speak with you.'

'What,' I said, opening the door.

She put a paper in my hand. 'Put name here,' she said.

'Where?'

'Here,' she said, pointing to the paper but nowhere in particular. I saw the space for 'Signature of applicant' at the bottom.

'No,' I said.

'Beti, my jaan, have pity, for God.'

'No,' I shouted at her pup-plaintive face and shut the door, quietly, not banging it, feeling immediately ashamed of myself.

She was doing only what she was told.

In the morning, during a pause in unfamiliar footsteps and voices of men, I went down.

'Who are these men?' I asked my father.

'Which men?'

'Men who have been coming here.'

'Only my friends. Why do you not co-operate?'

'Co-operate what?'

'Only you have to put your signature on one piece of paper, that is all. Is it too much to ask?'

'Yes,' I said.

'Then go back. I will determine further course of action.'

'No you won't, dad,' I said.

'What do you mean?'

'I will run away from home,' I said to him.

On his face appeared not shock or surprise as I had expected but horror, as if he had seen the face of death. Standing absolutely still, tiny surfaces of his cheeks quivered separately as if ants crawled under the skin. Suddenly, he moved a step back and turning to my mother, cried out,

'Shaitan – shaitan! Do you not see, Salma? This is not my daughter speaking but him, this is the actuality of shaitan I tell you, nothing but shaitan, do you not hear the change in her voice?'

He jumped forward and grabbed me by the neck, shouting, 'I will make you run, you cursed shaitan, how dare you enter my daughter, lahaulawallah quwwat – lahau-lawallah quwwat—'

I had not felt such rough hands on me before, dragging me to the cellar door, unlocking it and pushing me down the steps. Whatever light there was from the door turned into blackness as it was shut behind me and locked. I knew my way around the cellar, only prayed to God that the light was there; it was. There was an old mattress, two broken chairs, a wobbly chest of drawers and a small heap of old coaldust by the chute. I'm wet and sick . . .

I'm being starved, I know a little bit about these things, they think it's not me any more but the shaitan that they are starving, and if it gets hungry enough it will run away, bloody idiots. My appetite's gone anyway, days of semi-starvation making spaces full of pale shadows open up in my brain, leaf by leaf creating visions, not mad visions, real ones, like Martin looming over me in the park with the wet spot in the front of his jeans just beginning to soak through the fibre and become visible, then him turning and walking away with his fatless little bum moving roundly within its own space in the bright sunshine, giving me freedom from all hunger and fear.

I hear fresh unknown footsteps overhead. These are not all men's feet but mixed with women's, I can figure them out from their voices coming faintly through my ceiling which is their floor. It is night now. A smell of burning incense curls through down here. Who are these men? And women? I hear the top door opening and heavy feet treading the steps down and down, coming closer, and I shrink back into my corner. Now they are standing in front of me, three hefty women I've never seen, wrapped in heavy chaddars from head to ankles. Two of them bend down to me, constantly reciting holy verses under their breath, and lift me up in their hands like I was made of paper.

The back room is full of perfumed smoke given off by incense sticks smouldering in glass jars all round the room. In the room is our local mosque maulvi and with him is the fattest bloke with the biggest black beard I have ever seen, both of them wearing long kurtas and turbans. My father stands apart from them, looking out the window. My mother is sitting on the floor on one side facing the wall, reading from the open Quran placed in front of her. The maulvi mumbles some holy verses and blows on me three times. His breath smells like an open bog. I shrink back. Two women accompanying me sit me down in a chair and the third emerges from the kitchen carrying a metal cup placed in a tray. The cup contains glowing coal, with faintly visible blue flames spotted with yellow that appears and disappears leaping from it. The two women put their hands on my shoulders and press down as the third brings up the coal container right under my face. The maulvi approaches with a paper bag in his hand from which he produces small dry red chillies and crumbles them between his fingers. These he sprinkles on the firing coal. The chilli crumble catches flame and bursts into shards of white smoke that hit my nostrils as needles boring holes straight up into my skull, coming out in streams from my eyes and sneeze-rent nose while my squirming head is held in place by the elephant hands of the two women.

'What is your name?' asks the maulvi.

'Par-vin,' I say through a choking throat.

'O shaitan, you Allah-cursed devil, *your* name, your *real* name,' the maulvi asks harshly while his friend intones 'lahaulwallah quwwat, lahaulwallah quwwat—'

'Parvin – Parvin,' I cry.

'Right,' says the maulvi determinedly, 'you will not come out with straight hands.' He motions with his hand to the two women. The women lift me up off the chair and force me face down on the floor. I am lying on my stomach and feel a kind of relief to have got away from the biting chilli smoke. Immediately thin strips of dry wood begin to fall with force on my back, my hips, my legs. A memory returns of this being done to a jinn-entered woman way back in my village when I as a child stood among the crowd of onlookers, my eyes full of the twisted-faced screams of the woman lying on the ground under lashes of flexed twigs swishing through the air. I decide that I will not scream, choking them with a will within my chest, trying to bring back the vision of a sunlit park which is gone, as strips of wood fall all over my body. The vision doesn't come. After a few seconds I feel as if it's somebody else who is being beaten and just for a second I think that perhaps it *is* the devil and not me. The moment passes quickly as the pain seeps through my skin and becomes real in my bones. Just at this instant I see behind my shut eyes the vision of an animal inside me, a great big dog-like beast that raises its long snout to the sky and howls. Suddenly, it puts the strength in my back and with a heave I free myself from the grip of the women, rising on my knees, elbows, hands. I am on my feet, surrounded by faces loudly and rapidly reciting holy verses, the maulvi, his friend, the three women, joined now also by my father, all of them now beginning to fear the strength of the Satan inside me and attempting to finish it off with God's words. Only my mother sits bent over the Quran with her back to us all. There is no way for me to go anywhere or do anything, so I look at my father and begin tearing off my clothes. I keep throwing them off one after the other until there isn't a stitch left on me, my body exposed head to foot, hair down below and all.

'Look at me,' I say to my father.

He takes a step towards me and stops, a strangeness rising in his eyes.

'Look at me,' I weep, spreading my arms in front of him, 'look at my arms, I am a virgin.' Even as I say it I know it's daft, the two things don't go together, but can't stop myself from saying on and on, 'look at my arms, I am a virgin, nothing has entered me, look at my arms—'

My father stands transfixed, looking at my spread arms as I show him and then at my other parts with eyes full of a stare of strange definition. The other two men's eyes pop out, fixed with wonder at my body. They start shouting 'shaitan, shaitan, lahaulawallah quwwat—' and take a step forward with their arms half-raised to grab me. All of a sudden my mother jumps up like a flying insect from a sitting position and comes between us.

'Stop,' she says in a terrible scream, not even looking at them but at the ceiling, her eyes rolled up. She puts her arms round my waist and half-lifts me up the stairs and into my room. She sits on the floor with my head in her lap, dragging the sheet from the bed to cover me up with shaking hands, rocking from the waist up, to and fro, uttering long and low howls of mourning that seem to emerge from deep inside her belly. Downstairs I hear the foreign feet scurrying away and out.

'How could you do it?' I say to her, 'how could you let them?'

She doesn't answer.

'How could you, mum?' I say.

'I not like your father,' she says.

'What does it matter if you don't like him now, you were there and you let him do it.'

'No,' she says, 'I not like him before.'

'Before?'

'I like the other.'

Though I understand her grammar it still takes a few seconds for the words to sink in before they jerk up to my brain.

'What – what,' I say to her, 'you liked somebody else?'

She gives no reply, just looks at me and suddenly I know the secret of her dry-weeping eyes and her desert face.

'What—' I sit up, 'what made you live like this your whole life, mum?'

She still gives no reply, only takes the Quran from under her arm, kisses it, touches it with her forehead and opens it. She leafs through it as if with intent but no aim. I look at the words of this other language, familiar but not known or understood, coming to the sudden knowledge that they create a noise in others and a silence in those of our kind. My mother comes to a place in the book which has a peacock feather pressed between two leaves. This the holiest of all the holy feathers has the shades and colours of all the world in it from one end to the other. When my mother came over from home she carried the Quran with her and the peacock feather came with it. It shines today exactly the same as it did on the very first day that I remember setting eyes on it when I was maybe one year old or even less, never withering or fading in all the years I have known it. I stop my mother's hand at the page and put down my head on the glittering feather.

A click out on the landing and a quick alarm runs through my mother's sinews. She jumps up, sweeping me off the floor with her. Takes me years back when I was very small and she used to pick me up like a feather to settle me upon her hip, and riding on the dip of her waist I felt comforted that she had the strength of a buffalo in that slim body. Noiselessly she opens the door a slit and looks. It's all clear, my father gone into the loo. Flying down the stairs, the two of us are out the front door inside of thirty seconds. Sheltering me under her vast breasts, my mother goes round the gate and into Auntie Shirin's. She slaps the door repeatedly with the flat of her hand. Auntie Shirin takes one look at our faces and pulls us in. Immediately, a loud banging at the door. Auntie Shirin shoves us up the stairs and goes down. We stop at the top of the stairs, listening.

'Where is my wife and daughter?'

'No here.'

'Yes, yes, here, I saw, they are here.'

'No here. Go.'

'Why no here? Why go? You are harbouring my family.'

'No harbouring.'

'Harbouring, yes, harbouring.' My father's voice at once bullying and pleading. 'Salma,' he calls out, 'listen to me.'

'No shout here,' Auntie says. 'Go.'

'It is my family matter, you have no right, I will call the police.'

'No, I call police,' Auntie Shirin says firmly. 'You go.' She slams the door.

A pounding on the door one more time. Then silence. We wait, hearts leaping out of our mouths. Seconds pass. Then I hear the front door of my house closing with force. I can recognise this sound among a hundred other opening and shutting doors from way off. Auntie Shirin comes up, herds us into the box room and goes back down again. My mother finally falls in a heap by the wall. I sit down beside her. Through the wall that separates us from our house I hear my father's footsteps, going into his room, into my room, into the loo and up and down the landing, back and forth, like a journey without end, talking to himself, his voice faintly coming through. My mother pulls my head towards her, lowers her face on mine and says in a soothing whisper in my ear, 'Meri jaan, my life, what you want?'

What do I tell her, and how, that I want this, a language, like God has a language and my mother has hers and my father his own, even Jenny with a single tongue-wrinkle of a missed soft d has a separate voice, but not I, I have the verbs and nouns and adjectives and all the grammar but no language, I speak like everybody else and I am not everybody else; and this too (God of peacock, help me stop this clatter in my skull so I can know what I want), a nameless anonymous being to find its way into me, enter me, plunging head-first as a diver from a great height into an ocean, zealous and furious, shining like a great white fish in the bright sun, tracing perfect arcs in the air that stay visible against the sky long after the body has vanished, defining the time of the jinn, one of my very own. This is my hidden city. It has no past and no present, but what is not yet reached frames the world we shall inhabit. I can remember the future.

Suddenly the empty house begins to resound with the echo of the voice through the wall rising in layers as in a dome.

'What I have done wrong? Give me answer, Salma, I have traversed many worlds, done every man's job, Salmaaa, why do you not give me answer, what I have done wrong . . . ?'

Glossary

abbaji   daddy
assalam alaikam   traditional Muslim greetings
almirah   free-standing cupboard
ayeh (ayet)   A brief part (stanza) of the Quran
bibi   a respectful general title for a woman
beti   daughter
bolo   speak
chaddar   shawl (for covering upper body)
chacha   uncle
dhrake   common subcontinental tree
du'aa   brief prayer for blessing
Eid   Islamic festival
fateha   the final prayer for the dead
ghazals   Urdu poems of rhyming couplets
halal   conforming to Islamic dietary laws
haraam   not conforming to Islamic dietary laws
halwa   Urdu idiom for 'having a great time'; sweet dish
jaan   life (as in meri jaan = my life)
janaza   funeral
jinn   genie
kafirs   non-believers
karahi   Urdu idiom for 'having a great time'; an Indian wok
khlas   finished (or that's all, or final)
kurta   loose shirt

kutcha   mud-built (instead of normal burnt bricks)

laddoos   sweetmeat

Lahaulwallah quwwat   A phrase from the Quran to ward off Satan's evil influence

majlis   religious gathering

maulvi   Muslim priest

meri jaan   my life

mosque Imam   Priest in charge of a mosque

namaz   formal (five-times-a-day) Muslim prayer offering

namazi   regular offerer of formal prayers

namaz janaza   formal Muslim prayer prior to the burial of a dead body

paak   consecrated body – free of foul matter

pathan   a sub-caste, usually of people from North West Frontier region of India (now Pakistan)

peeng   the swings (for children)

pukka   strong, brick-built

quwalis   mainly Muslim devotional songs sung by groups of men

rugger (hore rugger)   rub it, or rub it down (rub it down again)

salan   curry, or curry gravy

shah ji   a respectful title

shaitan   Satan

sharab   alcoholic drinks

shias   sub-sect of Muslim religion

sunnis   also a sub-sect

suparas   sections of the Quran (30 in all)

surat (or surah)   a sub-section of the Quran

tasbeeh   worry-beads

taveez   amulet or charm for protection against evil

tawa   flat iron base for cooking flat bread (roti)

tobah astaghfar   Muslim phrase for begging forgiveness of God